ZÉ

ZÉ

Renée Smith

HONNO MODERN FICTION

Published by Honno
'Ailsa Craig', Heol y Cawl, Dinas Powys,
Bro Morgannwg, CF6 4AH

First Impression 1996

British Library Cataloguing in Publication Data

A catalogue record for this book is available from the British Library

ISBN 1 870206 21 5

Published with the financial support
of the Arts Council of Wales

Cover illustration by Justine Baldwin
Cover design by Chris Lee

Typeset and printed in Wales by Dinefwr Press, Llandybïe

For Peter

I

When my marriage ended I went to live in a derelict house in a town called Blaengarw; the local people said it was the end of the line, the last place God made.

My marriage broke up on the day I went to see the astrologer. He was as dark as a magician. He lived in Clifton on the second floor, in a room which smelt of muddy hiking-boots.

He sat down on the bed beside me and gave me a can of cheap supermarket beer, cold, weak and gassy, the kind which makes you wonder why you bother to drink at all. Then he drew me my own special pattern. It looked like an arum lily. He explained about afflictions: how Saturn was badly aspecting my Venus, and setting a time limit on all my love affairs.

'You have a problem with Uranus too, so your relationships are likely to be bizarre as well as brief. You keep falling for unsuitable men.'

'Yes.'

'Do you like travelling?'

'I do, but I've never been anywhere much.'

'You will soon. Travel shows up strongly in your chart.'

He was an ill-tempered, wintry little man with a strangulated voice and a sparse black beard. He had told me he spent all his free time walking in the Welsh borders. I could imagine him walking quickly from one youth hostel to another and carrying a painfully heavy rucksack to counterbalance the pleasure.

'You're attracted to dangerous men.'

'No, that's not true.'

'I have no personal interest in you, but speaking professionally I ought to warn you that you are. The Scorpionic side of your nature is drawn to the sinister, to the secrets of birth and death, to violent and vengeful partners. You need to be aware of these tendencies and to be very circumspect in the near future.'

I walked all the way back to Temple Meads Station, thinking about what he had told me, past green-painted restaurants with trestles out on the windy pavements like Continental cafés, all-night delicatessens selling greasy Greek pastries and cold battered vegetables. I crossed and re-crossed a network of roads beneath great clanking iron bridges and found my way into the station, which had an air of being half closed for the night. I wanted to do something Philip would disapprove of so I drank two cans of thick and bitter stout, which weighted my stomach like a cold stone, then one can of cider, sharp as vomit, which made my teeth shiver and my thoughts flick about spitefully.

The train slunk into the station. The window had a lacy pattern of station grime, through which I could see orange lamp-heads like rows of lollipops, dark fuzzy hedges, sections of flashing rail. At Weston-super-Mare there was a slow, friendly clatter, a couple of shouts; no rush. It was the end of the season. I met an ancient tottery tart with purple lips and skinny ankles. She looked as though she had arrived for a dirty weekend a decade ago and never gone home again. The sea wind along the promenade turned me inland, towards the main road, where I stopped to buy a lump of pale chips, half-dissolved in their own oil, another comforting self-indulgence.

I took the long way home, up a white-flagged hill, between escallonia hedges. One by one the wives came out with their milk bottles and the bright kitchen lights were extinguished downstairs, reappearing dimly in the landing windows. It was bedtime in Weston-super-Mare. I was expecting to see my own house in darkness but a light was showing through the curtains. I fumbled nervously for my key. As I hung up my coat I was confronted by my own reflection, with tightly clenched lips and bright pink patches beneath uneasy eyes. Encountering Philip was always daunting; it was like an interview with the headmaster.

I had thought he would be alone in front of the computer. The low, urgent voices took me by surprise. I could hear a nervous rearranging of chairs and legs and I guessed they were saying, 'It's her. She's back.'

I stood stock still for a moment, composing myself. The drunkenness was unfortunate. I needed to be in control. My feelings were swirling about inside me. As yet I was calm, but I knew I could become angry or hysterical at any moment; at best I would make a fool of myself.

As soon as I opened the living room door, Philip advanced on me, shuffling a little in his slippers. He said, 'Why didn't you ring up, love, I'd have fetched you.'

He shepherded me to a chair. 'You've met Vicky, haven't you?'

I saw a a folder lying on the table. I also noticed that he was wearing his soft, elasticated trousers with the spurious buttons, the kind worn by toddlers and teddy bears. This told me that he hadn't been expecting her, that she had called in to give him the report.

'Yes, I've met her,' I said, as if she were a film I had already seen.

Vicky had thin gingery hair falling to her shoulders in little ridges. She had a slightly deformed mouth. I couldn't describe the exact nature of the deformity because I made a point of never looking at her directly. She wore a khaki shirt and tight beige trousers; she always dressed in shades of mud, porridge and slush. Her voice sounded like a tape slightly speeded up. Like a child, she made little restless twirling, hopping and jiggling movements. I couldn't have explained why I loathed her, unless the above description constitutes a justification. I didn't think she was sleeping with my husband. I couldn't see why she would want to.

He said, with a slight whine, 'I thought you were stopping over.'

'I didn't go to Linda's. I told you I might not. I went to Clifton to have my chart drawn up.'

My hands were trembling but I managed to extricate the sheets of paper from the envelope. It should have been thick and grainy but it was semi-transparent, penny-pinching stuff.

Philip looked at my arum lily flower. He leered at me.

'Look, Sandy, this line is shooting off into nowhere. Does that mean you're at a loose end?'

When people call me Sandy I feel like a mongrel or a ginger cat. In fact my name is Alexandra, and my parents always called me Xana; the X is a shushing sound. It seems to me that the people who respect me call me Xana, and the ones who want to vulgarize me call me Sandy.

Before Philip met me he called astrology 'the stars' and he thought it divided people up into twelve categories, every member of each of which could expect the same fate on the same day; he had believed it to be rubbish. Now I realized that he hadn't changed his views at all. He had only pretended, to humour me. At this point I had a surge of anger. My head filled with pounding blood, I could hear it swishing in my ears. What I wanted to do was catch hold of Vicky by the shoulders and propel her to the front door, hissing:

'Get out! Get out of my house! Get out of my life! Don't come back!' I knew I was looking grim. My teeth were gritted, my neck was as rigid as a bitch's at bay, even my anus was clenched. I said loftily,

'I don't believe in predictions and I don't approve of them. But the full chart will give you a near-perfect analysis of character, and if you need a quick rough guide the sun sign is better than nothing. For instance, if I know a woman has the sun in Virgo I make a point of avoiding her. Virgo women are boring and bossy. They make frigid, self-pitying wives. Usually they're old maids. They take jobs where they can bully people.'

No one commented. There was a slightly disagreeable silence. Philip began moving restlessly about the room, re-ordering it while he composed himself, adjusting the plastic blinds and hessian lampshade. Vicky got up and shuddered, making a noise like a small motor starting up. Philip followed her into the hall. I could hear her saying something about a case meeting, in the voice of a baby duck on a cartoon film. When he came back he said,

'You knew very well when Vicky's birthday was, I told you we had a party at the office last week.'

'Oh yes, I remember now, you all clubbed together and bought her a bottle of dolly mixtures.'

'You're so smart, aren't you, so sharp. You can't resist the stinging rejoinder, you don't care how much you hurt.'

'How much I hurt who? Why should Vicky matter to you?'

He blustered, 'I have to work with her. She's a valuable team member. And,' he added defiantly, 'I like her very much. She's a sensitive, caring person.'

'She is an ugly, silly woman and I don't want her in my house, invited or uninvited.'

'This isn't your house.'

Of course I had known when Vicky's birthday was and I had known that we were going to have a row. Philip walked away and pretended to be tidying up the study. I followed him.

'I am supposed to be your wife and this is supposed to be my home.'

'It's supposed to be, but you're never in it. You're always out gadding about, wasting money on rubbish.'

'Do you expect me to stay here waiting for you, night after night, bored out of my mind, dusting somebody else's bloody gimcracks and answering the phone?'

'Do what you like.'

He sat down heavily in his basket chair, clearing his throat gruffly and fidgeting with his paper. I knelt down beside him and asked hopelessly:

'Do you just not love me any more?'

He complained, 'You keep using this word and I don't know what it means. All the warmth has gone. There's nothing left. I don't feel anything, anything at all.'

I said, 'Then I might as well go.'

'I don't mind. I don't care whether you do or not. I signed up for you so I'm stuck with you, but I keep thinking I'd be better off on my own.'

I said, 'I have loved you to the best of my ability. I really have tried.'

'Well it was a piss-poor effort then.'

After that I went. As I left I slammed the front door and cracked the glass panel. It was unintentional, but I wasn't sorry about it.

I stayed overnight with my friend in Bristol. She lived in a bleak new house on Plot 7, a wintry little patch of ploughed earth, rubble and labelled twigs. If I'd gone there earlier, as planned, I could have gone home sober in the morning to Furze Close: to the stopped British sausage clock and the mouldy gourds on the kitchen window-sill which had 'always been there', to the striped grass and trailing ivy in the bathroom, to the freezer full of large lumps of meat I had been instructed to buy, to the ghostly crying in the bathroom and bedroom.

He would never have left me or thrown me out. In time he would have grown attached to me as to the stopped sausage clock, as the bathroom had grown attached to the ivy. We could have gone on together into a grumpy, dependent old age. I had provoked the quarrel, and over Vicky; it demeaned me to know her name, let alone allot her a momentous role in my life. Until that time I had thought he must love me, because he let me sleep moulded around his humped, pyjamaed back and drawn-up legs, because I thought I was inherently loveable, but I had insisted on hearing the truth, which was perhaps not even the truth but only an expression of his need not to be bothered, to remain indifferent.

My friend Linda and I drank horse-manure wine which corroded the roof of my mouth.

'Don't waste time feeling guilty. Now you can go on and do something you really want to do.'

'I suppose so.'

I lacked the motive power and the sense of direction. I felt like a carriage in a siding, waiting for an engine to come and shunt me. I was surprised that I could go on talking, so extreme were my feelings of inertia.

When I woke up in the morning and realized that I wasn't in bed with Philip, and remembered what had happened, I felt so listless that I nearly didn't get up at all. In the end my panic got me out of bed, I found Southmead oppressive and I didn't want to be trapped there. I thought I would go to Wales. I felt like a dog which has just slipped its collar. It doesn't make purposefully for the nearest park or rubbish bin, it zig-zags about in a bewildered way, diving in suicidally amongst the traffic.

We went round after he'd gone to work, to collect my belongings. I took only necessities and friendly things: a favourite pen, letters to be answered, my Irish tape and Walkman, the clothes I wore constantly: soft dresses, cotton T-shirts and flat boots, nothing that lived on a hanger or folded in a corner. I took as much as I could carry in a big, black, green-trimmed canvas bag I had always had the use of. I dreaded that Philip would turn up but he didn't.

Instead, one of his clients appeared on the doorstep. I had never liked Jamie much and I wasn't inclined to waste time on him. I disliked his twee name and impertinent manner. I said, 'He's not here, I'm afraid. He's probably at the office.'

He wore a cheap plastic jacket with oil on the sleeve and something that looked like bird-droppings down the front.

'I've tried the office. I need to borrow some money.'

I said curtly, 'Well don't bother asking me. I've probably got less than you have.'

'No one could possibly have less than I have.'

He stretched his mouth into a smile without showing any teeth. He had a perfect face for clowning: a very wide mouth and a short , splayed nose, bright hazel eyes which he opened wide when he smiled, as infant teachers do to express bogus delight. I didn't find him amusing.

'You can leave a message if you like.'

He said smoothly, 'No, I won't do that. You can just tell him I'm going. It's OK, I'm over eighteen, I'm allowed.'

I doubted it. I said, 'Look, I don't care whether you're allowed to or not but I can't tell him because I shan't be here.'

He glanced at my bag and asked, 'Where are you going?'

'Why?'

'I thought perhaps you could give me a lift.'

Linda emerged from the kitchen carrying a bottle of Christ's Tears. She said, 'Oh, is this one of your dangerous men?'

I took the bottle from her and repressed her with a hooded look.

'This is old white port, you have to lay it on its side and decant it carefully or it goes rusty.'

Jamie gave her his bright, greedy glance. He said, 'Where are you going exactly?'

'I'm going as far as Bristol, then Xana's making her own way to Wales.'

He looked relieved.

'OK. Can I use the toilet first please?'

I didn't particularly want him in the house, although it wasn't my house any more, but I could hardly refuse. A few minutes later he found us in the kitchen. He'd shaved and washed. His hair was stubbly, his face was gaunt and his skin was sallow. I wondered if he had just come out of prison. He might well have done, I couldn't remember his case history at all.

I saw that Philip had not been too distressed to follow his usual routine. He had watered the lemon balm and set the video recorder. He'd found time to defrost a piece of pork tenderloin for dinner but he hadn't put the milk bottles out and he'd left the remains of his supper on the kitchen work surfaces: cold bacon pizza and potato salad. Linda was still trying to persuade me to come and stay with her, whilst absent-mindedly picking the bacon off the pizza. Seeing this, Jamie started helping himself too, and Linda poured us all a tumblerful of wine. To Linda, anyone is a potential dinner guest; she wouldn't recognize the distinction between clients and people one socialized with.

After the second tumblerful I gave up resenting Jamie. He was audacious, but the pickings were meagre after all. A lift, some leftovers, half a bottle of Sainsbury's; to begrudge them was like begrudging the birds my stale heels of Vitbe. After the third tumblerful of wine we all became frivolous. In the kitchen there was a whiteboard which we had used to leave messages on: in the beginning 'I love you', and in the end 'Gone to Bristol, casserole in oven.' On it Jamie wrote a message of thanks and explanation which he then erased, phrase by phrase, until it read:

'Goodbye, Jamie'. I added my own name, Xana, and Linda appended: 'Thanks for the wine!'

So we left, with as many bottles as we could carry between us. Linda took the white port.

II

Linda dropped us off in Bristol, where I took some money out of a cash dispenser. To remember my number I have to recite a little jingle. Jamie was standing behind me. I sensed that he was memorizing it. To someone who hasn't got one, a bank card appears to give unlimited access to cash. In fact I emptied my account and came away with twenty-five pounds.

I phoned my son at Hull University. When I came out of the booth Jamie was still there. He said, 'How are you getting to Wales?'

'Why?'

'Because I could hitch with you.'

'Why do you want to go to Wales?'

'Because I need to get away for a bit.'

I said, 'Look, there's no point in coming with me. I can't help you. I haven't got any more money. This is all there is.'

'Do you know how prejudiced you are?'

'Being prejudiced has got nothing to do with it.'

'It has, but you don't realize it. You don't see me as a person at all. You're a typical social worker's wife.'

After that I felt I had to let him come. He saved me money because I had intended to take the bus. I was too timid to hitch-hike alone. The first lorry-driver put us down at the motorway services and Jamie and I shared a teabag with unlimited free refills of hot water and little plastic pots of milk. He said, 'Tell me where we're going and we'll look at a map in the shop.'

'Ystradfellte.'

'Do you know someone there?'

'No, I'm going to the youth hostel.'

'Why particularly?'

'Because I met someone yesterday who said it was beautiful.'

'Are we on holiday?' he asked, blinking at me.

'No, we're at a complete loose end.'

We didn't buy the map, we studied it in the shop, spreading it out over the tins of glucose sweets and jars of jam with gingham hats. Jamie said, 'We'd better get a move on. I didn't want to say, but you took a very long time over lunch.'

We got two lifts in quick succession. I enjoyed being perched up high in the cabs of the wagons, with a broad view of the road. Jamie sat next to the drivers, quizzing them like a young TV reporter.

In the evening we became stranded on a verge at a quiet cross-roads. The few cars passing were driven by private motorists and they either ignored us or made turning-off signals. We waited on the verge for two hours or more. Periodically Jamie limbered up like an athlete, jumping up and down on the spot and shaking out his limbs. He managed to open a bottle of wine with a piece of wire he found by the roadside.

We decided to walk on, because, Jamie said, a change of position sometimes improves one's luck. I felt dazed after the wine; I hadn't eaten anything but a yoghurt all day. I followed Jamie through the dark pitted lanes. We didn't see a signpost, street light or house light. We didn't hear any traffic, only a few sheep coughing. Jamie said at last, 'We're not going to get anywhere tonight. It's very late, we might as well camp out.'We went in amongst the trees, stepping gingerly through the long grass. I didn't want to spend the night with Jamie but I preferred it to being lost on my own. We sat down, and Jamie said,

'Do you want some more wine?'

'Not really. I'd rather have a cup of tea and a sandwich.'

'Tomorrow we'll find a transport café that opens at 7.30 and we'll have the full English breakfast.'

I thought, 'And I can imagine who's going to pay for it.'

I lay down in the leaves and covered myself with clothes from my bag but I couldn't sleep. The leaf-bed was chilly and uncomfortable after a while and I shifted position and fidgeted restlessly. I rolled up a T-shirt for a pillow and made a mattress of jeans and a plastic mac. There was an odd dry smell which reminded me of smouldering bonfires and city alleyways.

Then Jamie startled me by shouting like a drunk. He was thrashing about in the leaves as if wrestling with an invisible opponent. I caught hold of his arm and shook it.

'Jamie! Wake up!'

He sat bolt upright. 'Oh heavens. It's OK. Lie down. It's nothing.'

After a few moments he said diffidently:

'Xana, would you hold me for a minute?'

He asked so humbly that I was touched and couldn't refuse. I said, 'Come here then,' and gathered him to me. 'What was it, a nightmare?'

'It was nothing, nothing happened, but I was afraid it was going to.'

'What did you think would happen?'

'It's not really a nightmare, it's more like the sort of pictures you get when you're just about to fall asleep. But sometimes I get it when I'm wide awake.'

'What is it like?'

'Have you ever looked in a mirror in a dream and seen your own face, but looking different?'

'I think so.'

'It was like that at first. He looked like me, but he wasn't me, he was darker and more sombre. Then he started coming right into me. When I was a kid I used to call him Zed, because he was like the end of everything, the ultimate awfulness.'

'What is so awful?'

'First there's a feeling of travelling down a long desolate road in the dark, the sky is clammy and closing in on me, and something wolf-like comes slinking out of the fog and attacks. I'm trapped and completely helpless, I can't breathe and I can't move. I struggle until my chest bursts open and my brain blows up. When I come to I'm on my feet, fighting and shouting, I'm full of pumping black energy, I could kick down walls or dive head first through windows.'

'It sounds horrific.'

'When I was a kid he only came when I was in bed asleep. Then it started happening at school. Now it can happen on a train, at work, anywhere.'

'And cause a lot of upset.'

'Yes.'

'Is that why you have to leave now?'

'Yes.'

I didn't ask about the diagnosis. I knew he would accuse me of wanting to stick labels on him. Instead I said, 'Can't anything be done about it?'

'No. When I was a child I was too frightened to go to sleep, I'd try all kinds of tricks to keep myself awake. So my parents found out. They're conscientious people so they took me round the clinics and child psychiatrists. They must have tried just about everything. I can take drugs to stupefy me. They make it easier for other people to deal with, but they don't do anything to help me.'

11

'And do the drugs stop it happening?'

'No, I'd take them if they did. They just make me lethargic. I act half-witted and I can't speak above a whisper.'

I felt sorry for him. I was stroking his hair. He said,

'Are you warm enough?'

'I am now.'

'Yes, it's better together, isn't it. Shall we sleep like this?'

* * *

I woke up because Jamie was kissing me insistently. It was pleasurable, so I kept my eyes closed and tried not to think, 'This is Jamie you're kissing. *Jamie!*'

We kissed hard for some unmeasured period of time, with lips, tongues and teeth. I didn't want to stop. I had cramps like the onset of labour pains. Jamie bit my mouth. He said 'Open your eyes and look at me.'

It was first light. His face looked long and pale and pointed. He said, 'Don't you think we kiss wonderfully well?'

We got up and I stuffed my damp sweaters and T-shirts back into the bag. We found that we had slept all night on the lip of a crater filled with domestic rubbish: bent pushchairs, stained mattresses, burnt cooking-pots and bundles of used plastic nappies. Jamie held out his hand for my bag. I said,'It's OK, I can manage.'

I was worried by this sudden shift in the relationship; afraid Jamie might become the indifferent one, that I might end up needing him instead.

We walked on into a buffeting wind, across a high plain. A few dirty sheep were eating the wiry grass. In the distance there were lime-green mountains scarred by streams and rock-falls. Only one car passed us. We reached the outskirts of a little town at nine o'clock. It was a self-conscious little town and the café had copper bowls with plastic poinsettias, wooden clocks and checked table-cloths. It looked homely but expensive. Jamie studied the menu.

'Good, we can have a proper breakfast and griddle cakes.'

'Jamie,' I said irritably, 'look at the prices. I can't afford it. You don't seem to understand, this is all the money I've got, it's got to last.'

'I can pay.'

'*You* can!'

'What's the matter?'

I said hotly, 'You came to the house asking for a hand-out. You asked me for money. You came along with me just so you could sponge on me. Now you tell me you can pay.'

His eyes had a critical gleam.

'I didn't have any money yesterday. But today I can go to the post office and cash my giro.'

'So you had a giro, but you still came round scrounging.'

'If you remember, I asked you if I could borrow some money. Your husband would probably have said yes because it was an emergency and because he knows I have an order book and I get my money every Thursday.'

I said 'Oh,' and then, 'I am prejudiced, aren't I?'

'Yes you are, but you're very nice to hold.'

'How did you manage to get an order book?'

'Well I don't have to sign on because I'm not considered fit to work. I get a sort of disability pension.'

'That's very lucky.'

He said wryly, 'I hoped you'd see it that way.'

Jamie had microwaved sausages, a pale battery egg and steaming tinned tomatoes. He called the waitress twice to bring more griddle cakes. He stared at her intently, raising and lowering his eyebrows. He meant to be disconcerting. The young waitress squirmed and combed her hair with a pencil. I watched her moving round the café and I watched him to see if he was watching her. He said, 'Don't you want your coffee?'

'No, it's got whitener in it.'

'We could have some tea, they don't put whitener in that.'

'No, please don't call her again. I don't want any tea and I want to pay for my own toast.'

When Jamie had finished his breakfast he went across to the post office to collect his pension. I said coldly to the girl,

'Could you bring me some coffee with fresh milk, please, and not powdered aluminium.'

I watched the door of the post office for Jamie's reappearance. I thought, 'I could insist that he makes his own way now he's got some money. I don't want to be there when Zed makes his next appearance, and I don't want to be endlessly watching girls' faces and watching him watching girls' faces until at last I'm right about one.'

He came back into the café with a map. He didn't look at the waitress. 'They said at the shop that Ystradfellte's not far. We could be there for lunch and somewhere else tonight.'

'I want to stay at the youth hostel.'

'You don't want to stay at the youth hostel.'

'Why not?'

'Because we won't be able to sleep together. And I need to sleep with you.'

My body reacted with a localized ache, but I said steadily, 'In case Zed comes?'

'No, not because of that. Xana,' he put out his hand and touched my fingers, 'who's Tim?'

'Tim? He's my son.'

He grinned. He had widely-spaced teeth, like a crocodile. 'I thought he might be your boyfriend. How old is he?'

'He's nineteen. How old are you?'

'Twenty-two. How old are you?'

I said, 'Well at the moment I feel about seventeen, but it won't last.'

We walked along the river at Ystradfellte. Jamie bounded over the stepping-stones, skidded, and pretended to sway and totter. I looked at his skinny legs in stained jeans, the balancing feet in battered trainers, and I thought, 'He's a boy, a scruffy boy. There's no rôle in his life that suits me.'

We walked through the dripping green valley; we passed at least seven waterfalls. At one place the path passed behind the falling water. We stopped and Jamie squatted down and gouged out the cork from our last bottle of wine. We crouched there like slugs, chilly and damp, passing the sour red wine and peering up at the dripping water. Jamie said, 'I've been here before, and yet I know I haven't. It's a funny feeling.'

I thought he was exaggerating for effect. I said, 'It's called *déjà vu*, it's a mild form of epilepsy, most people suffer from it.'

We climbed back to the road and took the first lift offered. This method brought us eventually to Bridgend, which was not a place we would have chosen to visit. We walked the streets looking in vain for a bed and breakfast sign, then we had supper in a pub. I sat next to a tank of fish who clamped their lips to the glass and watched me eat. I felt very tired and dirty.

A little back-street terraced house finally opened its door to us and I let Jamie talk. The landlady took us up steep staircases and across narrow landings to a low, twin-bedded room. I could hear the rushing and roaring of traffic through the shining black window.

Jamie said, 'My friend and I would rather have a double bed if you don't mind.'

She didn't smile. She said grimly, 'Certainly. There's a double room on the next floor up but you'll have to come down to the bathroom.'

'That's all right, we're not all that keen on washing.'

The double room had a light wood veneer and a blue nylon eiderdown. It reminded me of my sister-in-law's house, conjuring up the odour of stale roast dinners. I sat on a chair and felt thoroughly abashed. I looked at Jamie and for a moment he was a client again. I thought in dismay, 'I can't do it! I can't.'

Jamie was half stripped off. He had a thin, almost hairless body and spots on his back. He said, 'Come to bed.'

'I must go and have a wash.'

'I'll lick you clean.'

I took off my sweater and jeans and got into bed.

'Be a sport, Xana. Take the T-shirt off.'

I took the T-shirt off. I thought, 'I'll have to go through with it now.' His expression hardened and I received a minute signal from the pupils of his eyes.

'Take your bra and knickers off too, you won't be needing them.'

He got into bed beside me and pulled the sheet up over our heads. He had the kind of erection that isn't to be ignored. I had forgotten the rough urgency of young men. When he pushed into me, something strange happened. The room seemed to swing round and re-orientate itself, filling with thick, fizzing light and a noiseless rushing. We were lying on our sides and still kissing. Jamie held my nipples tightly in his fingers. I wanted to say, 'Oh love, oh love,' but I said 'Oh, oh,' instead, and then, 'Take it out, sweetheart, before you come.'

'It's too late, I'm sorry.'

We clung together clammily and kissed for an hour or more. I should have been worrying about possible pregnancy, or infection, but instead I was thinking:

'Please say you love me. If I have to say it first I'll always be the loser in this relationship.'

III

Jamie said, 'Good morning, naked lady, it's half-past nine.'

We got dressed and hurried downstairs. Unsmiling, the land-lady brought us our breakfast. She said, 'Would you vacate the room by ten, please.'

Jamie said, 'That's a shame, we were hoping to stay for a fort-night at least.'

She hesitated.

'Well the room is free, but we ask for payment in advance for long stays. And we still ask you to vacate by ten, for the clean-ing.'

'So we can't go back to bed.'

'I'm afraid not.' Her face was set but her eyes expressed her indignation.

'We won't bother then, thank you.'

As she left the room, Jamie said, 'I'm sure she'd like me if she got to know me.'

'She might like you better if you didn't wear that jacket. And if you didn't refer to me as your friend.'

He said, 'Should I have pretended you were my mother?'

We ate in silence. I was upset by his joke, and the landlady's disapproval, although I tried not to show it. The dining-room was tiny, but dark and oppressive. Jamie drew back the heavy curtains and uncovered the canary. He hadn't mentioned any plans for the day. I thought, 'If he goes off and leaves me now I can't complain. I'll be quite nonchalant about it.'

As soon as we got out of the house Jamie stopped dead and stood on the pavement shifting his weight from one leg to the other, slowly swinging my bag. There was a cold wind blowing and the landlady was watching us through the curtains. I felt like giving him a shove. I said impatiently, 'What are you wait-ing for, a bus?'

He said, 'I'm thinking what to do. The holiday's over, Xana.'

I gave a silent, desolate cry, then I said coolly, 'OK.'

'What did you mean to do after Ystradfellte?'

'I hadn't thought that far.'

'Do you want to go back?'

'No.'

He shook his head at me reprovingly. 'You really are irresponsible, you know.'

I said wearily, 'Jamie, I'm too old to play games.' His sense of humour was jarring on me. 'I haven't got the excess energy for fooling. I want to go now, and get out of this cold wind.'

He said reasonably, 'But where do you want to go to? We're running out of money. What we ought to be doing is finding somewhere for us to live.'

Relief soaked through like rain into my roots. I didn't really want to live with Jamie, the thought of it made my teeth tremble. I wanted to sit in the sun and drink cool green wine and listen to plaintive guitar music and dream about living with him at some future time, but I said bravely, 'OK. And what shall we do in the afternoon?'

Jamie led me to the estate agents in the main street. He said, 'Look at the prices further up the valley. We passed through places like that yesterday afternoon – decrepit mining towns, the shops all boarded up, houses collapsing.'

'But I haven't got the money to buy a house, however cheap it is. Did you think I had?'

Jamie gritted his teeth and closed his eyes. 'I know, Xana, I know I know I know that you haven't got any money. Stop telling me now, will you?'

'Have you got some?'

He laughed robustly.

'No. But this is the perfect place to find a cheap let, or a squat.'

I had never tried squatting. It sounded squalid and insecure. I thought, 'I mustn't stop and think. If I get off this ride I'll be too scared to get on again.'

We got a lift up the valley in the back of a delivery van. Jamie sat on an upturned plastic crate. He patted it.

'Xana, come here and be nice to me. You've been cross all morning.'

He rubbed my cheek and nose with his, kissed my ear with a wet, crackling sound. He smelt of hay and stale socks but his breath was pure, the whites of his eyes were clear. I stroked his hair roughly. When I held Jamie I felt confused. I couldn't separate my sexual hunger from maternal yearnings. I thought, 'When I look back on this affair, after he's gone, I must remember how shaming and uncomfortable it was, and how full of dread I felt.' I already knew it would end unhappily, and I wanted to spare myself the pain of looking back.

Blaengarw was the last town in the valley. There the main road petered out into a turning place for buses and a muddy rec' with a few children's swings. On one side the terraced houses backed onto the steep mountainside; on the other they backed onto a strip of waste land where the housewives threw their cabbage leaves and eggshells and stale sliced bread. Beyond the dirty river rose the half-grassed slag-heaps of the colliery tip.

We came to a little café where we sat down amongst the jars of boiled sweets and ate a meat pie, steamed between two pans on top of the coffee-maker. Jamie played the fruit machine.

The cafe owner told us about a house where they sometimes took in lodgers. It was round the corner from the school.

As soon as we had stepped inside Jamie said, 'We've changed our minds, thank you,' and hustled me out again.

'Xana, I can't live in a place like that. Did you see she had nailed a strip of clear plastic over her hall-carpet? She probably scrubs her doorstep every morning and hoses down the pavement as well.'

We walked back up the Blaen and sat on a roundabout in the children's playground. We saw two mothers with runny-nosed toddlers and a grandmother with a blanket wrapped around her and a baby inside it. The day was becoming dark and the buses had lighted windows. Jamie said, 'Now's the time. I have my eye on that empty block at the end.'

It was a forlorn row of houses with dim, cracked windows, crumbling sills, peeling brown paint and doorsteps gaping like graves. We went up a gulley and round the backs. The first house had been used for coal storage and the others were closed up. Jamie vaulted onto a lavatory roof and stuck his hand through a broken pane, then he jumped down again and dusted off his hands on his jeans.

'No, some killjoy has boarded it up. Let's try over the road.'

We investigated another derelict block. The mountainside had been cut away behind it at roof level, leaving a sheer, crumbling wall of clay soil and tree roots. Jamie tried the back doors. He said,

'Aha! This one should budge with a bit of luck. The lintel is parting company with the wall.' The door finally yielded to pressure from his shoulder and swung inwards.

Inside, it was pitch black. The hillside, rising steeply behind, blocked off all natural light. My groping hand encountered a clammy wall; the plaster came away under my finger-nails like cream cheese. We shuffled blindly into the middle room, where Jamie put his foot through a floor-board. He said, 'There's probably a defunct mine underneath.'

The wallpaper in the parlour hung loosely, like a petticoat. It had huge, tea-coloured stains. Jamie pulled off a yard or two. The wall behind was damp and friable like a dunked biscuit and frilly toadstools flowered in a corner. Jamie bolted upstairs, calling back, 'Watch out for the fifth one.'

The main ceiling had fallen in and the floor and landing were covered in chunks of plaster and soft black dust. Bits of broken lath still adhered to the roof beams, between which I could glimpse the sky. Jamie called, 'This room's OK.'

I went into the little back bedroom. There was a scrap of flecked lino on the floor, a china candlestick on the window-sill and a pile of cat's excrement in a corner. 'It's lovely,' I said sardonically.

We went downstairs again and out of the kitchen door. In the back yard there was a functioning water tap. A steep flight of rocky steps led up to the back gardens. We looked inside the shed; there, behind a partition, was a lavatory with a cracked wooden seat. Jamie enthused, 'This is the one, Xana. There must be nearly an acre of land here.'

'Are you going to grow roses?'

'No, but we could keep chickens. And as we've got running water,' he held his hand under the dripping toilet overflow, 'We could have ducks, *patinhos*.'

'*Patinhos*! Do you speak Portuguese?'

'No. These words just come, I don't know where they come from.'

'Keeping poultry seems a rather modest ambition for you.'

He said, 'I may look sophisticated but it's just a pose – I'm a peasant at heart.'

'What will we do with the ducklings if the council throw us out?'

'Eat them. Now we'd better go and buy some necessities before the shops shut.'

'Such as plaster, cement and ceiling-boards?'

'Some candles, a pan, mugs and dishes. And matches. If any of the chimneys work, we can pick up some firewood on the tip.'

That night we slept in a full embrace on the bare boards of the back bedroom, which overlooked a stained and dripping yard. The cracked window rattled all night and I worried about people bursting in. In the morning I crept downstairs and crouched below the front windows, putting on my eye make-up with the aid of a little handbag mirror. My eyes were dry with tiredness and my mouth was sagging. For a moment I longed to be in my kitchen at Furze Close, for my coffee pot and labelled canisters of dried fruit and grains. Then I heard Jamie coming downstairs and I sprang to attention like a dog.

He tugged sleepily at my ear and hair and pressed my nose into his T-shirt. When he had finished yawning he went outside and washed under the cold tap, as to the manner born. Then he set about unblocking the chimney of the kitchen range. He finally managed to dislodge an old bird's nest and we lit the fire with the sticks, and wallpaper pulled from the walls. We boiled up water in an open enamel pan. The wallpaper gave our tea a characteristic flavour, a little like lapsang souchong.

We scraped most of the mould and loose plaster from the kitchen walls. With Jamie's next giro we bought white gloss paint and covered them thickly. Beneath the sodden layers of lino, which had matted together like rotten leaves, I discovered undulating red tiles, which I scrubbed with an old vest. We bought a lamp with a frail gauzy mantle, which hissed comfortingly in the perpetual midnight of the kitchen.

Across the road lived a large disreputable family who called on us, bringing a bucket of anthracite, and lent us a single mattress and an armchair. The boys incited Jamie to steal coal from the colliery trucks. Near the war memorial was a brick-built working men's club, which was advertising for bar staff. I plaited my hair, put on my Marco Polo blouse and Portuguese boots and offered myself.

At lunch-time I served wheezing miners with pints of Special until it was time for them to go down into the dark. At night their wives and girlfriends came to drink Blue Moons and play bingo in the upper bar. Jamie said, 'Now I suppose I'll have to get a job too.'

'Why? You have your pension, I had nothing. I didn't want to be dependent on you.'

'No one would be foolish enough to depend on me.'

We were in the public bar, drinking Holsten to celebrate my new job. Holsten is a foul and potent brew – I couldn't decide whether I was getting drunk or poisoned. We sat close together, Jamie's hand rested on my inner thigh; I was aware of interested glances.

'If you got a job you'd lose your pension. Can't you stay at home and do some plastering or put up chicken-wire?'

'That's the second time you've mentioned plastering. Do you want to turn me into a home handyman like my father?' He went on reminiscently. 'He's a harmless, but irritating man, my father. He walks about on tiptoe in his socks. He's always pottering about the house, mending things awkwardly when they ought to be replaced, and injuring himself with his tools.'

I could see him clearly in my mind's eye. He had pale-framed glasses and untidy colourless hair, tiny genitals inside wide baggy trousers; he wore woollen gloves and carried a purse when he went shopping. I couldn't imagine Jamie being the son of such a man.

'Do you take after your mother?'

'Hardly. I'm adopted. My adoptive mother is a frustrated intellectual, or she thinks she is. She's very earnest. She used to be a primary school teacher; she's good at miniature gardens and pastry-men.'

'You sound as if you despise her.'

He flattened the hair on the top of his head and winced.

'She's so well-meaning; they're both very well-meaning people.'

'Do you go and see them?'

'I shall have to soon because I left my things in a box in their conservatory.'

I could picture his mother, too; she was tall with long mousey hair and corduroy jeans. She ate tahini and tofu. I said, 'I bet your mother chose your name.'

'No, my name is part of the legend.' He propped up his face in his hands and looked at me sideways. 'They used to tell me a bed-time story about a sad little boy called James, who was looking for a mummy and a daddy. Then he met Brenda and Roland, who needed a little boy of their own, and as soon as they saw James they knew he was the one. So they all went to the Judge, and little James became their Jamie.'

I said, 'Well I expect you enjoyed it at the time. They do sound very well-meaning.'

'Yes, they are. They didn't want to confuse me, you see, by changing my name. They let me hang on to that scrap of identity. They thought of things like that.'

I said, puzzled, 'But how old were you?'

22

'I was three when I was offered up for adoption. Then I was fostered for two years and adopted when I was five.'

'That's very unusual, surely? Do you remember your real mother?'

He shook his head.

'Have you ever tried to find her?'

'I've never particularly wanted to. She dumped me after all.'

I protested. 'But there may have been a good reason!'

He said, 'My real father was from Malaysia or somewhere thereabouts. I don't suppose they were married.'

I looked at his face, at the full, fleshy lips and delicate chin, the high cheekbones and felty black hair. I said, 'I'd never noticed. You look entirely English; it's the hazel eyes.'

He was shredding beer-mats, looking pensive and a little scornful. I said, 'Perhaps your mother gave you up for your own good, as she saw it. She may have been very poor or very ill. Perhaps she died.'

He said, sneering, 'And perhaps she just wanted to get shot of me.'

I said stoutly, 'I don't believe any mother feels like that. You just don't dump three-year-olds. The circumstances must have been exceptional. Can't your adoptive parents tell you anything about her?'

'They don't know. And they aren't the kind of people you could ask. My mother would get upset. She'd take it as a rejection and pretend not to. They're very self-critical. They used to keep asking the child psychiatrists where they'd gone wrong.'

I said, 'If it was me, I'd have to know. Are you afraid of what you might find out?'

'No, it can't be any worse than what I imagine.'

We were both drunk by this time. The noise in the pub had turned into a peaceful roar, like distant traffic. I was bemused. The to-and-fro of customers, the odd beady stare, were no longer threatening. Jamie said, 'You go ahead and find out if you want to,' and I thought, 'Yes, I will, and I won't tell you unless it's better than you think it is.'

That is how I came to write the first letter, and that is what took us eventually to the island.

IV

Jamie went down the road to Pontycymmer and got a job in a factory, making lids for plastic water-tanks. He was elated. I'd rather he'd gone on a Mickey Mouse project for the long-term unemployed, but of course I didn't say so. I didn't want to sound like a social worker's wife.

At the end of the week he decided to go home and fetch his box of belongings. He didn't invite me to accompany him and I didn't suggest it. I pretended to myself that I would actually enjoy a little relaxation and respite. I felt ill at ease when I was with Jamie; I watched him all the time, hungrily but surreptitiously. I took the bus to Bridgend and looked round the shops. I wanted to buy myself something consoling, like French cheese or green hair-dye, but instead I bought a striped cotton rug for the kitchen.

When I got home I settled down by the fire and wrote a letter to Philip. I didn't want to contact him. It pleased me to think that he didn't know where I was and couldn't find me even if he wanted to, but the letter was important. I made my words as sparse and chilly as I could. I said that I was living in a squat but he could write to me care of the club. I said that I was living with Jamie. It thrilled me to mention it, I hoped he would be outraged. I remembered the message we had left on the whiteboard, which implied that we had run away together; it had seemed a good joke at the time.

I said that Jamie was anxious to find out about his natural parents and wanted a copy of any relevant information in his case history. I was fairly confident that there would be some, dating back to the time when he was fostered. I thought that, as a social worker, Philip would feel obliged to send the information, whatever his personal feelings were. I didn't ask him for the name of Jamie's illness. It would have seemed disloyal.

Jamie came back long after I had finished work and gone to bed. He had walked the twelve miles up the valley carrying his clothes and tapes and a bulky cassette-player.

'How did it go? Were they pleased to see you?'

'Actually I think they were just getting used to not seeing me. Roland did his duty by asking me some searching questions about my life-style; Brenda was upset because I hadn't got my front-door key. She wanted to know where I'd lost it, if I'd told the police, if anyone knew which door it fitted. People like that force you to lie to them in the end. Then she wanted me to go up to the attic and look at my toys.'

'Your toys!'

'Yes, she'd sorted them all out into categories and she wanted me to say which I would keep for my own future children and which she could give to the WRVS. I said she could give them all to the WRVS but that didn't satisfy her. She wanted me to look in the boxes. So I went up to the attic and I found some of my old poems and read them for half an hour. They were better than I'd thought.'

'Were they pleased about the job?'

'They pretended to be but I think they were secretly rather worried. Now budge, Xana, I'm coming to bed and you're hogging the mattress as usual.'

Philip replied within the week. I felt nervous when the stewardess handed me the letter. I had to go on serving, but I was dithery; I over-filled the glasses and slopped beer into the drip trays. I sneaked a look at it while my customers had their eyes down for a full house. The tone was cheerful and practical. He might have been addressing a new acquaintance.

The letter chilled me little by little, like a cold wind on a warm day. I don't know what I had expected – pleas, or vitriolic accusation, but the even tone convinced me, more finally than rancour could have done, that my marriage was over. In the same friendly spirit he offered me £3,000 to 'tide me over'. Of course I knew what this meant. He had sought legal advice in a great hurry and had been told that he stood to lose a good deal more. My first thought was that I would be stubborn and refuse to accept it. My second was that I might as well take it.

The last paragraph read: 'Please give the enclosed envelope to Jamie and wish him luck. I have sent a copy of everything on file relating to his natural parents. His grandmother has more specific information and I would suggest that he contacts her. I have included her last known address.' I had no way of telling if the 'wish him luck' was sincere or sardonic. It seemed a curious message for him to send his wife's young lover.

He had sealed the envelope, and that irritated me because I was the person who had requested the information, and he had seemingly acknowledged my right to do so. I didn't look at it until we'd dried the glasses and swabbed behind the bar and the staff were sitting down for a cigarette. Then I ripped it open. I had to know if it was good news or bad before I passed it on to Jamie, and to be honest I was curious.

The news was neither good nor bad, but it was surprising. Jamie had been born on the island of Macak, in Indonesia. At the age of three he had been removed from an orphanage by an RC priest, Padre Emanuel, and taken to the British consulate on the mainland of Kawalinggan. The British consul had issued him with documents in order that he could be flown to Britain. He had been subsequently offered up for adoption by his maternal grandmother, Mrs Elizabeth Anne Hodges, resident in Sutton Coldfield.

His original name was given as Tiago Joaquim Jesus Coelho da Silva. He was the child of married parents: João Jesus Coelho da Silva, aged 18, a forestry worker, born in Costassol, Macak, and Amy Elizabeth née Hodges, aged 19, a British subject.

I was particularly intrigued by the names. My parents had loved Portugal and all things Portuguese. We'd seen the bones of Évora, the port cellars of Gaia, the mountains of Gerês. We'd even eaten Portuguese food, octopus and chicken's claws, whether we liked it or not, and we'd tried to learn the language from tapes. I'd been much the best student, being the youngest. That was how I knew that Tiago was the Portuguese version of James, and João Coelho was John Rabbit.

The Portuguese, like the British, were once explorers and colonists. I thought that Costassol could be a corrupt form of the Portuguese for Coast of Sunshine. Costassol sounded to me like a tourist trap and I hypothesized that Amy had gone there on a package holiday, fallen in love, and got pregnant by João.

I was excited and I thought Jamie would be too. As soon as I saw him, I said, 'Do you remember telling me to go ahead and find out about your parents?'

He said warily, 'No, I don't remember saying that.'

'Well you did.'

'I must have been drunk.'

After a show of reluctance, he whisked the proffered paper from my hand. I felt sure the indifference must be feigned. He read it through two or three times and said, 'So much for the legend.'

'Tiago is the Portuguese for James. I think Macak must have been a Portuguese colony.'

He was reading his own name again, I could see him mouthing it experimentally. At length he said lightly, 'It's a bit hard to swallow, isn't it?'

'Is it? I expect that's just a first reaction.'

'Why would a married couple send their child to an orphanage?'

'They must be dead, Jamie.'

'Both of them? They were teenagers.'

I said, 'This is Indo-China we're talking about, not Britain. Surely your grandmother couldn't have given you up for adoption if your parents had been alive.'

'Then why doesn't it say so here?'

'I don't know.'

Jamie thrust the paper back at me. He smiled at me with wide-open eyes, but coldly.

'It stinks.' He flicked the paper hard with his finger-nail. 'Why does this priest go to so much trouble? Why did he send me to England anyway? What happened to my father's family?'

I felt as though I had given him a present which had turned out to be unsuitable or insulting. I said, 'I don't know. Write to your grandmother, perhaps she can tell you.'

'My grandmother! My grandmother seems to have had as little to do with me as possible. Please don't tell me she thought it was for my own good, it's so patronizing.'

He tugged open the kitchen door and I watched him climbing the steps to the garden. For a moment I wished I hadn't interfered. After all, Jamie could have had access to the same information at any time during the past four years, if he had chosen to. I had done it 'for his own good'; I had been patronizing. Nevertheless, I folded up the letter and put it in my pocket. I decided that I'd write to Jamie's grandmother, person to person, without involving Jamie. I meant to find out if she wanted to be put in touch and if she had anything useful to say.

The next day Jamie had an accident. I was standing on the front room window-sill, scraping the loose plaster from the walls, when the car pulled up outside. Jamie got out awkwardly. He was holding a carrier bag which he put down in the hall. He was the colour of cement.

'What's the matter?'

'I fell into the machine. It's OK, Xana, don't fuss, I've been to the hospital and everything is still intact.' I followed him down the hall and into the kitchen thinking, 'Don't smother him,' because he had said 'Xana, don't fuss.' I had absent-mindedly picked up the carrier bag. In it was Jamie's T-shirt, cut to shreds and stiff with dried blood.

'What happened? Where are you hurt?'

'It's only cuts and bruises, on my chest and back. I didn't have any stitches, they just X-rayed me and strapped me up.'

'Wouldn't you be better lying down?'

He had lowered himself into our one armchair.

'No, I want to sit here and have a cup of tea.'

As I passed his chair to put the pan on the fire I caressed his head and said, 'Poor love.' Jamie started to cry.

I knelt down by his chair and stroked him and kissed his wet face. When he could speak coherently, he said, 'Oh God, Xana, why did it have to happen just now?'

'It was an accident, accidents can happen any time, it wasn't your fault.'

'I needed that job so much.'

'You can go back when you're better. And if you can't, it doesn't matter all that much.'

He sobbed, 'It does matter. Now you think I'm sick. You think I'm not capable of doing a job.'

I did think he was sick, he had told me as much himself, but I said, 'No I don't, darling, of course I don't. Hush.'

I soothed and petted him until he quietened down. He said, 'Xana, I need to make love to you.'

'Not now. You're injured, you need to rest.'

He insisted. 'No, now. Please. You undo my jeans for me.'

I unzipped him very carefully and pulled his jeans down. I took my clothes off and dropped them on the mat. Then I climbed up on top of him. He was red-eyed and snuffling, he kissed me with cold damp lips and that repelled me. I had to take the more active role. I felt ridiculous bouncing up and down. At the same time we had never been more intimate.

He often said to me, 'Xana, you're a very careless and irresponsible woman. You've forgotten your cap again.' Sometimes I suspected that I did it on purpose. This time he clutched the arms of the chair and said, 'Now I'm going to give you a baby.'

I washed myself in a plastic bowl by the fire. Normally I didn't do anything so inelegant in front of Jamie. Then I fried him a piece of thick Welsh bacon. I had to leave him and run down to the club to be on time.

Towards the end of the evening Bryn Howells came in. He said: 'How's the boy?' and I said, 'He's OK. Just cuts and bruises.' He didn't listen to the answer. He demanded, 'What happened?' 'He fell into a machine at work.'

I didn't know until that moment that Bryn worked in the same factory as Jamie. He said, 'Fell in the machine? He was *fightin'* with the machine. I never seen anything like it, man, he went berserk.' He picked up his pint, shook his head at me indignantly, and took a swig. 'We thought at first he was having an asthma attack – he was clutching at Dennis and gasping. I took a look at him then: his eyes were crossed and he was dribbling at the mouth like that boy of Mansel's, the one in the wheelchair.

'Dennis said he turned his stomach, his skin felt all clammy and he had a funny smell about him, like a drowned dog. He was crying and hanging onto Dennis and Dennis was trying to shove him off. He really upset Dennis.

'Then, all of a sudden, he yells in Dennis's ear and nearly shatters his eardrum. Diawl! Next minute he's on his feet, flying across the shop. It happened so quick, nobody had a chance to stop him. He charges at the machine and starts laying into it; flailing his arms, he was, and carrying on. And the machine pulled him in, you see, it had him round the chest. Dai Thomas jumped up and switched it off before it could slash him to pieces.

'Christ! If he hadn't been cut to ribbons they'd have put a strait-jacket on him. It was all we could do to haul him off, and he's as skinny as a rat.'

He glared at me. He said truculently, 'What is it? Fits or something?'

I nodded and bent my head over the sink, ostensibly washing up glasses, but he wasn't deterred. He went on, repeating himself, shaking his head in bewilderment, and drinking his beer. Then, to my relief, he started talking to someone else.

When I got home Jamie was still sitting in the chair, and he'd let the fire go out. I propelled him up to bed; he couldn't sleep because his ribs were hurting him, and neither could I. I thought, 'As soon as I can I'll go to Bridgend library and take out some books on abnormal psychology. I'll get information about alternative treatments. I could pay, with the three thousand pounds.' As a social worker's wife I had no faith in conventiona̅ care. I knew how little was available and how ineffective it was.

The next morning Jamie was listless. He sat all day, sighing and staring up the chimney.

'What shall I make for supper? Would you like a curry?'

'I don't mind.'

'Do you want some music, Jamie? What shall I put on?'

'Whatever you like.'

As soon as I could I went to Bridgend library. There was only a handful of books in the Psychology section, and most of them didn't deal with psychiatric disorders. I took home two of them and with the help of the librarian I ordered some more. I looked at the first book on the bus. It had tiny print and was long and abstruse. I abandoned it after the first chapter. The second contained a series of case studies of psychotics. A few of the symptoms described broadly resembled Jamie's but there were no striking similarities. Nor did Jamie seem to suffer from the gross personality malfunctions common to the other patients. Over a period of time I read every book I could find on the psychoses without ever discovering what Jamie was suffering from. Neither did I discover anything definitive about the cause, nature or treatment of psychosis, or learn how to distinguish one kind from another. Some of the writers of the books admitted to a similar confusion.

Jamie's grandmother didn't reply.

Jamie's cuts were healing, but he spent all his days hunched up by the fire or lying half-clad on our mattress. He gave up washing and shaving. He gave up cleaning his teeth, too, and his mouth smelt of eggs. He wasn't interested in making love, and if I spoke to him, he answered, after a long pause, in a voice which was barely audible.

One Saturday, after scanning the local paper in the bar, I went to Caerphilly and bought twelve point-of-lay Warren pullets. I sat on three buses with the box of hens on my lap. They had been bred in a small enclosed space and were very docile. Now and again one of them would crane its neck and peer over the side of the box, briefly scanning the bus.

When I got home, I dropped the box of chickens on the floor by Jamie and lay down on the mat in pretended exhaustion. I thought, 'I can stay here all day if necessary.' I lay on the floor, Jamie stared up the chimney, and the chickens murmured to each other in astonishment. At last Jamie stood up and looked at them. Then he lifted the box and took it up to the shed. When he came back, he said, 'I'm just going over to the tip to get a bit of wood to mend the shed door; otherwise a fox could get in.' It was the longest sentence he'd spoken all week.

Later, when I was back from work, Jamie said, 'Those hens you bought are ignorant. They don't know how to roost, they don't know how to scratch. They just stand around and burble and gawp at the sky and trees. You know the man who keeps chickens on the tip, the one they call the Talking Horse? He's given me some layer's mash to start them off. They really need a rooster. We could have one with long orange hair and a green tail.'

'Why do they need a rooster?'

'To keep them in order. He jumps on their backs, like this, and he bites their necks, like this, and however independent they are they have to grovel in the dust until he's finished with them.'

He pounced on me and pushed me down onto the mat. When we had gone to bed and he was holding me, he asked,

'Why are you reading books on exorcism now?'

I had planned to evade questions like this, but I said, 'Don't you think we should look into every possibility?'

'My last girlfriend thought it was eating E numbers that was making me crazy. I used to drink a lot of orange squash at that time, she was particularly suspicious of the orange squash. Another one I had used to take me to therapy groups. She was a nurse in the mental hospital, I met her there. The Reichian groups were the most fun: lots of massage and screaming.'

He took his hand from my neck and passed it over his hair.

'Then I met someone else at one of the weekends. She was my partner in a trust-game. After, I was lying on the floor pretending to be a seed in winter and she came over and lay down beside me. Her name was Sophie. She was little and she had a sort of naked face and very short blonde hair. Her body was covered in yellow fuzz, like a peach. She had nowhere to go so I took her home with me.'

He rolled away from me, onto his back. I could tell from his voice that this anecdote wouldn't have a funny punch-line. 'We made love a lot but I don't think she really liked doing it, she just didn't know how to tell me. She said she had to go to Bath and fetch her things. She made it sound convincing but I didn't think she would come back and she didn't. After that I spent a long time looking for her. She had a lot of problems and I wanted to make sure she was all right.'

'Did you find her?'

'No.'

His little story touched me unbearably. Sophie made me sick, but I longed to be her. I wanted to talk to him about his illness and the effectiveness of the techniques he had tried, but instead I asked the question uppermost in my mind.

'Have you had a lot of relationships?'

'Of course I have, Xana, I'm twenty-two years old, although you treat me like a boy of fifteen.'

I said huffily, 'I'm sorry. I didn't realize that. I don't normally sleep with fifteen-year-olds.'

'It's just that you never seem to forget the difference in our ages. I never think about it.'

'I have to think about it. I have to bear in mind that this is only a short-term affair.'

'Why does it have to be a short-term affair?'

'Because one day you'll meet a young girl and fall in love with her.'

He sighed.

'I won't be falling in love with any young girls. I don't like young girls, they giggle and talk a lot of nonsense.'

That was the wrong answer. He should have said: 'I won't fall in love with a young girl because I'm in love with you.' I wondered how long Jamie would spend looking for me if I went missing. Something told me, even then, that I would be the one to do the searching. I wanted to ask him if he loved me, but that was probably the kind of nonsense the young girls talked. Anyway, the answer could have made no difference. I knew that I would stay in his life as long as I could, whether I was invited to the banquet of love or fed only the scrapings of his affection.

V

Jamie brought home a little cockerel which flew at me whenever I went to the toilet. I hated going out to the shed. It smelt of dried peas and the straw was squelchy – slimy-black on the underside and teeming with thin red worms.

Jamie fenced off the field with old bedsteads, wooden pallets and corrugated iron from the tip. Our innocent pullets soon grew into wily voracious birds who would tug a sandwich from my hand and sprint up the field with it, tackling one another like a rugby pack. At first they laid tiny, dirt-mottled eggs in the hedge, but they soon learned to use Jamie's boxes which he filled with curly straw from the hillside. My upstairs customers vied for the privilege of buying their eggs: the outsides were caked with droppings but the yolks were orange and viscous.

One Sunday evening, as I was leaning on the bar and listening to a live rendering of 'Don't Cry For Me, Argentina', Tim appeared, flushed and beaming and carrying a big sports bag. He greeted me facetiously. I was pleased, but appalled to see him. I had to arrange my face in a smile. To make up for it I hugged him ferociously. I said,

'How did you find me? I was going to write to you at Christmas. The house is unspeakable. It's not really fit to visit.'

'I heard you were in a squat.'

'Did you hear I was living with someone?'

'No?' he said in an inquiring tone.

The stewardess came up while we were talking and offered kindly: 'You can get off home now, Siân, if you want. We can manage.'

I wasn't sure that I wanted to go. I took Tim back with me and introduced him to Jamie. Tim said hello in a pompous voice. Jamie grinned awkwardly. Tim was wearing thick, drab-coloured cords and a diamond-patterned sweater from Marks and Spencer's, paid for, and possibly chosen, by his father. Jamie had on a matted cardigan and a tee-shirt wider than it was long. His wellingtons smelt of the chicken coop.

We took Tim on a tour of the house and showed him our bedroom. All the signs of our intimacy were there: the single mattress with a rumpled green cover, the candle on the floor, my cap

35

in a plastic case, pretending to be a powder compact. My book and reading glasses on one side of the bed, a tangle of Jamie's underclothes on the other. I shut the door on it quickly.

'And this is where you'll be sleeping. The indoor snowstorms are an unusual feature of the guest bedroom.'

Jamie said, 'Xana thinks we should do it up but I think we should preserve its original character.'

Tim laughed coarsely to cover his unease. We went back to the kitchen and he politely declined our single armchair. 'Jamie, why don't you show Tim the chickens?'

He gave me a droll look, shooting his eyebrows up and down. I said, 'Do you like chickens, Tim?'

'Roast?'

'No, to share a toilet with. Jamie will show you.'

'OK.'

As they went up the steps I heard Jamie say, 'If she says we've got to look at the chickens we'd better look at the chickens.' Tim laughed again.

I wiped my brow and fidgeted nervously around the kitchen. I wanted to talk to Tim in comfort and make him welcome; I sensed his embarrassment and hurt feelings. I wished I could send Jamie out on his own for an hour or two but instead I suggested that we all go down to the pub. The boys walked ahead of me down the hill. Tim was asking political questions about squatters' rights.

We had a pint of beer each. Tim insisted on buying. After a while the conversation perished. I became aware that Jamie was craning his neck to look out through the curtain onto the street. After a few minutes I touched Jamie's shoulder and said his name. He made a loud noise, somewhere between a groan and a whimper. I wasn't alarmed, because Jamie played the fool so often. I caught hold of his shoulder and twisted him round.

The face was not Jamie's. The jaw was hanging loose, the eyes were brutish and malign. He gave a mighty shudder and heaved himself up, catching the table with his knee; the table overturned and our ashtray and all our glasses hit the floor. There were a few ironical cheers from the other corner of the saloon.

He reached the bar in a couple of unsteady bounds. He hung onto it with one arm, holding himself up. With the other he swept it clear of glasses. He had seized something, a beer bottle I think, and this he lobbed ineptly at the mirror. The publican whirled around the corner of the bar, protesting, and at the same time a customer from the annexe advanced on Jamie, brandishing a snooker cue. I said to Tim, 'Let's get him out, quick.'

We took one arm each. Jamie looked at us blankly but suffered himself to be led. He was breathing fast through his nose, like a boxer.

We marched him out into the street. The publican and a couple of customers followed us to watch. Jamie made as if to lurch into the main road and Tim imprisoned his left arm. Jamie pulled his right arm free of mine and swung at him, catching him a blow in the mouth. Tim has always been frail and slight and this was more than I could bear to watch. I shouted angrily, 'Let him go! Just let him go!'

Jamie lumbered out into the middle of the road, causing a car to pull up sharply. He stopped and leaned on the bonnet, staring in at the driver, then hammered on the windscreen with his fists. I could hear the driver expostulating. Then he blundered off down a dark side-street which could only lead to the river or the mountain.

Tim said in amazement, 'What's the matter with him? Is he drunk?'

'No, he's only had a pint.'

'Shall I go after him?'

'No.'

'What shall we do?'

'I don't know, Tim. I suppose we'd better go home.'

We walked back home and sat in the kitchen. We were both shaken, and Tim kept pressing his fingers to his lip. I explained as best I could about Jamie. After an hour or two I brought the cider out of the pantry and made fried egg sandwiches. We drank and made an effort to talk and joke as we would normally have done, but we were both listening out for Jamie and hoping he wouldn't come. Once the front door blew open and we both leapt out of our seats.

'What was that?'

'Just the wind, I think.'

When it got very late I sent Tim up to lie on the mattress and I lay down on the mat by the kitchen fire. I don't think I slept. Jamie didn't come home and I was very glad of that.

In the morning we got up early and I lit the fire with the aid of some lollipop sticks I found in the gutter outside. We had a cup of tea then we set out through the dark. I went down the valley with Tim and saw him onto his train. He said,

'Please be careful, Mum. Please.'

It was eleven o'clock when I reached the house. The chickens were still shut up and I was ashamed that I'd forgotten them. When I opened the shed door Jamie was there, lying in the straw.

I wasn't afraid of him. I sat down by him and said, 'Hello. Why don't you come into the house now and I'll make you some tea.'

He shook his head. He said in a low voice:

'I shall have to go.'

All night I had been dreading that he would come home and now I dreaded that he would leave.

'Why do you have to go?'

He turned away his face and said, 'Because I am just an embarrassment and a handicap.'

I took his hand. It lay inert in mine. I said, 'No you aren't. I don't want you to go, Jamie.'

'I don't want to go either.' His eyes filled with tears. He said, 'I don't mean to be pathetic. But I don't want to get locked up again.'

'Listen , don't worry about the pub. I'll go round this morning and offer to pay for the glasses.'

'But how long can we go on like that? It's getting worse. Ever since that letter, it's been like living through a nuclear winter. The weather is always dark and menacing, everything is poisoned.'

I felt dismayed and guilty. I said, 'I'm so sorry, Jamie. I thought it would help. I should never have interfered.'

He said, 'I've been thinking that instead of using all my energy to fight him and keep him out, maybe I ought to just let him in and try to find out who he is and what it is he wants.'

This was an experiment I was not prepared to make. Although I'd talked to Tim about Jamie's 'delusion', last night I had shared it. I felt that I had just met Zed for the first time and I was sure that I didn't want to meet him again. I remembered the noise, like a donkey's hee-haw, that had come out of Jamie. I shuddered and said, 'I don't think he can talk, Jamie. And whatever he wants, it isn't anything good.'

'No, I know it isn't. But I can't go on like this.'

'Perhaps it's all to do with your parents and whatever happened to you when you were little.'

'I know that's what you think. But I can't remember anything at all before I came to England.'

'But perhaps that's because you can't bear to remember!'

He said drily, 'Yes, perhaps it is. You don't give up, do you, Xana. You want me to write to my grandmother.'

I winced and confessed, 'I *have* written to her, but she hasn't answered. I checked her address with Directory Enquiries but they said they didn't have a subscriber of that name.'

'When did you write?'

'About three weeks ago. It was on the day of your accident.'

'When is your period due?'

'My period?' I said in surprise. 'It's about two days overdue, but that's not unusual.'

'No, I'm sure it's not unusual at all.'

I said, 'Would you mind very much if I was pregnant?'

I said it as if nothing depended on the answer, but there was a hissing in my ears like the hollow sound you hear on the long distance telephone wire. Jamie said, 'No. I want us to have a baby.'

We made love lying on the dirty, prickly straw, with chickens scratching and warbling around us. I thought, 'Only last night I hoped I might never see Jamie again, and now, for the first time, I'm beginning to believe we might have a future together.'

On the way to the club I called in at the pub and offered to pay the landlord for the broken glasses. He was not disagreeable. He took the money, but he was quite sure that he didn't want Jamie in his pub again. When I got to the club there was a letter waiting for me. It was from Philip and it contained a cheque for £3,000.

All evening I thought about what I could do with the money. I could buy a camper-van. I could buy Jamie a leather jacket. I could buy him a motorbike too, for that matter. I could take him on holiday. When I got home I said, 'I've got my cheque for three thousand pounds. What do you think we should do with it?'

He was sitting by the fire, looking strained. He said apathetically, 'I don't know. Do whatever you like.'

'Well I think we should go on holiday: somewhere very warm and out of the way where they don't celebrate Christmas all through December.'

'Sounds like Macak.'

'Macak! Are you serious? Would you really go there?'

'What else is there left to try? But it's your money, and your holiday. We must find out first if it's the kind of place you want to go.'

I said, 'OK,' but I had already decided. I thought, 'I'll go and get the tickets tomorrow before he changes his mind.'

VI

Before we went to Macak we paid Jamie's grandmother a visit. We bought Jamie the clothes which I considered suitable: a heavy wool jacket, a dark green denim shirt and suede boots. I trimmed his hair and he shaved and washed carefully in our plastic bowl by the fire. The scars on his back were purple and puffy, but by the time he was dressed he looked like a grandson that no old lady would be ashamed of. In the event it was all wasted time.

We took the train to Birmingham New Street, emerging from a network of sooty tunnels into an underground station smelling of pickled onions. We took a little diesel out to the prosperous suburbs. The house had changed owners, but the new occupant directed us next door to a neighbour who knew Mrs Hodges. We had decided not to reveal Jamie's relationship, in case Mrs Hodges didn't want it known, so we prevaricated.

The neighbour gave us tea in china cups. She said, 'Mrs Hodges has got the what-do-you-call-it, premature ageing. They don't know what causes it, do they?'

Jamie said, 'Too much tea.'

'Too much tea? Is that what it is? Well, I don't know.'

She ate a biscuit, dropping the crumbs into her lap between her splayed legs. 'I've been in to see her a couple of times but she doesn't really know me. She might be glad to see some young faces. Her grandchildren are all out in Canada, but perhaps you know that.'

Jamie said: 'No, we didn't know that.'

Jamie's grandmother looked very thin and wobbly but she smiled at us with big perfect false teeth. She said to Jamie, 'Hello, dear, have you got a ciggie?', and Jamie said, 'Hello, grandma.'

She held out her arms and we both kissed her cheek. She seemed to be expecting a present, so I gave her a half-used bottle of perfume. On the chair beside her was a sponge-bag, from which she took a picture of a middle-aged man. She said, 'He wasn't a handsome man but he had beautiful hands. Do you remember how nice his hands were?'

I said that I did.

Two girls in overalls brought in her tea. It was egg and cress sandwiches, with a little jam smeared on top. One of them explained, 'She'll only eat it if it's red, otherwise she just pulls it apart.'

At one point Mrs Hodges said quite clearly, 'Where's Amy? I haven't seen her for ages,' but a moment afterwards she asked, 'Where's Mother? Shall I put the boys to bed?'

As we were leaving she said accusingly, 'You must have been past this door a hundred times and not dropped in to see me,' and Jamie said, 'We're living in Wales now, grandma, but we'll try and come more often.' We kissed her again. When we were outside I said to Jamie, 'What do you feel like doing now?'

He said, 'I think we should go to a café and have a good strong cup of tea.'

Booking a holiday in Costassol did not prove as easy as I had anticipated. No one in Bridgend was able to help me, so I took a train to Swansea and visited the big travel agents there. They had never heard of Costassol and they had no information about the island of Macak. They gave me the address and telephone number of a small agency organizing adventure holidays and expeditions through the rain forest by jeep. This turned out to be an informal, amateurish concern operating from the back room of a cycle shop. They had never heard of Macak either, but between punctures we looked for it on a map. There were a number of specks in the sea off Kawalinggan – some near the shore, like bathers' heads, some sticking up like reefs in mid-ocean. They were all too small to be labelled. The boy said, 'I think your best bet would be to buy a ticket to Kawalinggan, and then take a ferry out to Macak.'

I went back to the big travel agents and I booked two weeks in Kawalinggan in a hotel depicted in the brochure. The picture showed a blue swimming pool surrounded by palm trees, lounging women in bikinis and smiling waiters in sarongs. The smiling waiters were carrying hollowed-out pineapples festooned with paper maypoles and sprigs of herb. The lounging women had flowers behind their ears. The hotel itself looked exactly like any other four-star hotel and boasted the same facilities.

While I was in Swansea I bought myself a Benetton sweater and I bought Jamie an Iceberg shirt. I phoned Linda. She said, 'I wish I had a gorgeous young man and money to dress him up.'

I had to revise my hypothesis about Amy. She hadn't gone to Macak on a package holiday. I said to Jamie, 'I expect she met João when he was visiting Kawalinggan.'

'She probably said, "Hello, dear, have you got a ciggie?"'

'You once accused me of being prejudiced, but actually you're a social snob yourself.'

'Yes. That's why I like you, Xana. I need a woman of taste, to take me to places like this.'

He was studying the brochure. I said defensively, 'We probably shan't spend any time there; we'll be on Macak. But a package deal with accommodation thrown in is always cheaper than making your own way. And we get a free week because December is monsoon time.'

Jamie laughed. He said, 'Don't forget to pack the wellingtons.'

Secretly I was looking forward to a stay in a hotel, to meals in the Bamboo Restaurant as a complete contrast to blackened bacon and wallpaper tea, warm showers instead of a greasy bowl, carpets underfoot instead of grit and broken tiles and chicken turds.

Before we left, Jamie hid his music machine under a floorboard in the middle room. He gave his chickens and a sack of whole corn to the Talking Horse. I wanted him to put coloured rings on their legs so that he could reclaim them but he didn't do it, and because of that I wondered if we were coming back to stay. The local men had started to treat Jamie with a sneering jocularity, in the manner of policemen on the beat. The local women sometimes offered me their old acrylic dresses and plastic shoes. The teenage boys called after us in the street and once, when we were at the top of the garden, they burst in through the back door and stampeded round the house.

I was relieved to be going; at the same time, I was sorry. I had grown so used to living in the lamp-lit kitchen that the daylight seemed harsh to my eyes. I'd grown accustomed to the single mattress I shared with Jamie; even in our sleep we signalled our intentions and turned in unison, like dancers. I'd come to enjoy our own eggs and the hot white bread from Teg's. I would put it under my jumper to keep me warm as I struggled against the sleet-laden wind blowing down from the mountain.

We got on one of the big buses that ply the valley. I was half awake and shivering. The morning was so grey and cold that I felt nothing but foreboding. I carried my green-trimmed black bag and Jamie had a space-age rucksack containing stiff new jeans and T-shirts pinned to pieces of cardboard.

We travelled all afternoon by British Rail. Jamie read the papers and I lay back on the opposite seat and tried to warm my cold

43

stockinged feet between his thighs. The plane was warmer but considerably more cramped. We ate obediently at scheduled intervals, like infants in a maternity ward. The menu seemed inappropriate; we were served smoked mackerel and white wine in the early hours of the morning when I longed for coffee and toast.

When we touched down at Kawalinggan, blue and red lightning flickered in a low grey sky. We were enveloped by a warm fug as we walked down the little covered corridor between the plane and the airport building. It was rush hour and the hotel bus could barely crawl through the streets for the throngs of waving, wide-smiling youths who pressed against the bus windows offering cigarettes and bottled water. We drove out through shanty-towns into the countryside, sounding our horn at the little cart-pushers, bicycle rickshaws and scurrying workers.

At our hotel we were greeted by a smiling employee in a sarong who carried our luggage to our suite. He was smiling in expectation of a tip. Jamie ate the fruit in our complimentary basket and played with the light dimmer while I took a shower. Then we went out on the balcony to listen to the cicadas and feel the heat of the air. Afterwards we went to dance at the disco. It was my idea. We wandered out under a glittering multi-faceted globe which sent little puff-balls of light bowling across the floor. Jamie was a supple dancer and took up a lot of floor space. My feet and ankles had swollen on the plane and he made me feel clumsy, like the middle-aged women at the club on a Sunday night, who hopped steadily from one foot to the other, moving their arms in marching rhythm. I soon realized that Jamie was exaggerating his movements, parodying the dancers he had seen on TV. He meant to amuse me or embarrass me; with Jamie I was never sure which. The women watched him openly. The men threw him closed and critical glances.

When Jamie went out to the toilet a girl spoke to him. She had very short stylish hair with an improbable cerise tint. As he came back she spoke to him again and this time he turned and answered her. I looked at them and I sipped my drink and then I looked at them again. Sideways on they were as slim as a pair of ferrets. Jamie was posing, with one hand in the back pocket of his new jeans. The girl was swaying slightly on her high heels and undulating her body. I thought, 'I'll wait five minutes and then I'll leave.' Five minutes seemed a long time. I sat staring at my face in the bar mirror; it wore the stony, disapproving look I use to repress badly-behaved children. I rubbed my puffy feet together and drank with quick, angry sips. The wine tasted like cider vinegar. Then Jamie came back and said in the manner of an over-attentive waiter, 'Can I get you another drink, madam?'

'No. This is German. It tastes like apple juice and it's full of chemical additives.'

The red-haired girl came boldly to the bar. She turned her stool so she could watch Jamie. I said bitingly, 'Your friend is over there, don't you want to talk to her again?'

Jamie glanced at her in the mirror. 'Why should I want to do that?'

'Well, she's about your age, and she fancies you.'

'So I ought to go outside and have sex with her?'

In fact the girl was not very pretty; she had pitted skin and a short upper lip. I said, 'She's rather coarse-looking at close quarters.'

'She can't help it, she's Australian. Do you want to dance again?'

'No, not to this computerized music.'

'What do you want to do?'

'I want to go to bed.'

Jamie said, 'OK.'

He put his hand lightly on my neck as we left the disco. He said in my ear, 'I warn you, Xana, if you bite me tonight I'm going to bite you back.'

He didn't glance at the red-haired girl.

The next day Jamie tried his hand at water-skiing. That kept him occupied for most of the day and used up most of the spending money I had allotted for our two-week stay. I lay on the beach and watched him through our brand-new binoculars. After dinner we went to see the mythical shadow-show in the courtyard of our hotel. The play was enacted by two-dimensional leather puppets on sticks, bobbing and nodding across a lighted screen in silhouette. The villain entered, heralded by a series of drum-rolls, like the comic turn on a variety show.

It was a history of rape; the heroine was flung down and violated to the frenzied beating of a gong. A female voice was raised in protest and lamentation. Her avenger appeared, a battle-scarred warrior with an oversized dagger in his tucked-up skirt. He sprang, shrieking, into the air and swooped down upon his opponent, clawing and scrabbling with his long, jointed arms.

The adversaries flew at each other, uttering harsh cries. They clanged together in combat. From behind the screen came the fierce clashing of cymbals. I looked at Jamie and noticed that he was staring down at the flag-stones. I whispered, 'Are you OK?'

'No.'

'Come on, let's go.'

We were in the middle of the second row but we squeezed out in a panic, trampling heedlessly on people's feet. We hurried through the courtyard to the gate, where a hotel employee was handing out flowers to latecomers. I held Jamie by the hand. My contingency plan was to take him to the most secluded part of the beach, where there was little damage he could do and where he would attract least notice. He came with me amenably. We sat down on the artificial sand. His breathing and posture seemed normal.

'Are you all right?'

'No. I think my hearing may be permanently impaired.'

'What happened? Did the show bring back any memories?'

'Yes. I once watched two children fighting with lollipops. It reminded me of that.'

I laughed, exasperated, but I sensed that the performance had unsettled him. I said, 'They seem to be a smiling, friendly people. Why do they put on such crude, ferocious plays?'

'Perhaps they are a crude, ferocious people and the smiling is put on.'

'Do you think so?'

'I don't know. Go back and watch it if you want.'

'I don't, especially.'

I did want to watch the show, but I didn't want to leave Jamie cruising the discos and young people's entertainments on his own. I felt a little peeved. I thought that Jamie's behaviour since we came to Kawalinggan had been inconsiderate and ungrateful. I said, 'I think we ought to go to Macak tomorrow and not waste any more time and money here.'

'We could go camping instead if you like, it would be a lot cheaper.'

That made me feel uncomfortable. I thought, 'I've been grudging the money I've spent on Jamie, expecting him to give good value for it. Perhaps it's just as well I don't have much.' I said, 'No, I want to go to Macak. But it may take more than a couple of days to find Padre Emanuel or someone who knows your family. I think we should start now.'

I also wanted to put some nautical miles between Jamie and the pink-haired girl. She had appeared briefly on the beach that morning, her face lardy white, her mouth plastered with lurid, sun-blocking lipstick.

Next morning we inquired about Macak at the hotel Information desk. They told us it was one of the smaller and more distant islands and so the ferry service was infrequent. According to their timetable there was no sailing scheduled for the next two weeks. Jamie was undaunted. He said, 'There must be someone who'll take us. I'll go and chat up the boatmen on the beach.'

We had no language problem on Kawalinggan; even the street-traders, peddling their puppets and fake Cartier watches, could speak English after a fashion.

Jamie came back an hour later. He said, 'I went for a beer with the little speed-pilot from yesterday. He said the island's real name is Macacoh Silveng Iah. It means Wild Monkey Island.'

I said, 'It's bloody awful Portuguese.'

'He says there's nothing on it but wild monkeys. He wouldn't believe I wanted to go there. I kept asking him to take me and he kept on laughing and shaking his head. Finally he said he'd bring his friend to the beach bar this evening. His friend has got a powerful boat and he might take us, for a price.'

We went down to the beach at sunset. A low-grade employee was raking the sand; another was wading through the water with a big net, trawling for rubbish. The pilot and his friend appeared with suspicious alacrity. The friend had well-oiled wavy hair and a short-sleeved shirt with a pattern of creepers and large red flowers. His name was Ib. He flashed us a smile and shook our hands but his mouth turned down sarcastically at one corner. He named his price, a stupendous amount of rupiahs.

Ib agreed to take us to Macak in his motor-boat, and he told us how fast it could go. He said that he would leave us at the port and come back for us five days later. He knew the island and he drew us a map on the back of a cigarette packet. I watched his hands; he wore a complicated watch and the watch reassured me that he was competent to handle a powerful boat. We studied the map; there was a direct road from the port into Costassol, or a track along the mountainside which was steeper but quicker. I asked if there was a bus and both men exploded with laughter.

We asked Ib where we could stay. He said the people of Costassol were Christians and were friendly to strangers; they would

47

certainly offer us food and shelter. I should take some presents but I shouldn't offer them money. They didn't speak English but they all spoke Portuguese, as well as Bahasa and their own particular island language which resembled Japanese. I asked what kind of presents I should take. Ib said 'toffees' and his friend said 'monkey-nuts'. They laughed again and banged us on the back.

When they had gone we sat and stared out to sea for a while. I said gloomily, 'I knew a man who visited some primitive people in Borneo. They gave him bony river fish to eat and then they expected him to sing and dance for them.'

Jamie said, 'We'll rehearse a couple of numbers in our hotel room tonight.'

'Do you think Ib can be trusted? He could leave us there and not come back.'

'I think he can be trusted to come back for the second half of his money.'

We started ambling slowly along the beach. Jamie said, 'What I wonder is why I have to keep swallowing malaria tablets and you don't.'

'I'll tell you by the end of the week.'

'For sure?'

'Yes.'

We didn't go back to the hotel, we went down into the village. On the way we were accosted by traders and taxi-drivers and menaced by slinking dogs. We had dinner in one of the many restaurants catering for foreign visitors. Jamie had a steak which he insisted was either dog or buffalo. During the meal he said, 'If we're pregnant, shall we do it all properly?'

'What do you mean?'

'Do you want to get divorced and marry me? We can if you like.'

I had fantasized about this moment. In the fantasies I had always said yes. I looked at him and I thought, 'In ten years' time Jamie will still be an attractive young man, and I shall be a fast-fading menopausal woman. If he's married to me he will feel trapped and guilty and I shall never know where he is.' So I procrastinated, wanting to go on pretending that it was possible.

'Shall we get the next five days over first, and then talk about it?'

Jamie nodded. He said, 'Tell me one thing.'

'What?'

'Do you *want* to marry me?'

Tears came to my eyes. I said, 'Yes, very much.'

We walked back to the hotel. Jamie put his arm round me and rubbed his face on mine. At length he said, 'If I have food poisoning tomorrow we shan't be able to go.'

'Is that why you ate the dog?'

A group of Chinese musicians were staring at us balefully from the floor of the hotel lobby where they squatted in front of their instruments. We stayed and listened for a while, then I went into the shop and bought some bags of toffees. I also bought a cassette-recording of the Chinese musicians. I thought, 'I won't play it often, I'll just play it when I want to remember tonight.'

We gave in our passports and plane tickets and travellers' cheques at the reception desk and saw them locked away in a box for safe-keeping. Then we booked an early call because we had to be on the beach by sunrise, which was six a.m. We went up to bed and made love very slowly. I think we were both nervous. We were overawed by the magnitude of the adventure we were undertaking. As it turned out, we were totally unprepared for it.

VII

Neither of us slept well. We were in the twenty-four-hour coffee bar by five a.m., drinking coffee and eating pre-soaked muesli with lumps of mango and papaya. Ib was waiting for us on the beach, his smile gleaming in the dark. A young boy paddled us all out to the motor-boat in a pleasure canoe. The boat was small but jaunty; she looked like a new Matchbox toy. We left Kawalinggan harbour at dawn.

The temperature on deck was tolerable till about eleven o'clock, when we retired below. In the little cabin there was a small battery-fan and there were cans of fizzy orange and cola in a bucket of melted ice, drinks which I normally despise, but for which I now discovered an insatiable craving. In the late afternoon we put in, briefly, at Weh Tuluk and Ib recounted to us the bloody history of the island, which had once been a Dutch possession. Having rid themselves of the colonial oppressors, the natives had turned to genocide and fought each other in a protracted civil war.

I asked if there had been unrest on Macak and he said no, it had all been amicable. The Portuguese had sent in their missionaries ahead of them and the natives had been accepting. They had simply grafted the new religion and culture onto the old, interbred with the 'conquerors' and translated their old names into Portuguese. The Portuguese had left in the end because they didn't really want the island, but the natives continued to believe Macak was a Portuguese colony. He went ashore at Weh Tuluk and brought back bottled water, biscuits and fleshy green figs.

After dark we turned down the little oil lamp and tried to sleep, sharing a bunk designed for one standard-sized Indonesian. My cramped-up leg developed a spontaneous twitch and Jamie grumbled continuously, 'Stop kicking me. Stop sticking to me, Xana, it's like sleeping with a boiled chicken.'

Before dawn I crawled up on deck to feel the sea breeze and Ib told me we were approaching Macak. He boasted that it took considerable expertise to land. We had to circumnavigate the island, describing a wide curve, by-passing whirlpools and a stretch of sea where the water boiled and spurted up in jets. I listened incredulously – it sounded like a tale borrowed from the *Odyssey*. Ib explained that Macak was a volcanic island with active geysers in the sea bed. He said that sometimes ready-poached eels and turtles floated in to shore.

I stayed up on deck while we made a smooth circuit of the island and I watched the steam rising from the water. Then the boat swung round and sped in to port. Presently it slowed and chugged gently towards the jetty, where Ib tied up. I went to wake Jamie, who was sleeping soundly. We put the remainder of the biscuits and water into the rucksack and strapped it on Jamie's back and then we climbed out onto a ladder. Ib called a cheerful goodbye and turned the nose of his boat towards the patch of white steam on the horizon.

The port consisted only of the jetty and a single low building on the waterfront with no lights showing. We walked towards the shore. We were in a dark, buzzing, humid place with a smell of stagnant water. Jamie sat down on the glinting black shingle and rubbed his eyes. He said, 'Jesus, this is eerie.'

I asked curiously, 'Have you been here before?'

'Only in my worst nightmares.'

The air was clammy but I saw that he was shivering and I gripped his hand. He said, 'I wish we hadn't come. I hate this place, it scares me sick.'

'It'll be OK when the sun comes up. It's nearly half-past four already. Shall we try and find the road? It'd be better than sitting here.'

The track was not hard to find. It began behind the port building. There was no doubt about which direction we should take; our track led east and the other led directly up the mountain. I said, 'Now let's find the bus stop and look at the timetable.'

He didn't respond. He said, 'This is it, Xana, the road I told you about. It's long and lonely and you walk down it in the dark, the sky is clinging all round you, and then something creeps up and attacks ...'

I said, 'Jamie! It's like any other road in the dark when you've just woken up and you're tired and on unknown territory.'

They were empty words. I knew what Jamie was afraid of: of Zed, and the nightmare which had become a daymare, and which might turn real on this island. There was no way of reassuring him.

We started walking. I said cheerily, 'If we come to a transport café we'll have the full English breakfast, and a strong cup of tea. Or perhaps your other grandmother will make us one when we get to Costassol.'

He didn't make the expected joke about ciggies. He said tiredly, 'You're always so optimistic, Xana,' and after that we walked in silence.

As the sun came up, the mountain turned swiftly from black, to grey, to the jubilant green of little seedlings. It was tamed, right to the top, neatly marked out in terraces and sown with rice plants. To our right were densely forested hills, the trees crowding each other out like jostling children. Birds, or perhaps monkeys, were waking up, whooping and howling fiercely to one another. We stopped to drink some tepid water. Jamie said, 'I think we're coming to the village. Look.'

Ahead of us was a steep flight of steps, a couple of hundred, cut into the hillside, and on the other side of the track was a log bridge across a little pond with red fish swimming in it. We soon came to a patch of bare dry earth the size of a football pitch. In the corner was a stage, or bandstand of the kind you often see in Portuguese villages, and all around it were thatched wooden huts with verandas. I thought, 'This is where Jamie was born.' I asked,

'Do you recognize it?' and he said, 'No, not any more than you do.'

Outside one of the houses a woman was winnowing grain in a big basket. She stopped when she saw us and I called out a polite greeting in Portuguese. She stood gripping her basket and averting her face as if overcome by embarrassment. Presently children came tumbling out of the houses, some goggle-eyed, some hanging back coyly, soon followed by the adults. The bravest approached and stood in a semi-circle confronting us, the others watched from a safe distance.

I opened a bag of toffees and handed them out to the children. They asked me my name, how old I was, how many children I had and whether I was a Christian. One little girl told me that Doutor Xico and 'Stora Rute were Conquerors like me. The adults laughed, so I did too. Another child reached out curiously and felt the dark fuzz on Jamie's legs. I explained, 'He doesn't talk.' The young women edged closer, some smiling, some giggling, some bent double with laughter. They fingered my clothes and one handed me a little knife. It was a basic little knife which she said was for cutting rice; she signed that I should give her something in return. I opened the rucksack to take out some more bags of toffees but she spied the new blue and green striped sweater I

53

had bought in Swansea and took a fancy to it. I wanted to keep the sweater but I let her take it. The other women began to cluster round my bag as if it was Father Christmas's sack so I strapped it up again in a hurry.

I had been half-expecting them to look Portuguese, but they were much tinier and they were scrawny and skimpily-clad. Most of the children were naked. They had small broad faces with flat noses and curvaceous mouths. The women were smiling but the men had fierce, impassive stares. A little boy had incongruous light blue eyes and another had matted, honey-coloured hair. They spoke in an oddly syncopated Portuguese with glottal stops. They didn't stress one syllable and swallow the next as the Portuguese do, thereby making their language virtually unintelligible to foreigners; they gave each syllable equal weight, even the final vowel. They spoke Portuguese like Welsh cockneys.

Jamie was letting the children look through his binoculars. Clipped to his belt he had a key-ring with a little torch attached. He gave it to a little boy who was fiddling with it. The other children scowled and held out their hands; we had to pacify them with toffees. Jamie said to me, 'Ask if Padre Emanuel is here.'

I spoke to one of the young women, but she was too shy to answer and covered her face with her hands. Instead one of the men answered. He said that Padre Emanuel had gone to heaven. I translated for Jamie. He said, 'I suppose that's only to be expected.'

'Shall I ask him about your family?'

'Yes, go on.'

I said, 'My friend was born in this village. He has come here to look for his family.'

Their glances flickered speculatively between my face and Jamie's; they murmured incredulously to each other. The man who had spoken to us was small, and the flesh on his face had shrunk into hard ridges, but he had a strong chest and a resonant voice. He said, 'What is his name?'

'His name is Tiago Silva.'

I had their full attention. All the nudging and wiggling and whispering had ceased. Only the children were unaffected. They went on chasing each other between their parents' legs, swinging on their mothers' skirts. One little girl was about to put a toffee in her mouth but her mother smacked it from her hand and it fell in the dust. The child yelled.

The man who had spoken before made a noise between a snort and a spit. He jerked his hand at Jamie and said contemptuously, 'That is not him!'

If you went to Lisbon and walked up and down the Rua Augusta calling for Tiago Silva, you would have four or five volunteers within the hour. I thought I understood the problem; it was a case of mistaken identity. To resolve the confusion, I said, 'His name is Tiago Joaquim Jesus Coelho da Silva.'

The spokesman jerked up his chin and tossed his head. He demanded roughly, 'Who is his father?'

'His father is João Jesus Coelho da Silva, his mother is an Englishwoman.'

Even the little children stopped moving and stared, poking at their gums. The women's hands fluttered rapidly around their faces. One said faintly,

'*Ninguém*. Nobody.'

The girl who had taken my sweater thrust it back into my hands, disappearing quickly into the ranks.

'There is no such person!' He chewed on the lining of his mouth for a moment then said aggressively, 'How did you come here?'

'By boat.'

'To the port?'

'Yes.'

He narrowed his eyes.

'Go back there.'

When we didn't move he shouted ferociously, 'We don't know him. You can't come here. Go away.'

Jamie didn't need a translation. He said, 'Come on, let's go.'

As we walked two missiles landed behind us. He said disbelievingly, 'Are they throwing stones?'

'No, it was your key-ring, and what looks like a leg of lamb.'

'A leg of lamb! Pick it up, Xana. Ib said they were hospitable.'

'I expect there'll be a hail of toffees next.'

I picked up the key-ring. We laughed frantically. We laughed for about five minutes. I could hardly speak or breathe for laughing. It was manic laughter; I was not amused. At length Jamie said, 'If we'd been ordinary tourists do you think we'd have done better?'

'Yes.'

'It was my father's name, wasn't it? He is definitely *persona non grata*.'

I said, 'I'm not sure. They said they didn't know him.'

'Well I think they did. Where are we going?'

'I don't know. We'd better camp out, hadn't we? We've got bottled water and biscuits and lots of toffees.'

'But we haven't got a tent. We'll be eaten alive by mosquitoes and it's beginning to look like rain. There must be another village somewhere on this fucking island.'

In the end we decided to go back to the port and look for another road. The sky was overcast but we were ready to expire from heat exhaustion. We zig-zagged ponderously along the track, taking it in turns to carry the rucksack. Jamie soaked his T-shirt in bottled water and tied it round his forehead. I took off my drenched underclothes and stuffed them in the bag. I kept wiping my brow and neck and bosom with baby-wipes. Jamie said, 'You can't complain, Xana, you said you wanted to come somewhere warm and out of the way.'

When we got to the port I said, 'Do you see inside the building? I think it's a shop. Shall we go and look?'

It was more of a warehouse than a shop; nothing deliberately tempted the eye. At one end sat a very elderly and infirm Chinese. We clumped up and down the bare boards, poring over the rolls of batik cloth, poking into boxes of wooden figures packed in shavings, playing with sets of bamboo pipes which clattered together and chimed huskily. I said to Jamie, 'Shall I talk to the man?' He said resignedly, 'If you must.'

'Good day, Senhor. Is the Senhor from Costassol?' He considered, then shook his head.

'My friend was born on this island. He doesn't talk. His name is Tiago Silva. His father was João Jesus Coelho da Silva. He is looking for his family. Do you know where we can find them?'

He reflected for a long time, as though I'd asked him to voice an opinion on some obscure and baffling paradox. Finally he shook his head.

Jamie said: 'OK. I can follow. Ask him if there's another village near here.'

The old man spoke. He said that the village of Yogung lay inland to the north west; we could reach it by midday.

I asked him if he knew where we could stay the night. He got up very slowly and walked to the door, then he grasped my arm and pointed up the mountain. He said if we followed the track we would come eventually to a pilgrim's bothy. Everything was there: lamps and oil and matches, rugs and firewood, and there was water nearby.

We debated whether to head for Yogung or toil up the mountain. We decided to make for the shelter because we thought, mistakenly, that it would be nearer than the village. When we had been climbing steadily for an hour or more Jamie said thoughtfully, 'I bet there'll be a good view of the island from the top.'

'From the top! You don't think the shelter's going to be at the top?'

'Well, I've been thinking: what on earth would we need rugs and firewood for unless we're going up so high that it's much cooler?'

I said, 'Oh God!' and flung myself down by the side of the track. There was a good view of the port building, the turgid grey sea, and the foaming green forest. Jamie said, 'When we get up a bit higher we should be able to see Costassol.'

'I don't particularly want to see Costassol.'

'Well I do. I want to work out the quickest way to get there.'

I said, disbelievingly, 'You're not going back there, surely!'

'I am,' he said firmly. 'Did you notice the church behind the houses?'

I had seen it, a little white, square built, Portuguese-type church, lacking only the patterned blue tiles and big green bell. 'Next to it there's a cemetery and the graves have headstones. I want to see if my parents are buried there.'

He looked at my face and said, 'Don't be miserable, you don't have to come.'

'I don't want you to go either.'

'Don't worry, I'll go after dark and I won't let them see me. I'll be perfectly all right.' He added reasonably, 'We can't come all this way and then go home without finding out anything at all, can we?'

'No.'

'It was your idea, remember.'

'Yes. But I didn't mean us to go off on an adventure, like the Five Find-outers. I just thought that it would be good for you to confront the Indonesian half of yourself; I thought it might help you to understand how the split occurred.'

Jamie chewed on a seed-head, twisting his lips to one side.

'I see. You think I'm schizoid. You think Zed is a split-off part of me.'

'Schizoid is just a word, isn't it? Just a way of talking.'

'Schizoid is not just a word and it isn't a way of talking. Xana, if we are going to stay together you had better understand one thing. I am not schizoid and Zed is not a split-off part of me. If you don't understand that, it's a waste of time trying to tell you anything.'

He had never been angry with me before. I wanted to say that I believed him but I felt like an agnostic compelled to recite the creed. I said, 'When I saw Zed, at the pub, I felt as you do, that he was a separate entity. But my reason told me he couldn't be.'

'What does your reason tell you he is?'

'The embodiment of your anger, the resentment you feel against your parents for abandoning you.' I added quickly, 'But I don't have any answers. I'm not saying it's true.'

He sighed.

'All I do know is that you were born on this island, and half of you, half your genes, half your ancestry, half your rhythms, are Indonesian, and I don't think you should go through life denying half of who you are.'

Jamie said, 'Do you remember the puppet show?'

'Yes, vividly.'

'It stirred up something in me that I didn't know was there. You know, I always thought I believed in non-violence. Anyone brought up by Brenda and Roland would have to be a pacifist. We weren't church-goers but we adhered to Christian principles; we had the worst of both worlds, I suppose. We practised self-denial and non-retaliation in this life but we didn't expect to get to heaven to eat our pie.

'Religion here is something quite different. There's no hanging about on crosses. If someone offends you, you drop on them out of the sky like a black eagle and rip the flesh from their bones. Do you know, Xana, I find myself much more in sympathy with that way of doing things. I think I am Indonesian after all, and I think that's what Zed has been trying to tell me. But the part of me that's English is shocked. It wishes we hadn't come.'

It was mid-afternoon when we reached the shelter, which was a small log cabin, empty but for a wooden box and a wood stove shaped like a top hat. We were very high up but not at the top of the mountain and the air was not noticeably cooler. We washed in the stream and filled up our water bottles. I went into the shady cabin and lay down thankfully on a thick blanket I found in the box. Then Jamie came in and said, 'We're very near the top. Shall we go up and have a look? Unless you're tired.'

If I had been twenty-two I would have refused to go, but I didn't want to appear middle-aged, so I said, 'Oh no, I'm fine,' and after a moment's inner struggle I sprang up. I ate some toffees to give me energy. The toffees were soft and bendy like tough jelly.

The top of the mountain was not as near as it appeared from the cabin. There was not one peak, but a series of peaks; each one offered a view of the next. We came upon a partly dilapidated stone building which I thought was an abandoned shepherd's hut. I said, 'It looks like our house at Blaengarw.'

Jamie opened the door and peered inside. He seemed puzzled for a moment then he said, 'Look, Xana. The ducklings slept in here. In the morning they came out and marched along to the stream in single file – to the stream which is just round the corner.'

As he spoke he took my arm and drew me around the corner of the rock. There was the promised stream, pouring out of the rockface and running down onto a small plateau which had once been a garden with fruit trees. Jamie said, 'That's all I can remember, the little ducklings coming out and walking in a line. And I went with them, carrying a very tall stick.'

VIII

Jamie stood on a precipice, facing east. He was looking down through the binoculars. He said, in a satisfied tone, 'Aha! There they are.'

Below him was a wall of bare rock, and at the base of it the green folds of rice terraces. In the cleft between the mountain and the coastal hills we could see what looked like scattered grain and long scratches in the dirt, the tracks and houses of Costassol. Jamie said, 'I could climb down there and get to the village much quicker.'

I looked at him to see if he was joking. 'Jamie, it's a sheer rock-face.'

'It's not, there are loads of footholds.' He said convincingly, 'Xana, I'm a good climber. Once they sent me to this place in Scotland, an adventure centre for problem adolescents. We did abseiling and pot-holing; I was brilliant at both. They're the only things I've ever been good at. I kept trying to get sent back there.'

I argued, 'But there you had all the equipment and a trained instructor with you.'

'I don't need any equipment, or an instructor. It's not a diffi-cult climb. Just go back to the cabin and wait for me. I promise I'll be OK.'

If it had been Tim I would have forbidden him to go, but I couldn't forbid Jamie. I didn't want to watch him climbing, so I went back to the cabin. It was dark before I was half-way there. I hoped that Jamie was safely down amongst the rice terraces. I fumbled in the box for the oil lamp and the jar of matches and managed to light the lamp. A tall flame shot a foot into the air, blackening the chimney-glass.

The air had turned cool. I put on my blue and green sweater and set about lighting the wood stove. I sat on the rug and watched the flames. I thought about Jamie herding the ducklings and I wondered what I would do if he didn't come back. After a while I took my book from the rucksack and tried to read but I read the same words over and over again without taking in the meaning.

I didn't hear her approach. It was ten o'clock and I was still watching the flames when I heard a woman's voice calling urgently: 'Amy! Amy!' I threw open the door. She was hovering, balanced on her toes as if ready to flee at a moment's notice and she was shivering, her bare arms crossed over her thin chest.

She looked at me in utter dismay and said, 'You're not her!'

I said, 'I'm looking for Amy too. Please come in and talk to me.'

'I can't.'

'It won't take a minute.'

'Who are you?'

'I'm Tiago's girlfriend.'

She advanced cautiously and peered into the cabin.

'Where is he?'

'He's not here. He's gone for a walk.'

I didn't think I had seen her before but I couldn't be sure. She was so thin that her bones looked brittle and her mouth had a disappointed droop. She said mournfully, 'Amy is dead, isn't she?'

'I don't know. Were you Amy's friend?'

She said thickly, 'When I heard you'd come, I thought you might be her,' and began to cry noisily, wiping her face with her hands. She was not a young woman but she was little and skinny. Her body was the size of Tim's at the age of ten or eleven.

After a moment I said, 'Won't you come in and get warm by the fire?'

'When will he be back?'

'I don't know. He won't hurt you.'

'Why did they give him that bad name?'

I said in surprise, 'It's a saint's name.'

'No, it's a dirty name. You had better not stay here, you are too easy to find.'

'Why? What could they do?'

She looked up with angry, suspicious eyes, 'They could set fire to the cabin. They set fire to Amy's house. I know they did.'

'Who did?' I said in amazement. 'Why would anyone want to do that?'

She said, speaking rapidly in a tinny little voice, 'There was a crazy old woman in the village called Fátima; she went crazy because she was old. She got in a rage because she was put out of her house. She went round the village shouting and threatening and spreading lies, no one could shut her up. In the end people got frightened and they believed the lies.'

I stared at her and said, 'I don't understand. They fired Amy's house because of an old woman's rambling?'

'You mustn't say who told you.'

'I won't, I promise.'

She looked at me distrustfully as if she regretted having told me anything, then she skirted the cabin and disappeared uphill. I could see the pale oval of her skirt vanishing into the dark and the soles of her feet flapping rhythmically as she ran, like a duck paddling through water. I thought, 'Perhaps she'll meet Jamie on the cliff face,' and the thought encouraged me. 'If she can climb it probably he can too.'

When she had gone, I put out the lamp as a precautionary measure and let the fire die down. She had said we were easy to find and she had proved it was true. I thought that we could not afford to ignore her warning.

Jamie got back at half-past twelve. He said, 'It was a piece of cake, that climb, only one hairy moment when I over-stretched myself a bit.'

The fire was still glowing; he slumped down in front of it and finished off the biscuits. He said, 'I'm so hungry I'm getting light-headed. Well, I crept round the churchyard flashing my little torch on the headstones. There were plenty of dead Coelhos, but none of them recent. Joaquim Jesus died twenty-seven years ago and Maria Madalena died the year I was born. They were the last two.'

'So Amy and João weren't there?'

'No. I found Padre Emanuel; he died in 1975, but there were bunches of flowers on his grave. And I saw something interesting.'

He was fiddling with the oil lamp and I said quickly, 'Don't light it.'

'Why not? Why are we sitting in the dark?'

'I'll tell you in a moment. What did you see?'

'A very ornate and palatial house, just by the church, flying a Portuguese flag.'

I said, 'Doutor Xico and 'Stora Rute. One of the children in the village told me they were 'Conquerors'. That means Portuguese.'

'Well I think we should pay them a call.' He paused and said, 'I remembered something when I was walking down the mountain but it didn't make much sense. Do you want to hear?'

'Of course I do.'

'I had the feeling that I'd been there before, walking around in the dark. It wasn't *déjà vu*, I really did remember.'

'What didn't make sense?'

'Well, when I saw the duck-shed door I didn't recognize it because it was too small. Then the door swelled in my memory. It got thick and huge and the bolt looked like something very interesting and enticing to handle. I was seeing it as I did when I was a tiny boy. On the hill it was the opposite: I remembered feeling very tall and ambling about unsteadily like a drunk. The sky was tilting and the ground was revolving under me. And somebody was there with me, someone who was always there, like a part of me.'

I knew enough now to take Jamie's recollections seriously. That is how, in the end, I came to find the waterfall. I pondered and said, 'Could it be that your father used to carry you on his shoulders?'

He snapped his fingers.

'You're right, Xana! That's it. Once,' he went on, 'once he started racing madly down the hill with me. My head was nearly shaken off my neck. It was like clinging to a runaway horse; I couldn't breathe for crying. I can still see the patches of black turf spinning, everything was out of focus. The sky was flickering, all the trees were lurching and the rocks were jumping. He must have been insane to run like that.'

I said grimly, 'Perhaps the house was on fire.'

He stared at me.

'I had a visitor from Costassol while you were away, Amy's friend. She was very nervous and agitated and I couldn't get her to talk much. But she told me that the villagers fired Amy's house. She said they might do the same to us. That's why I put the lamp out.'

I told him everything she had told me. He listened, then he said, 'In a way this is no business of ours. We could head for Yogung and lie low until the boat comes, just stay out of it.'

'Is that what you want to do?'

'I don't know. I don't think it's fair to involve you in anything dangerous, particularly now. I think you ought to decide.'

I asked, 'If we don't go and lie low, what do we do?'

'Tomorrow we go and see the people in the big house. I'd need you to come with me to talk to them. We could move up to the shed if you like, it'd be safer than here.'

I thought that if the cabin was the first place they looked for us, the shed would be the second, but I said, 'You really want to find out what happened, don't you?'

Jamie said, 'Up till now I never cared what happened to Amy. She rejected me so I rejected her too. I never thought about João at all; he was just the guy who got her pregnant. But tonight, for a moment, I remembered being with him, and now I feel differently, I do want to know what happened to him and I think it may explain what has gone wrong with me.'

I said: 'OK. Let's take the blankets up to the shed.'

We moved our belongings up to the shed. The floor was of stone with a few dusty wisps of grass and some dirt that had blown in under the door. One end of the shed was intact but we had heavy showers in the night and the water came in through the broken part of the roof. It was not a comfortable place to sleep but we both dozed because we were very tired. As soon as it was light we got up. We planned to walk into Yogung in search of food. Jamie hid the rucksack amongst the trees. I took out my little Portuguese dictionary and Jamie pocketed the little rice knife which I had unthinkingly slipped into a zipped compartment.

When we arrived at Yogung we saw that a market was in progress. We sat on the grass beside a kiosk and had a meal of hot fish in a thin chilli sauce with beansprouts and fried noodles. The cook was squatting by the track cooking over a charcoal fire. I was dubious about his hygiene but Jamie expostulated, 'You can see it all seething in the pan, nothing could breed in there.'

We had decided to ask no questions and to act like tourists. The meal had a soporific effect. We strolled slowly about the market bargaining for starfruit and mangosteens by holding up fingers. We also bought rice, lentils, meat, spinach and spices, which Jamie said he would cook in the pot on the cabin stove. We sliced up the fruit with the rice knife and shared it as we walked along. Everywhere we went the stallholders took hold of our arms and tugged insistently at our clothes, soliciting custom. One of the men made a playful snatch at my purse; the women called out after Jamie in loud flirtatious voices.

In the late afternoon we started back. We hid our bag of food in the dark hole beneath the port building, rather than carry it with us. We planned to walk to Costassol along the mountain track which Jamie had discovered on the previous night. It skirted the village and dropped down through the trees to the gates of the walled house. We expected to arrive at about eleven. At midnight in any Portuguese village you can see the café still lit and crowded, boys playing football in the street and babies running screaming around the square, so I felt sure that Xico and Rute wouldn't be in bed. I explained to Jamie that in Portugal 'Doutor' is a courtesy title denoting respect for the educated.

Jamie said, 'What are the educated Portuguese like?' and I said, 'Snobbish and very flashily dressed. You should have worn your Iceberg shirt.'

It was gone eleven o'clock when we reached Xico's house, which was surrounded by tall palm trees and enclosed within a high stone wall. Jamie shone his little torch on the gate; there was a metal plate such as you might see by the doorbell of a superior dentist, and I read out, 'Francisco Frederico Lobo Pureza dos Anjos. He is a wolf with the purity of the angels.'

Jamie said, 'Or is he an angel with a streak of pure wolf?'

He seized the knocker and rapped on the wooden door. In response two servants came. One opened the gates and the other lurked in the courtyard behind him.

We asked to see Dr. Xico, giving the English versions of our names: Alexandra Beale and Jamie Darkling. Presently we were escorted into a reception room. It was in keeping with traditional Portuguese taste, sombre and crowded with heavy, dark furniture. Xico rose to greet us. He wore a superb silver-grey suit in a lightweight but creaseless material. He had a sultry mouth and a look of 'saudades', a word used by the Portuguese to convey hopeless longing for the homeland. I asked him if he spoke English and we established that he didn't. I explained that Jamie had come to trace his family, and Xico said regretfully, 'I'm afraid I won't be able to help you. Let me make my position clear. I came to Macak in 1976 when I inherited certain business interests on the island. I have no official status. I am not the Governor, although the inhabitants,' he smiled indulgently, 'would like to think I am. I propose that we find one of the villagers who was here prior to 1976 and see what he can tell us.'

At this point his wife came in, preceded by a servant carrying tea. She kissed us formally on both cheeks. Her features were masked by thick make-up and her hair was rigidly styled in a baker's twist. Xico left us, to go and summon a villager. We drank tea and Rute chatted to me in Portuguese, asking how the weather was in England. When we had exhausted this topic I talked to her about the regions of Portugal I had visited and she described to me her long stay in South Africa, from which she had just returned. I asked her where the orphanage was and she said she thought I must mean the house of the Irmãzinhas da Misericórdia; it was up on the hill to the north of Yogung. Because the little girl in the village had called her 'Stora, I asked her if she was a teacher. She stretched her glossy, damson-coloured lips into a smile, and told me that they had made a little school in the old housekeeper's annexe; she was teaching the babies in the village to write their alphabets.

Jamie said, 'What the hell is keeping him, he's been gone nearly an hour?'

When Xico came back one of the villagers strutted into the room behind him. We recognized the man who had yelled at us in the square. Xico said,

'This is Mateus. He should be able to tell you what you want to know.'

Jamie and I exchanged looks. I felt sure that Mateus wouldn't tell us anything we wanted to know. Mateus began at once. His tone was glib and his expression was cold and sneering.

'His parents are dead. They lived in a shack up the mountain. The shack caught fire and they burned to death.'

Xico said suavely, 'I'm sorry, I wish Mateus could have given you better news.'

I translated for Jamie. He said, 'But they aren't buried in the churchyard.'

Mateus shrugged insolently. 'They did not live in this community.'

Jamie said, 'If they both died in the fire, ask him who took me to the orphanage.'

Mateus wore a secret smirk, like a wilful child. He said, 'I expect your mother took you there and left you with the Little Sisters as soon as you were born. It commonly happens to the sons of unmarried parents.'

I translated for Jamie and he said, 'Tell him he's a son of unmarried parents himself.'

I didn't relay the message. Instead I said, 'Jamie's parents were married. He has documents to prove it.'

Here Xico intervened smoothly to ask, 'Does he have them with him by any chance?'

'No.'

He nodded and I detected faint scepticism, so I added, 'He needed a passport to fly from Kawalinggan to England. Naturally full proof of parentage had to be furnished before he could obtain one.'

Xico asked, 'And how did he manage to furnish this proof?' I felt like saying, 'What business is it of yours?' but I said, 'As I understand it, Padre Emanuel took him to Kawalinggan and provided the proof.'

Xico said thoughtfully, 'Ah yes, I remember Padre Emanuel. An unorthodox priest, but very highly regarded.'

I went on, 'Jamie was not left at the orphanage at birth. He remembers living in the house on the mountain. He was probably taken to the orphanage after the fire.'

Mateus said, 'If he remembers so much, perhaps he can remember how he escaped from the fire and whether it was a miracle, or just the opposite.'

I took a break to translate for Jamie; he had been following this exchange impatiently, like a spectator at a tennis match. He said, 'This little bastard does nothing but needle. And the slimeball is lying. He made a big point of how he came here in 1976 but he remembers Padre Emanuel who died in 1975.'

I said, 'Is there any point in going on with this?'

'Ask Mateus why he hated my father and why he told us there was no such person.'

Mateus smiled. He said, 'Your father, if he was capable of the act of fathering, was beneath my notice. He was too small to merit my hatred.'

I translated for Jamie. He was beginning to look riled. He said, 'Teach me a good Portuguese word to call him.'

I said, 'There's no point in having a slanging-match. This is unproductive. We might as well go.'

Jamie said obstinately, 'Ask him if what Fátima said was true.'

Xico reacted to the mention of Fátima, I noticed. He glanced up, with widely-spaced, watchful eyes, then covered his displeasure with a show of polite interest. Rute, on the other hand, was yawning behind closed lips and examining a finger-nail. Mateus was standing behind Xico's desk. He pressed down on it with the heels of his hands and leaned forward, pushing his face close to Jamie's. He said slowly and emphatically, 'I don't know, *Sacana*, why don't you tell us?'

Xico rose to his feet. He said urbanely, 'I'm so sorry we can't be of more assistance.' He shook hands then said to me, 'Will you ask Senhor Jamie how long he intends to stay on Macak?'

Jamie said, 'Tell him I intend to stay as long as I like. Tell him I also have "certain inherited interests" on this island and mine go back before '76.'

Rute kissed us again. She said in clear English, 'Goodbye. I hope you enjoy the rest of your visit.'

We were escorted across the courtyard and the gate closed solidly behind us. We made for the trees and scrambled up amongst them looking for the path. I said, 'Now Rute will be telling Xico you called him a lying slime-ball.'

'I hope so, but I don't think she was attending. She was imagining she was back in South Africa.'

I was annoyed with Jamie; I thought he had made a serious tactical error. He had allowed Mateus to provoke him into saying things he should not have said. I said severely, 'What do you think we gained by all that?'

'A cup of tea and a new enemy. Xico and Mateus are in cahoots.'

'Xico may not have lied about Padre Emanuel, you know, he may have met him at some previous time.'

'No, it was a conspiracy. Xico didn't like me. He allowed Mateus to insult me, and as soon as I mentioned Fátima he threw me out. I wish I knew what she said that frightened them so much.'

I suggested, 'Perhaps she said Amy was a witch.'

'That might frighten the villagers but it wouldn't frighten Xico. I don't think it was Amy they hated, I think it was João.'

We soon realized that we had found the wrong track. It was too steep and overgrown to be the one we arrived on. Jamie said, 'Let's follow it anyway and see where it goes. We might as well make for Yogung. I want to go and see the Little Sisters when it gets light.' We climbed steadily upwards through the thick shrilling darkness. I scratched at my arms and neck, tearing at yesterday's mosquito bites with my finger-nails. I thought, 'Three more days to survive then we can go back to Kawalinggan.'

Eventually we sat down on a flat ledge near tumbling water. Jamie said, 'What was it all about, Xana? It wasn't to do with money or power because I'm sure they didn't have any. Could it have been about jealousy? Love, or sex?'

I said, 'No, not if it frightened the whole village, surely.'

'What else is there that makes people hate each other and burn houses down?'

I said, 'Family feuds? Revenge?' I groped around in my mind for a sentence I had read somewhere recently. 'The sinister secrets of birth and death, violent and vengeful partners.'

Below us was a bridge across a cleft through which the water was rushing. Jamie said, 'I think we ought to cross that bridge and head north west.'

He grasped my shoulders and pointed me in the right direction.

'Further down, can you just make out a clearing? That's the centre of the village. We could sit here with the binoculars,' he said bitterly, 'and watch them, see what they're up to.'

'We are going back on Wednesday, aren't we?' I said anxiously.

'Yes, I suppose so. But we won't be much wiser than when we came.'

As we clambered down over the boulders I remembered where I'd read the phrase about sinister secrets and violent and vengeful partners. It was in my horoscope.

IX

The house of the Little Sisters was easy to find. It was perched on the hillside, high above Yogung. It was builpt of grey stone and had green wooden shutters like a Portuguese house; it lacked only the wrought-iron balconies. A young native nun in a white cotton habit admitted us and listened while I explained what we wanted. She came back a few moments later to say that the Irma Superiora, Maria do Ceu, would like to talk to us.

The Reverend Mother was sitting in a dark room with all the shutters closed. She had a grave, heavy face with vertical lines, like a Portuguese peasant. She stared at Jamie for a moment, then she said, 'Come here and kiss me. What's the matter, have you forgotten how to speak Portuguese?'

I said, 'Tiago has been living in England, but we think he was here in this orphanage when he was a little boy.'

She said, without taking her eyes off him, 'I know. Come here, Tiago.'

When he approached she pinched his cheeks hard and then kissed him; they were not token kisses like Rute's.

I said, 'Tiago came here to discover what he could about his family.'

Ceu said tartly, 'Can't he speak for himself?'

I felt rebuked. I told Jamie 'She doesn't want me to speak for you.'

'In that case this is going to be a very short conversation.'

Ceu took hold of his hand and beat with it on the tray attached to her chair. She continued to talk to him in Portuguese, mouthing the syllables carefully and increasing the volume as one does when talking to the deaf or foreign. Jamie looked embarrassed. He said to me, 'I don't know why old ladies like me so much. I never give them any encouragement.'

Ceu was reminding him that he used to hate soup, and asking if he remembered feeding the pigs. She was working hard to elicit the answer 'yes'. Finally Jamie shook his head and she laughed. She said, 'When you were here you never stopped asking questions. Now you don't talk at all.'

Jamie said: 'Who brought me here?'

'Quem é que me trouxe cá?' I murmured in the muted tones of the interpreter.

Ceu said, 'The Padre Emanuel brought you. He found you sleeping in the church one morning.'

'What happened to my parents?'

'They are dead, *filho*. The Padre went straight away to look for them. The house was burnt to the ground.'

Ceu didn't look at me, or speak through me, as Mateus and Xico had done. She spoke directly to Jamie.

'Who rescued me and took me to the church?'

She extended her hands, palms upward, as though comparing the weight of melons. She said, 'The Saints were watching over you, they guided and protected you.' I remembered Mateus saying: 'Was it a miracle or was it just the opposite?'

Ceu went on. 'Padre Emanuel asked us to keep you until he came back for you himself. He said he would take you on the next ferry to Kawa and send you to England. He insisted that we should keep you inside the house and tell no one you were here.' She spread her hands again. 'That's all I can say. Padre Emanuel was a sensible man. He usually made the right decisions.'

I translated for Jamie. Ceu interrupted, 'Now tell me how you got on in England.'

He said with a trace of self-pity, 'My grandmother gave me away for adoption.'

'So you had new parents. Were they kind to you?'

'Yes, they were.'

'Were they good Christians?'

'They didn't go to Church but they were conscientious people.'

'Did they give you an education?'

'Yes they did,' he said drily, 'a great deal of education.'

Ceu frowned at him and said, 'So, what's wrong with you, boy?'

'I want to know my history and what happened to me on this island.'

'Why do you want to know?'

'Because it is bothering me.'

They gazed at each other, then Ceu sighed. 'I don't know, and I don't know of anyone who could tell you. Padre Emanuel is dead. If you take my advice you will go back to England and consider it your home, and consider the people who have brought you up and shown you kindness, and educated you, as your family.'

We left shortly afterwards. I felt uncomfortable because Jamie hadn't shown her any reciprocal warmth, so I said, 'Thank you for talking to us. Could we make a small contribution to the work of the orphanage?'

Ceu said, 'You may if you wish. Money is always useful.' She was still watching Jamie. I gave her some money, rather less than an appropriate contribution and rather more than I could afford. As we walked away Jamie said, 'The ones that know won't talk and the ones that will talk don't know. What shall we try next?'

'I don't know,' I said glumly.

'Are you very tired?'

'Of course I am. I must have sweated off about a stone. My clothes won't stay up any more.'

'Let's go back to the shed and rest. This evening I'll cook you a meal if the meat is still fit to eat.'

I said, 'Why do we have to go back to the shed? Why can't we stay in Yogung or go to some other village?'

He looked at me in surprise and I said sharply, 'Did you understand what she said? Padre Emanuel wanted you kept out of sight. I think he shipped you off to England for your own protection. Now you're back and making sure everybody knows it.'

'Xana, that was nearly twenty years ago.'

'Do they like you any better now?'

He said, 'Mateus is just a yob. If he was Welsh he'd join the rugby club and shout, 'Oggy! Oggy Oggy! Oi! Oi Oi!' on a Saturday night. He'd like to push my teeth down my throat, that's all. He told us he didn't hate João, he despised him, and I think that was the truth. He's not dangerous.'

'What about Xico?'

'Can you imagine Xico scrambling up the hillside with a gallon can of petrol, to set fire to our shed?'

'No, I can imagine him sending Mateus to do it for him.'

He stopped and turned me to face him. Then he pulled me close. I was stifled; his shirt felt wet and tepid, like a dishcloth.

'Look, we have to go back to collect the rucksack. We'll sleep at the shed, or in the trees, and tomorrow we'll go and be tourists on the other side of the island. OK?'

'OK.'

'I wish there was some easier means of transport. Xico has got a jeep but I haven't seen another motor vehicle since we arrived.'

'I can walk,' I said despondently.

We walked to the port and collected our bag from the dank, briny hole beneath the shop. The old Chinaman watched us impassively. Jamie said, 'Let's get away from here. This place makes me nervous. I keep looking over my shoulder to see what's stalking me.'

We walked all afternoon and we reached the cabin at sunset. We'd long since stopped talking. Jamie put his hand underneath my hair and caressed my neck. He said, 'Go up to the shed and lie down. Take the blankets and a lamp. I'll bring you a wonderful dinner in an hour or so.'

I wasn't hungry, but I didn't argue.

I picked up the blankets and started up the hill. The furry touch of them was intolerable; I shifted them from my hip to my shoulder to my head. I thought about ditching them by the side of the track. The lantern swung, rattling, from my finger. When I reached the shed I dropped the blankets and lay down in the rescue position. After half an hour I got up to drink at the spring. The coldness of the water made me whoop. Then I went back to the shed and fell asleep in peaceful expectation of my dinner.

I woke up feeling cold, cramped and disorientated. My watch glowed greenly: 23.05. I knelt up and crawled to the door. I stuck my head out and called 'Jamie?' The moon lay on its back like a thick slice of melon with a dark red centre. I lit the lamp and looked round the shed. There was nothing there but an inert pile of blankets and a pot of matches. No sign of the promised meal.

'Jamie? Jamie?' I got up and stumbled round the garden. I could hear my own breath panting beside me like a pursuer.

I looked at my watch again. I thought, 'Dinner is just taking longer than expected, that's all, he couldn't get the fire to light.' I waited there in the shed until midnight, then all at once I jumped up and started walking fast down the hill. I half-expected to meet Jamie at any moment. I kept calling out to stunted trees and running to meet blowing bushes.

As soon as I got to the cabin I could smell smoke. The door was open and the cabin was dark inside. I turned up my lantern. The big pot was on top of the wood-stove but the food inside it was black and brittle. It had stuck to the pan at the bottom like treacle toffee. The fire was out and the second lantern was rolling about on the floor. I took my lamp and paced around outside. Just behind the cabin all the flowering bushes were flattened as though an elephant had disported itself there. I raised the lantern and saw something lying among the roots. It was the little rice knife given to me in Costassol.

I thought, 'Someone has been here, several of them, and there was a tremendous struggle.' Through my mind flashed a succession of unbearable images: Jamie being jumped on as he prepared our dinner; Jamie being dragged from the cabin; Jamie fighting for his life in the bushes; Jamie dropping his knife.

I started to run round the cabin, trampling clumsily over creepers, thrashing through the undergrowth. I travelled in frenzied circles, like a demented rat. As I went I yelled 'Jamie! Jamie! Jamie!' as if the sheer urgency of my shouts could compel him to answer. I searched in ever-widening circles, covering the entire flat fold of hillside on which the cabin stood. I found nothing, no blood, no marks, no clue at all. I heard nothing but the whirring, clonking and squawking of the night creatures, and the sawing sound of my own breathing. I thought, 'If they've dragged him down the slope and beaten him up I'll never find him, or hear him, there's too much hillside for me to cover', but I was thinking it to encourage myself. I was afraid that he was already dead.

Then a new idea occurred to me. Was it Zed who had come and not Mateus? Was it Zed who had attacked the bushes, as he had attacked the lid-making machine, and had he then gone blundering away over the mountain? If it was Zed, perhaps I had only to wait and Jamie would find his way back to me by morning. I went back to the shed to see if Jamie was there. The shed was exactly as I had left it; the rucksack was still hidden among the trees. I sat cross-legged on the floor and waited. It was so like the night in Blaengarw when he had broken the glasses and smacked Tim in the mouth; but then, I remembered, I had hoped he wouldn't come back.

Dawn was breaking. I went out and sat down at the door of the shed. Ironically, I watched the sun come up on the first unclouded day. I saw that our mountain peak was shaped like a dented horn, the tip smothered in trees. I saw from the date on my watch that I was exactly two months pregnant. I thought, 'What am I going to do now, and how am I to get through the rest of my life?' As it grew hotter the mountain began to steam and the sunlight, reflecting off the water vapour, created a blinding white fog at ground level. I went down to search below the cabin, zig-zagging through the smoking, streaming fog. I couldn't see my legs below my knees. It was like an exhausting dream, in which one is already hours late for a vital appointment and struggling with some intractable hindrance, the telephone dial or a lost key.

As the sun climbed, the mist evaporated and I scanned the eastern slope. I saw a vast plunge of featureless hillside. I knew it would take a line of policemen with tracker dogs to make a search of such magnitude. I would have gone at once for help if I had known where to find it, but I trusted no one except Maria do Ceu, and to run to the Irmazinhas would have cost me twenty hours, twenty hours of time which might be crucial if Jamie was lying injured on the hill. I twisted the slack of my waistband into a loop and knotted it. I fetched the little rice knife and charted my progress down the mountainside by hacking channels in the waist-high grass. I was afraid that I might otherwise retrace my steps and leave wide areas uncovered. By midday I was too dejected to call out any more. My calves protested at every step, my skin felt stiff and scalded; my head and neck throbbed and the mountain shimmered before my eyes. I went up to the cabin to rest. I drank water and forced myself to eat some of the fruit we had bought in Yogung. I took the burnt cooking-pot and hurled it down the slope with all my force. I wondered why they hadn't killed me too. I had been there alone all night, crying out my whereabouts at one-minute intervals.

When it got dark I gave up searching. I went back to the shed to see if Jamie was there. No one had been there, nothing had changed. I would not allow myself to cry, but I put my head under the spring and when the water ran down over my face I opened my mouth and wept silently, rocking on my haunches. I didn't believe, any more, that he was lying, beaten, on the eastern slope. I thought he was dead. Yet there was still a chance that he was alive, that they had spirited him away to Costassol and kept him there, or that he had wandered off into the jungle of his own accord. I thought, 'I've wasted a whole day when I should have gone for help.' And I thought: 'Ib will be here soon; he will tell me what to do.' In the meantime I took the binoculars from the rucksack. I meant to be at the waterfall by dawn, to keep the village square under surveillance and see if that provided any clue.

I walked all night. As I walked I had waking dreams and moments of euphoria. I reached the waterfall just as the sun was rising. A little colony of brown rats was already active; there was constant traffic to and fro at the roots of a wizened bush beside the pouring water. I trained my binoculars on the rats to adjust the focus. Then I sat down on the grass and pointed the glasses at the village square. A woman's face came into clear view. I followed her progress to the stream, where she lifted her skirt to the waist and squatted in the water. A boy appeared with a shining black goat on a leash. The goat was wagging its tail and tugging him across the square. The villagers came out and went about their business. On the hillside opposite, over a hedge bright with frangipani flowers, I could see the pointed hats of tea-pickers. A gaunt old man in shorts waded barefoot through the rice fields carrying two baskets suspended from a pole. The young mothers came out on the verandas to suckle the babies.

An hour later I focused suddenly on a face I recognized. Mateus was sitting idly on the wooden bandstand, kicking slowly at the stage with his heels and talking to a couple of men. I felt a great thrill of rage when I saw him: it was a violent, convulsive emotion, like love. I wanted to swoop down like Superwoman and annihilate him. I couldn't believe that he could sit there, placid and insouciant, after what he had done. I scrutinized him through the binoculars; I couldn't see any cuts, bruises or grazes. The boy with the goat reappeared and Mateus flashed him a smile.

I watched the village square all morning and I detected nothing, no sign of excitement or unusual activity. Several times I dropped my glasses and fell asleep with my eyes open, and the people in the square turned into slinking, sniffing brown rats. I was in a fugue induced by sun or shock, or the lack of food and sleep. At the back of my brain a confused image formed insistently: the rats, the brown rats of Costassol, what were they up to?

I left my post and stood under the water. My temples ached unbearably from the cold. It was like the pain I used to have as a child when I bit into a hard ice-cream. I looked up at the high ledge over which the water was cascading and from which two bleached tree roots were dangling. I remembered Ystradfellte, and how Jamie had said: 'I've been here before, yet I know I haven't', and suddenly I knew where the rats where going.

I tried to climb the rocks. My body felt light but I judged the distances poorly. The rocks zoomed down to meet me and retreated as I grasped at them. I was like someone in the middle stages of drunkenness. Eventually I reached the dead, bristly bush and embraced it. The rats had all fled.

I was looking into a rocky hallway, the shining, steel-grey curtain pulled aside for me to enter. I stepped in and walked along the passageway between the mountain face and the water, running my hand along the rough rock wall. Jamie's voice said, so clearly that I jumped, 'Let's open the last bottle of wine.'

When I was half-way along the corridor I saw that I was not alone. My companion was sitting silently on the ledge, his spine lolling against the rock wall. The bleached tree roots I had seen from below were his two yellowish legs. One arm had fallen from its socket; the fingers were lazily extended towards a dull metallic object lying on the ledge.

As a child, I'd peeped into the Chapel of Bones at Évora, gripping my mother's hand, and the skeletons had peered back at me, crowding forward, climbing on each other's backs to get a better view. For years afterwards, I used to pray: 'For Évora and Évora, Amen'. The name 'Évora' still tolls in my mind with the knell of death. But I was not afraid of my skeletal companion. He looked quite relaxed, as if he'd been sitting fishing on the ledge and grown too lazy to move, like the cats that lie sleeping peacefully at the roadside until the ants crawl through their eye-sockets.

He was not a fisherman. I saw that the object he had failed to grasp was a long curved dagger. I didn't touch the knife. I had not the least idea who it was that I had found.

X

Long before I reached the port I could see Ib's boat, floating on the dark water like the belly of a fish. I ran the last lap with the pack on my back; I ran partly from relief that help was now at hand. The rucksack was bruising my spine and shoulders like a specially-designed instrument of torture. I was carrying all Jamie's things as well as my own, including the Iceberg shirt, still unworn, and impaled on pins like a shining yellow butterfly.

I reached the jetty at six a.m. It was my last appointment with Jamie; he didn't keep it. Ib listened while I explained about Jamie's disappearance. There was a look in his eyes which accused me of lying. At any rate he was dissociating himself from my troubles. He said, 'I can wait another two hours for him, but that's all, then I must go.'

'I was hoping you would tell me where to get help.'

He said, 'You should have gone to Costassol at once. It's probably too late now.'

I thought, 'A fat lot of use it is to tell me that!' I said, 'I don't trust the people of Costassol. They weren't at all friendly. Are there any police on the island?'

He shook his head with a slightly sneering smile. He said, 'No. They make their own law here. The nearest police are on Kawalinggan.'

'Then you had better go and fetch them at once and I'll stay here and carry on searching.'

He considered for a moment with his hand in his pocket, then he said, 'I don't want to go to the police. They will ask a lot of questions and I am not supposed to transport foreigners from island to island. The best thing is that you come back with me now and talk to them.'

I shook my head angrily, 'No, I'm staying here. If you won't go to the police will you go to the British consulate and tell them what has happened?'

'OK. But if you want me to come back here to fetch you the price will be the same. And I would like the other half of what you owe me already.'

I didn't have the money to pay for a second trip. I said, 'My money is all in the hotel safe deposit at Kawalinggan.'

He said, without any further attempt at charm, 'Then you had better come back with me now and get it.'

We waited at the port until mid-morning. In the end I climbed aboard the boat and we headed at once for Kawalinggan. Ib and I didn't speak again. When we reached Kawalinggan, Ib came with me to the hotel and I gave him his money. Jamie's passport was still in the box, as was all the money, and everything else we had left.

I went by taxi straight to the British consulate. The consul, when he could be found, was sympathetic but regretted that there was very little he was empowered to do, beyond notifying relatives in England. He telephoned the police and made an appointment on my behalf. I went by taxi to the police station. A high-grade policeman took me to his air conditioned office. On the way we passed through the sweltering public room, buzzing with flies, where people sat around listlessly as they do in DHSS waiting rooms. The policeman listened politely to my story but he didn't appear moved or impressed. When I had finished he asked my forgiveness and explained to me that people commonly disappeared of their own free will, often on impulse. Sometimes they reappeared at a later date and sometimes they didn't.

I asked if they commonly disappeared leaving their passports behind. He said Jamie had returned to the country of his birth; perhaps he had decided to stay there. I felt like shrieking, 'On Macak! You think Jamie wanted to stay on Macak?', but I held my tongue. He said he saw no reason to believe that the people of Costassol had harmed him in any way. As for the flattened bushes, the dropped knife and burned stew, I myself had provided the explanation: Jamie was subject to brief episodes of insanity. In this way he disposed of all my objections before I raised them.

I stood up and said emphatically, 'Look, I know Jamie. He didn't leave of his own accord.' I added wildly, 'We were going to get married. I'm expecting his baby.'

Too late, I saw from his raised eyebrows that this disclosure had had the opposite effect from the one intended. I had just given him a good reason why Jamie would want to disappear. He gave me a long assessing look, rubbing his neck, then he glanced down at his paper.

'The young man is twenty-two.'

I said acidly, 'Yes, he is twenty-two.'

I waited for him to ask me my age, but he didn't. I said desperately, 'Listen, I am absolutely certain that he didn't disappear of his own free will. If he is not dead he is kidnapped or injured or lost in the mountains or the rainforest. Whichever it is, he urgently needs help.' The policeman looked up at me. He had mild eyes with long lashes. He said, 'Please sit down,' and waited until I had obeyed.

'You see, we are not a mountain rescue service. We are concerned only with serious crime and what you are telling me is village tittle-tattle. The village women are not to be taken seriously. They are like small children, they love to invent new scandals and stories.'

I shook my head speechlessly. Then I raised my arms and let them fall again. I was near to tears of frustration and despair. The policeman went on explaining quietly that each island was to some extent autonomous. Someone in Costassol would be in charge of policing the area and it was to him that I should have made my complaint. I said, without raising my bent head, 'But I didn't, so what can I do now? I can't afford another trip to Macak.'

'I can believe that it was very expensive.'

'I would gladly pay any price, however expensive, if I had the money, but I haven't and that's that. What shall I do now, leave him there to die? Won't you help me at all?'

'I didn't say that I wouldn't help you.' When I looked up, he continued, 'We are obliged to investigate your complaint. We will go out to Macak on the next ferry and inform the proper authorities and we will help them to make enquiries, if appropriate.'

'When is the next ferry?'

He said stolidly, 'In a few weeks' time.'

'A few *weeks*! Then there is no point in going at all.'

'You must understand that I cannot proceed with any urgency on the strength of village gossip.'

'Then will you go and talk to the Portuguese governor?'

'There is no Portuguese governor, Madam.'

'He is not the official governor but the natives think he is. His name is Francisco dos Anjos and he inherited his uncle's estate on the island. Ask him where Mateus was on the night Jamie disappeared. Ask him why he allowed Mateus to insult Jamie and Jamie's father, and ask him why he lied to us about his date of arrival on the island. He told us twice he arrived in 1976, but he couldn't have done; he remembered the priest who died there in 1975.'

The policeman narrowed his eyes and stared through me at the wall. He held his pen between two fingers and tapped with his thumb on the pad. He had made some very sparse notes. Underneath them he scribbled Macak 73? and drew a circle round it. He got up and said, 'Leave it with me. I can't say any more at present.'

'Well I am not satisfied. I want to make a complaint.'

'You may, of course, if you wish. But, believe it or not, I am trying to help you. In the meantime, if you hear from your fiancé, please let me know.'

As soon as I had left the police station I went to the British consulate. I wanted to borrow the money to go back to Macak. The consul had left so I spoke to a thin and rigid old lady; she said she was afraid that they didn't lend money. I asked her if there was a way of pressuring the police to act quickly. She said shrilly, nodding her head for emphasis, 'Bribes and influence. Bribes and influence.'

I said I had neither money nor influence, was there nothing the consul could do to help? She promised she would speak to him as soon as he got back. I also asked her to look through the files for any entries concerning Jamie. I thought they might contain the reason why Padre Emanuel shipped him off secretly to England and that this might help to convince the police. She said, 'Twenty years ago, that's a tall order. I don't think we keep them that long. Wait a minute, this isn't about the girl interned on Weh Tuluk, is it?'

I said patiently, 'No no, not Weh Tuluk, Macak.'

I went back to the hotel, and I rang a journalist friend at a national newspaper office. My friend wasn't there; by the time I'd held the line and been put through to his extension, the brief call had cost me such an alarming amount of money that I couldn't afford to make another. I wrote letters instead, to my MP, and to the British newspapers.

I sat out on my balcony. I couldn't eat or drink or sleep. I was burdensome even to myself. I would begin to go somewhere, to the coffee bar for instance, and then I would lose heart and run out of energy. I couldn't rest, but every kind of activity seemed intolerably futile.

The next morning I was paged by tannoy. There was a visitor

for me in the lobby. At first I didn't recognize the policeman. He looked very slight and he was smiling. He said, 'I have some good news for you.'

I stared.

'I am authorized to visit Macak tomorrow.'

He sat down close to me on the window seat, like a friend. He was not wearing uniform, only a white cotton shirt and trousers. He explained, 'Normally we would go on the ferry with the Range Rover, because, as you remarked, there is no transport on Macak. But tomorrow we are going by special boat and taking a motor cycle.'

I managed to sound grateful, which was what he seemed to expect.

I waited out the next two days, sitting in the hotel lobby and watching the doorway. I made contingency plans: 'If he's injured I'll have him flown back to hospital in England.' Really I knew that if he flew at all he would be flying in a box. I felt another, unspecified dread, as though there could be something even worse to fear than this. I kept phoning the police station and eventually I learned that my policeman was back and that I could call round to see him. I knew that this was not promising. He would have come to see me if the news had been good. I sped round to the police station at once. The policeman was sitting at his desk, ostensibly rearranging papers. He wasn't smiling. He greeted me formally and began without preamble, 'We investigated your complaint and we went to talk to the people of Costassol. We found nothing at all to suggest that they had harmed your fiancé in any way or had even wished to harm him. They remembered that he had visited the village twice to enquire about the fate of his parents, that was all they could tell us.'

He paused, perhaps expecting a tirade of questions, protests, abuse, but I was silent. The finality of his tone had already convinced me that my worst fear was about to be realized. There would never be an end to this, I would never know. He went on, 'It is common knowledge that there are groups of bandits in the forest who sometimes prey on travellers. To pursue such people through the jungle is an impossible task, I'm afraid. I am not saying that this is what happened to your fiancé, but this was a suggestion made to me by several of the village people. Now,' he said, patting his papers with both hands as though coming to the crux of the matter, 'in case your fiancé is lost or injured, the people of Costassol have mounted an extensive search, and have sent their own excellent mountain guides. These mountain guides are truly skilful, I commend them to you very highly.'

I forbore to comment but I think my expression was commentary enough. He must have felt guilty because he glared at me and said,

'That's all. We will keep you informed.'

Two days later I went home. My time was up, my luck had expired, my money had run out and there was really nothing more that I could do. Brenda and Roland were expected to arrive in Kawalinggan on the day I left. I was glad that I didn't have to face them. Before I went I took Jamie's passport to the British Embassy, just in case he should be needing it, and a letter for Maria do Ceu, which they promised to send out on the next ferry. I left forwarding addresses for the police. I gave my old address in Weston and the address of the club at Blaengarw, but I didn't expect to hear from them.

When I left the office the stiff old lady pursued me down the corridor and caught up with me outside the Ladies' toilet. She laid her hand on my arm and said, 'Alexandra, don't ever reproach yourself, you did everything possible.'

Tears came to my eyes. I said, 'I wish I thought so. I bungled it. I should have gone for help right away.'

'No, it wouldn't have made any difference. It was all over before you even knew he was missing.'

I stared at her. 'How do you know?'

'I know these islands. There was a case some years back, in the seventies. The Portuguese governor was killed, a particularly brutal killing. Well, the first the police in Kawalinggan heard about it was when the relatives from Portugal turned up and started breathing down their necks. They were very embarrassed. They went out to the island, one of the distant ones, it might even have been Macak. No enquiries had been made, nothing had been done. The islanders all said, "It was the bandits from the hills." They stick together, you see, and you don't always know which side the police are on.'

'You think he's dead, don't you?'

'Yes, I think he's dead, otherwise he would have found his own way back by now, and I think you should try to accept that and not torment yourself any more.'

I flew back to Britain. As the plane accelerated, accumulating energy for its great leap into the sky, I had a sense of impending separation as though I were leaving a vital organ in Kawalinggan. Once we were in the air I became passive. The detachment of flying suited my mood; I didn't want to land, I wanted to fly on, surrounded by sleeping strangers and impersonal cabin staff.

*   *   *

I went back to Blaengarw because I wanted to be left alone. As soon as I entered the house I knew it had been violated. I walked from room to room, making a tour of inspection. My kitchen equipment was strewn across the floor as though a toddler had been making merry with it, a half-burnt, maggoty pigeon was rotting in the kitchen fireplace, the mattress was soaking wet, they had found my bottle of ink and splashed it up the bedroom wall. Jamie's music machine had gone from under the floorboards. It was mischievous damage and I thought that the vandals were probably pre-teenage boys.

I was bitterly cold. I had been shivering convulsively ever since the plane landed. I went down the road to buy some milk. I walked down into Pontycymmer so that I could go to a supermarket where no one would speak to me. On the way back I ran into the stewardess from the club. She said, 'Diw! Look at the colour of you!'

I had to stop and tell her about the weather in Kawalinggan. She said, 'There's a parcel for you under the bar, Siân, recorded delivery; I had to sign for it.'

It was not a parcel but a large padded envelope, and it had an English postmark. I went back to the house and lit the fire. I heated up some milk and cleared a space in the kitchen, where I lay down in a nest of clothes. I wrote to Philip, asking him to send on any letters as a matter of urgency and explaining what had happened because I thought that otherwise he might not bother. Then I opened the padded envelope. I opened it carelessly and half a dozen exercise books fell out. The covers were dirty and all the pages were closely written in pencil. The pencil writing was very faint and barely legible.

There was also a typescript in a clear plastic folder, and clipped to the front of it, an envelope addressed to James and Xana. I took the typescript out of the envelope and with it came a couple of press-cuttings and a scrap of paper. I flipped through the typescript and I read, 'At the end of the three days the young man lay sleeping and his bride reached down and stroked his hair. As soon as she touched him, he knew that she was his mother.'

I said, 'What the hell is this?'

I went on turning the pages, making little sense of the contents, until I came to two names I recognized:

'Who wants to offend the most powerful man on the island? More prudent to slander Tiago and victimize João.'

I said, 'Oh God, what's this?'

On the last page I read,

'I thought Zé would rear up out of the stinking mud. Then the bubbling ceased. I saw João running towards me along the edge of the water.'

I pulled the letter free of the paper-clip. Now that I could read the opening paragraph of the manuscript, I saw that it began, 'My name is Amy Elizabeth Hodges. I am eighteen years old.'

XI

I had known all along who Amy Hodges was, but her name had slid from my memory. I had read the newspaper reports, but they hadn't interested me at the time. Now I looked at a press photograph of Mr and Mrs Hodges clutching stiffly at one another, and I remembered the story.

I opened the letter. Its writer introduced himself as Richard Hodges, Jamie's natural uncle. He apologized for the delay, explaining that his mother was no longer capable of dealing with her own correspondence and this was kept for him by the staff of the home in which she lived. At the time my letter had arrived, he had been out of the country visiting family in Canada.

He went on: 'The enclosed exercise books are part of a diary written by Amy, James's mother. When I first read them I considered destroying them. When you have read them yourselves I think you will understand why. I concluded that I had no right to do this. Instead I made a fair copy on the word-processor and I have sent you this along with the originals, as I feel they rightfully belong to James. I hope you will not find them too distressing.

'I should like to explain how I came to be in possession of them and at the same time I should like to explain the circumstances leading up to James's adoption. My mother first learned that Amy was still alive when she received a visit from a ferry-captain who had met Amy on Macak a few days previously. He brought a letter, in which Amy made it clear that she was remaining on Macak of her own free will because she was now married. At that time my father was very ill with a heart condition and required constant care. Although my mother was naturally overjoyed by the news she was unable to attempt to visit Amy. In her letter Amy did not mention any of her difficulties and we assumed that she was happy. We contented ourselves, therefore, with writing her letters and we were not particularly concerned when we received no reply as Amy had forewarned us that communication with the island was extremely difficult.

'When my father died, my mother suffered a mental collapse.

It was at this point that she was contacted, via the British Embassy in Kawalinggan, and asked if she would take responsibility for James. She was told only that he had been found wandering, that his house was burned to the ground and his parents presumed dead. On hearing that James was currently in an orphanage, my mother agreed that he should come to England.

'While visiting the scene of the fire, the same priest who had found James had uncovered Amy's diaries in an outhouse, some of them partly burned. Recognizing only that the language was English, he sent them to my mother. She was too upset to read them and gave them into my keeping.

'My mother was clearly quite unable to care for a young child, and my wife and I, with our own small children, were living in Canada and unable to offer much support. Since James was still so young we felt that the best solution was to offer him up for adoption. We sincerely believed this to be in his best interests. If we were wrong I must accept most of the responsibility, as the decision was mainly of my making.'

Richard concluded with good wishes.

I stayed awake all night reading Amy's diaries. Like Jamie she had a facility with language. She had edited her writing and Richard had faithfully copied the corrected version. She hadn't interspersed her narrative with dates, perhaps she hadn't known the date; but she had kept track of the moons. From time to time she had doodled in the margin at the beginning of the entries, indicating the number of moons she had already spent on Macak, and the number that were still to go before the boat was due, the boat that would take her home. Richard hadn't copied the moons, but he had typed in italics: *two and a half moons gone, ten and a half moons to go*. At first I didn't take to Amy. I thought she was a silly, spineless girl, but by the end I felt differently.

When I'd finished reading I sat and held the typescript in my hand. Like Richard, I considered burning it, but not out of distaste. I believe that a child has a right to its own family history, I think family history is important. I fed a big, tarry railway sleeper into the fire and I debated: 'Shall I keep this document for Jamie's child, or shall I get rid of it now and put an end to this once and for all?'

I had overlooked something. The scrap of paper had fluttered down to rest on the pitted tiles of the hearth. It had been screwed up and thrown away but retrieved, and it was still legible. It was written in thick black ink in a laborious, semi-literate hand, and I now knew that it was the testament of Joaquim Silva, who, having nothing to bequeath but his knife, had left us a riddle instead.

'*Eu deixo-vós dois companheiros na vossa escuridão:*
João-ninguém para vos guiar,
Zé-ninguém para vos chamar de voltar.'

I had forgotten Zed.

I went through the roll-call of Joaquim's issue, four generations of Silvas. I counted six victims: Tiago, the twins themselves, the two girls, little Conceição and Amy Elizabeth; Jamie. They had all come to a violent end, knifed, burned, drowned, or battered and thrown in a gulley. Now all the Silvas were dead, all dead, every one of them, all except for the one inside me.

Burning the diaries might not rid us of Zed.

*   *   *

'My name is Amy Elizabeth Hodges. I am eighteen years old. It's too hot to sleep and the mating frogs are making a noise like a hundred football-rattles in the flooded padi-field. I think I'll write a diary. I feel the need to communicate in my own language, if only with myself. I've got one soft pencil and a cheap school exercise-book, half-full of vocabulary lists, in a language which I suppose is Spanish.

I'll begin by explaining how I came here. I was a voluntary worker at the Children's Project on the island of Weh Tuluk when, one morning, three excitable soldiers with guns drove into the camp. The leader was swarthy and bandy-legged. He was sweating profusely and appeared agitated. The brown of his eyes overlapped the irises and leaked into the whites. There were three of us on duty at the time and we were ordered to get into the jeep. I went the wrong way. One of the soldiers was expectorating; without looking up he hit me on the leg with his rifle. It was the hardest blow I've ever sustained. We got into the jeep. I was snivelling with pain but I wasn't as frightened as I should have been because I felt so sure that it was all a mistake and showers of explanations and apologies would shortly follow.

We drove along the coast road until we came to something that looked like a motorway toll-booth. The Dutch students talked to the official inside. I had been in the country for barely a week and I could only shrug and shake my head in answer to his questions. For failing this test, or perhaps for passing it, I was separated from the others and sent to a kind of zoo compound where distorted messages were broadcast in some unintelligible language.

I sat near the wire by the door, ready to leave. The compound looked like the Birchfield Harriers Sports ground during a particularly long interval and I almost expected to watch some minor event like the long jump at any moment. Nothing happened except that I became hot and thirsty, and rocked my injured leg, and wanted to go to the toilet; but there was no shade and no sanitation and I wasn't given any water.

For the first two days I assumed that we were all waiting for something. Then I realized that we weren't. More people came but no one left. There were a few skirmishes, nothing worse than you see outside the pub on a Saturday night. It was like an open-air pop festival except there was no music and no beer and we couldn't leave. After a while I ran out of fear and indignation. My heartbeat drummed despairingly on my empty stomach. My thigh swelled up, hard and red, around the injury. Even the light touch of my clothes hurt me.

One group of prisoners was privileged because they could speak to the guards in their own high-pitched, tonal language. Sometimes the guards brought them extra water and cereal biscuits and even cracked jokes with them. In the midst of them a young girl lay still on the hard earth, swathed in scarves and rags to protect her from the sun. During the fourth night she died and I lay listening to the noises of death and muted grief, followed by muttered prayers in Latin.

I sank back into a half-stupor. Suddenly one of the women gripped my arm. She was squatting beside me, pinching it with her sharp fingers and shaking me awake. Her breath was tainted. She spoke to me in a European language bearing a resemblance to French. When I did not understand, she became impatient. She mimed that I should take off my clothes and dragged at my T-shirt. I did as I was told because by now I was too listless to argue. I took off my jeans and T-shirt and shoes and put on a skirt and slippery blouse which the woman thrust into my hands. She held me by the arm and towed me across to join her group.

I looked round at their faces. I felt dazed. I didn't know if they intended me harm or not. They motioned me to lie down, so I sank to the ground and they covered me in rags. An hour or so later, just before the sun came up, the soldiers clanged open the compound gates and stirred us up with sticks. One of the women threw a light cloth over my face and they lifted me and carried me towards the open gate. For all I knew I could have been going to my own funeral. I didn't protest.

With an armed escort we descended the stony incline to the beach, where a sailing-boat awaited us. It was a long, narrow boat, tall in the helm. At either end a long talon pointed upwards into the dark blue sky. It had once been carved, and painted with sunflowers, but the sea had licked off most of the paint and smoothed the pattern over. The boat looked well worn and was barely big enough to contain our party.

I was lowered into the bottom and I lay rigidly on the boards. I lay like the dead, not anticipating my fate. When we were well out to sea some of the men let out howls of triumph. Hours later I worked out what they had done; they had substituted me for the dead girl, for reasons I could not guess at. Some of them were kindly and smiled and passed me water, but some looked surly and clearly regarded me as an unnecessary encumbrance. The sun made me sick and gave me feverish nightmares; my leg festered and hurt constantly. I no sooner lay down in the bottom of the boat than I wished fervently to be propped up again. Even now I can't look at swelling blue water without feeling nausea. When I had to urinate, which fortunately wasn't often, I hung over the side of the boat like a rag doll and had to be hauled in again.

We sailed for two days and nights, or three perhaps, before a cabbage-green island came into view. There were war-cries from the men as the boat scraped ashore. I stepped out onto land but I fell and lay in the shadow of a rock. The rest of the party, chattering now, moved up the beach and sat in the shade of the coconut palms. I watched through half-closed eyes. The trees quivered and seemed to be hopping nearer.

Late that afternoon a party of men arrived, leaping and slithering down amongst the trees. I dimly saw, or dreamed, that some kind of conclave was in progress and that my own fate was under discussion. One boy, a long, faded blue cloth tied round his hips, stood apart, with his arms wrapped protectively about his body. At a peremptory shout from the men he came down towards me carrying a bamboo stretcher. I looked up into a tight, scowling face and bleak eyes, but he handled me gently, despite the furious expression. He, and the little priest they called 'Pai', lifted me up between them, and we set off up the mountainside through the trees.

At first I closed my eyes and gripped the poles of the stretcher, but then I started to trust in the agility of the boy. He climbed the mountain as swiftly and unswervingly as I might have climbed a staircase. The other man puffed in the rear, sometimes tripping on meshed roots or stumbling over creepers like telephone cables. The exuberant vegetation provided plenty of overhead shade, but the air was stifling. We proceeded through green gloom. The ferns had a sweet, fetid smell like damp biscuits. Shut off from the sky by taller, pushier neighbours, the trees had all produced tumorous masses of fungus and scabs of lichen. Loud, heckling cries came from the bushes beside the track.

We stopped at intervals to drink water from a hide bag; my stretcher-bearers brushed the ants from their legs and then at once resumed their swingeing pace. Big butterflies settled on my arms to suck my sweat, excreting stickily. At dusk we stopped on a grassy lip of the flat-topped mountain and Pai picked off two leeches which were fastened to his ankle like little wobbling balloons of blood. Presently the rest of the boat party came toiling up, three of them carried on stretchers, and set up camp about a hundred yards away. The boy went off, but returned and crouched over me holding an orange-red fruit like a tomato. He pulled out the leaves and stalk and deftly fed me the pulp from his fingers. It was sweet and slippery and the first food I had eaten in several days.

The boy knelt down beside me and tried to lift my skirt away from my thigh. I jerked out of his reach and struggled to sit up. For the first time he spoke. I understood – 'no … bad, no … bad, no … bad,' from the resemblance to French. The wound on my leg had oozed and stuck to my skirt; trembling, I submitted while he soaked the cloth and peeled it away. He was perhaps as old as I am – they are a deceptively small, slightly built and hairless race.

I still wonder why none of the women came to attend to me. I don't understand why none of those who gave me water on the boat and smile at me now at the washing-place would come near me on the mountain. During the whole of the journey through the jungle I was left alone with the priest and the boy. I have to call him 'the boy' because I don't know his name.

After he had cleaned the wound he made a poultice of leaves to cover it. He disappeared into the trees and came back with some long, slim limbs of wood with which he constructed a raised platform, lashed together with creepers. He floored and roofed it with bendy young branches and then he fetched some big palm leaves to lay on the lattice-work of the platform and roof. This was my bed; he lifted me up carefully and put me in it. From the other group came the sound of chatter and whistle music, but the boy lit a smoky fire and lay down near it.

During the night I was woken by my own groans. I felt clammy and my heartbeat thundered through my skull. The night air smelt of singeing and it was full of the churring of harsh little voices. At once, the boy was there, wiping my face and speaking softly in my ear. I didn't understand anything except the word for 'sleep', but his presence comforted me. I wanted to keep him near me and on impulse I held out my hand, which he took and clasped tightly in his. Then we must both have fallen asleep. In the morning he was still sleeping next to me on the four-poster bed. He was lying on his front, with his arm lightly across my waist. He woke and sat up, his eyes wary.

While the morning was still cool the boy brought me some mushy rice in broth and I ate it with my fingers. I tried the English and French words for thank you, but he didn't understand, so I smiled instead, through stiff, sun-blistered lips. Before we left, he caught a fat female mosquito and popped it to show me the human blood inside. Then he gave me a handful of leaves, chewed one himself and nodded to me to do the same. I was curious about the medicinal properties of the leaves and kept them carefully. At that time I believed, ironically, that I was being transported to a hospital and from there to the local airport.

We went on as before. I travelled on my dais like an Egyptian queen. White mist was boiling up out of the valley below us. Once a loud howl came from the trees to the side of us and an animal could be heard crashing around in the foliage. We climbed more tall pointed hills and skirted the bare crater of the volcano, which sat on the soft sand like a blancmange turned out from a mould. The top was wreathed in sulphurous smoke which blew in our faces and made me wheeze.

In the afternoon the three of us stopped by a waterfall. Below, I could see cultivated land, a patchwork of padi-fields in pink, gold and green. The other party carried on down the hillside and over a rope bridge. As he passed, one of the stretcher bearers looked sideways and made a rough, jeering comment. The boy, stung, cried out loudly in indignation and the priest made placatory gestures. As the man turned away, he surreptitiously crossed himself. I was startled to see the little priest aim a hard kick at his bottom.

I was left alone with the boy again. This time he didn't busy himself with tasks but sat with a bent head, plucking disconsolately at stalks. I reached over tentatively and touched his arm. He turned and gave me a look so fixed and intense that I held my breath. Then he jumped up and signed me with his hand to wait and watch. He ran lightly over the rocks to the waterfall, pulled aside the branches of a tree and disappeared, seemingly into the falling water. He re-emerged, dry, and stood poised on a boulder, as though waiting for applause. I was puzzled and shook my head. I was slow to understand. Since then I have looked for the waterfall a dozen times.

We heard the sound of two men returning. They had changed into brightly-coloured shirts and cotton trousers and smelt clean and spicy. Without a word they picked me up between them and trotted off down the path to the swaying bridge. I looked up at the boy. He had shrunk back against the rockface and was again the wretched creature I had first seen at the beach. I wanted to call out to him but it all happened very quickly and no words came.

XII

two and a half moons gone, ten and a half moons to go

This little book lies on the floor and every so often I pick it up and re-read it. I read what we did, the boy and I. It was little enough, and perhaps it has been changed in the remembering and writing of it. I think about him, especially at night, when I am trying to sleep and trying not to make the floor creak. I wish I could see him again.

If I ask Dona Dalu about him she says she doesn't know, in a tone which suggests that I shouldn't have asked. I sometimes suspect she is a man-hater and widowhood suits her well; she never speaks of her late husband and, in this most fecund of communities, she has no children. I don't mean to suggest that she likes women better. Her cronies often remark, smiling, that she is like a mother to me, or that I am like a daughter to her. She is not, and I am not, except that I live with her and obey her. I think they say it to please her. They are afraid of her and so am I.

She never calls me 'daughter' as the other old women do; that word is locked up somewhere behind the puckered mouth and gooseberry-green eyes. I certainly don't call her 'mother', either, although I am used to calling Māezinha 'cousin-sister' and am apparently more or less adopted into the family.

I don't mean to be ungrateful, and she is not ungrateful either. Once she gave me a new-born nanny-kid, a limp, quivering, beige-coloured scrap, the smaller of twins, with a pat and a leer. I had to force-feed it hourly, and by the time it could raise its head its mother had forgotten it. I stood it near her and she butted it across the shed. So I went on feeding it and the kid lived in the house with us.

Fortunately for me, but not for her, Dalu can no longer climb the ladder, so the upper storey of the house, or hut, is mine alone. It's small but fragrant. Downstairs some of the walls are wooden, but up here they are woven bamboo screens. The dawn light shows through them in pinpricks. The window has no glass and the hut backs onto the mountain-side, so I can look out, or climb out, at any time and watch the green thundery light of evening turn to night and listen to the insistent insect chorus.

Most days Dalu can dress herself, but her knuckles and finger-joints are knobbly and her knee and hip hurt her so she is not really capable of much more; a bit of winnowing perhaps. The rest I do. My feet are rotting between the toes from paddling through the rice field. I have to squat to transplant the seedlings. My back doesn't seem made to bend like the backs of the native workers. Sometimes I make ironic jokes to myself about voluntary service overseas and how this was not really what I had in mind.

When I first arrived, Mãezinha tended both myself and Dalu and we lay groaning and creaking side by side on the floor. Happily I didn't know then that this baleful old woman was to be my constant companion, and this hut not a stopping-off place but my destination. After a few days I got up and stood in the doorway of the hut. The heat enveloped me like a blanket but the sky was low and grey. In one place beside the track the sun was beaming through like a searchlight, and there the vegetation glowed fiercely. On the veranda of the opposite hut squatted three old women, their skirt-tails pulled up between their legs to pre-serve their modesty. They nodded gravely in greeting and all the passing children paused and stared at me, waving and smiling widely, or averting their faces, squirming with laughter. Presently the ever-giggling Mãezinha appeared with an exercise book. Excited, but chewing her lip with apprehension, she settled down beside me for our first lesson.

Mãezinha came every day at dusk. At first we wrote down all the words she taught me but I found numerous puzzling incon-sistencies. I realized after a while that Mãezinha couldn't spell and in fact could barely write. So after that we had conversation les-sons, turning the pages at intervals to convince Dalu that we were working and not wasting time. Pai, who doubles as priest and primary-school teacher, gave me a children's alphabet book, from which I learned that the letter 'm' has four little legs, like a table.

Because we have goats and a rice-field, we have some stand-ing in the community and we don't hob-nob with the tea-pickers from up the Steps. One day Mãezinha took me round to visit Sr. Onorusco, who is the big landowner and the most prestigious person in the village. His house is an august relic of the colonial days, stone-built and flying the green and red flag. The outer door was opened by a servant, who led us across a cobbled courtyard. In the middle was a defunct fountain, and climbing up it, a stone dwarf wearing a black and white checked cotton skirt.

Sr. Onorusco had on a white shirt and cream trousers. He had well-oiled wavy hair and a mildly harassed expression. Mãezinha addressed him respectfully as 'Tuan'. She had brought my exercise book in which I had sketched a family group and an ocean-going vessel to convey the question I could not ask in words: 'When can I go home?'

Sr. Onorusco looked at the drawings. By gestures, he conveyed 'sleep, sky, circle, *moon*' and then drew a whole row of thirteen moons. He briskly tapped the ocean-liner to make his point. I felt sure he hadn't properly understood my query. I sketched a little plane: Sr. Onorusco permitted himself a smile but shook his head, looking pityingly at my stricken face. He circled the boat and shrugged apologetically, to make me understand that there was no other way to go home.

Mãezinha walked back with me, pouting mournfully in sympathy with my obvious chagrin. We climbed up into my warm little loft beneath the grass thatch and sat on the floor. I felt trapped and despondent. I half-suspected I was being lied to, that no one wanted to take me to the boat, it suited them better to keep me here. I was only being churlish. Mãezinha, silent for once, began lifting strands of my hair, combing them with her fingers. I was soothed, and closed my eyes. Tears of self-pity threatened. After a few minutes it occurred to me that, like a mother monkey in the zoo, she was actually checking me for nits.

Sometimes I'm convinced the boat will never come and I'll never leave this island. At other times I can believe that my parents will locate and rescue me. They will almost certainly have learned how the three of us were taken prisoner on Tuluk; but there my optimism falters. I can't imagine any sane communication coming out of that dreadful compound.

I think about the boat perhaps once a day, and I fill in Onorusco's moons like a child with an advent calendar. I think about the boy perhaps once or twice a day too, and how the same mosquito perhaps bit us both as we lay together, and mixed our blood inside it. Mostly I have to concentrate on the job in hand – rubbing the firm warm udders of the goats, squeezing the speckled teats alternately until the first fierce stream goes rattling like marbles into the bucket. Dalu is teaching me. She is an exacting and implacable tutor. She seldom needs to comment on my slowness and stupidity. Her expression does it for her.

I've only once seen Dalu at a loss. Isti, our senior goat, was straining; her vagina pulsed, wide open and bright with blood. Dalu could not get her stiff hands inside and so I had to fumble around instead, encountering two little hooves and a huge rump: no, twin heads. I turned to signal 'two' to Dalu and as I did so the goat gave a high-pitched bray of pain and delivered her kid into my fluttering hands. I stared at the little creature in that calm moment of disbelief which precedes shock. It had two heads, joined at the muzzle, four eyes and two mouths, one set sideways and both bleating independently.

I looked at Dalu. Her pupils were contracted and her mouth hung open. She picked up a rock in her arthritic hand and dashed it ferociously on the little beast's forehead. Then she gripped my wrist and shook it, urging, 'Don't speak of this! Don't speak of this! To no one! Understand?'

To reassure her I put my finger to my lips. It smelt of rusty iron and sea salt.

We took the little monster and carried it out to the hillside and buried it deeply. It was a normal little nanny but for the Siamese heads. Dalu crossed herself. That evening she sat propped up like a dummy against the screen, her hands twisted together in agitation and pressed against her mouth. Before I went to bed I knelt down beside her and stroked her cheek. I don't think she noticed. Perhaps such freaks are common amongst goats, I don't know. I pitied Dalu for her superstitious fear, but I was a little awed myself. It was as though the Devil had paid us a visit.

✳   ✳   ✳

five months gone: eight months to go

As my command of the language improves I like Mãezinha more and more. At first I thought of her as a tiny mechanical doll, working and smiling, working and smiling. But Mãezinha was not so prejudiced; she treated me from the first as she would treat any other girl.

Once, when we were sitting cross-legged on the veranda, drinking the milk from a green coconut, she looked at me slyly from the corners of her eyes and asked,

'Amy, do you like any of the boys in the village?'

'The boys in the village?' I said in surprise. 'Yes, of course.'

'Which one do you like?' she asked, simpering.

'They're all OK. But I don't like any one of them especially.'
My stomach lurched, already queasy with coconut milk, as I felt
a tremulous need to confide my secret. 'The one I like is the boy
who carried me over the mountain.'

'I know.' Mãezinha stood up and wriggled in her tight cotton
skirt.

'How can I find him again, Mãezinha?'

'You've asked me that a million times already.'

'I could ask Pai who he is. I'm sure Pai knows him.'

I thought she would offer to go with me, but she didn't. She
just held out her little hands in a graceful gesture of resignation.

Until then I hadn't dared to go and ask Pai, but now I was disappointed in Mãezinha and it became a point of pride to show
her I could manage without her. So I set off haughtily down the
rutted track, despite the coconut milk sloshing heavily about
inside me. Under my breath I was rehearsing the question: I can
communicate well enough with Mãezinha, but with Dalu and
some of the others I still have to resort to mime.

Pai should have been a cricketer; his talent lies in patient
blocking and deflecting.

'Pai,' I said in my best Hispanic, 'who is the boy who carried
me over the mountains with you?'

'Why do you ask?'

'I would like to thank him.'

Pai smiled. 'It's not necessary. Thanks are not necessary.'

'But I would like to see him.'

He considered me thoughtfully, and said, 'If you were an
island girl you would be married by now.'

This idea frightened me very much. I could imagine Pai and
Dalu getting together and selecting a mate for my perpetual
entrapment. Nevertheless I persisted,

'Father, I only want to know his name, and where he lives.'

He nodded, smiling shrewdly, but continued as if I hadn't
spoken. 'But you aren't an island girl. When the boat comes you'll
go home and marry a young man from your own country. And
forget all about us.' He laughed, and made a sweeping-off-the-
table gesture.

'Of course I won't forget you. I owe you my life.'

He stood up, smiling and embracing me, but shepherding me
towards the door.

'Do you know him, Father?'

'Patience, daughter. Be calm, be calm.'

'Why won't you tell me?'

His answer was more genial laughter.

'Father,' I said desperately, 'where is the waterfall you can pass behind?' He protruded his lower lip dubiously. I went on, 'We stopped there, you, me and the boy, near the bridge. It was the last time we stopped. There was a waterfall and you can pass behind the water and enter the rock.'

'No, there is no such waterfall.'

'But I saw it.'

He tapped the top of his head and pointed upward, saying, 'A touch of the sun'.

'You don't know it?'

'There is no such waterfall.'

'How long have you lived here, Father?'

At this he threw back his head and laughed uproariously.

'All my life. And there is no such waterfall. And you, daughter, must go home to Dona Dalu. And be calm, the boat will come.'

I didn't go home. Instead I went up to sit with the goats. Matahari, my own little mongrel kid, laid her head on my lap, belching gently and chewing the cud, blowing her foul breath in my face. While I sat there it came to me that what he had shown me was a refuge. The waterfall was his hiding-place.

The next day I went to look for Māezinha and found her at the washing-place, vigorously scrubbing linen on a stone, her entire skinny body moving back and forth like a piston. When she saw me, she smiled widely and began to chatter about the coming festival when the boys of the village would declare themselves to their sweethearts and the left-over girls would perform a dance of longing called the Gandrung. The weather was better, and as we spread out her washing several lizards tickled the grass and a large zebra-striped butterfly sailed by like a flying convolvulus flower. Hand-in-hand we walked to the batik factory, Māezinha's work-place. I liked to watch her work. She heated up the wax over a little spirit stove and dribbled it onto the cloth through a tiny copper pipe in whorls and spirals. Benício, the owner's son, was printing shadow-puppet motifs onto tracing paper: they were fearsome angular deities with skinny arms and pointed elbows.

On the way home I spotted ahead of me a naked human figure veering from one side of the track to the other like a rabid dog.

By cutting off the corner I arrived at our house in time to observe his arrival. He was a squat, ill co-ordinated brute; his eyes squinted and his lower jaw protruded like Javaman's. As he lurched along the path he crowed and cuckooed fiercely. At our door he stopped and nosed in, so that Dalu and I had a clear view of the undershot jaw, low brow and dull feral eyes. But he withdrew at the sight of us and scampered to the open door of the goat shed, where the goats paused fractionally in their masticating to look at him sardonically.

'Be quick,' Dalu commanded, 'and fetch a fresh bone.'

I went and found a leg-bone. It was not all that fresh but some hairs and hide still clung to it, and we flung it to him. He licked the dried blood on it, and chewed on the gristle of the knee cartilage, then sped off with his meal. Dalu crossed herself. 'We must protect our goats, girl,' was all she said.

I sometimes feel that I don't understand these people at all.

XIII

six and a half moons gone, six and a half moons to go

I began the day as a traveller in a lampshade hat, sitting in the back of the cow cart with Benício and Mãezinha. We were taking the bales of wax-printed cloth to the Port Stores, and I was going to do some shopping. While the others went in, I stood holding the cow and looking out at the tepid wavelets slapping on the beach. The sea looks like satin, but just outside the port there are serious hazards for small boats and swimmers: sharks and drop-off, whirlpools and hot water spouts. Dalu told me this as though she suspected me of plotting my escape.

The door opened and a boy emerged in a hurry. He stopped dead, but poised for flight in an attitude I remembered. For a moment he hung there in the corner like a crane-fly, his thin arms spread out against the walls. Then he said,

'It's you.'

I said eagerly, 'Olá! Where have you been? I went to look for the waterfall lots of times but I couldn't find it.'

'I left some things there for you.'

'What things?'

'Medicinal leaves. Things of no importance.'

We stared at each other. I noticed that his mouth was beautiful, with a long curving upper lip and a full, straight lower one. He said,

'Are you well? Is your leg better?'

I unwrapped my skirt to show him. He didn't touch me, but the skin of my thigh was sensitive to his gaze. His eyes met mine in a long sombre look.

'It's better,' I said breathlessly.

'Now you speak Portuguese.'

'My cousin Mãezinha is teaching me. But she didn't tell me it was Portuguese.'

He said, 'It is. My great-grandfather was a sailor once. I have his maps and a picture of Portugal. I could show you them.'

I would have agreed to anything. I said at once, 'I'd like to see them.'

He slowly reached out a hand and stroked the curve of my

waist. Then he looked at me half-fearfully. I took his hand and said winsomely, 'Are you coming to the festival at our village tonight?'
'No.'
'Oh,' I said in disappointment. 'Can't you come? Please come.'
'No. No!' he said in a tone of dismay. The door opened, and he moved round the corner and into the shadow. I thought I had never met anyone so nervous. Benício came out and said, 'Tie up the cow and give me a hand.' I tied her to a rail and helped him carry in and stack the rolls of cloth. When I'd finished the boy had disappeared and he didn't come back, although I went stumbling around and calling in the rough area at the back of the stores.

I was upset. I didn't know when I was going to see him again, I hadn't asked his name, I still didn't know where the waterfall was and I wanted to get my 'things of no importance'. If we'd been alone I'd have told Mãezinha, but Benício was there, bragging and blustering as usual, so I sat pensively in my corner, watching the shadow of my pointed head bobbing above the cart and wanting to cry out childishly, 'But you promised, you promised to show me the maps!'

Mãezinha looked unusually serious; she barely responded to Benício, who needed no encouragement anyway. I had never seen her before with her mouth out of action. She had a pretty, sultry mouth. It was very like my boy's mouth, which I had just thought so beautiful. I suppose that such marked resemblances are not surprising on an island such as this where there must be continual inbreeding. As though she had guessed my thoughts, Mãezinha turned to me and whispered in my ear, 'Don't tell Tia Dalu!'

By this time we had reached our house and I scrambled down, wondering, 'Don't tell Tia Dalu what?' The warning was unnecessary, as I never told Dalu anything if I could help it.

It was one of her good days. She had lit a charcoal fire and was squatting down by it making *gado gado*, beansprouts in peanut sauce, for the party. As we are a comparatively well-off household, we also took along some little wobbly jelly-covered cakes wrapped in a leaf. They tasted a bit like bread pudding, a bit like marzipan.

Dalu was in unusually good humour. In fact good humour is so unusual for Dalu you might almost have called her manic. She held my arm and as she hobbled along she filled me in on the mythological background to the dances I would see. She is very hard to understand, but requires little response beyond a few wide-eyed nods. She told me that the masks the dancers used were so powerful that the wearers had to be revived with holy water afterwards. Mãezinha had made the festival sound like the St Valentine's hop at our local church hall; I found her descriptions of romping around the fire hard to reconcile with Dalu's version of the festival. I thought that perhaps the old ones watched the cultural events and then left before the fire was doused and the serious courting began.

We reached the party late. We had missed the first procession, but all made way for Dona Dalu and her basket. A shower of huge furry moths and beetles were battering themselves against the lanterns around the little stage, on which stood Mãezinha in a Christmas-tree head-dress, her legs slightly bowed and bare feet splayed, her face intent, her braceleted arms moving like fronds of weed underwater. I had never seen Mãezinha dance before and had thought of her little body as neuter, unlovely but functional.

The musicians sat cross-legged around the stage. One played a xylophone which sounded like a cracked bell, one a gong, one a gamelan, and another a bronze drum in the shape of an hour-glass. They chimed and jingled tunelessly in a steady trotting rhythm or with slow, widely-separated notes. It made a soothing sound, like water dripping.

After Mãezinha came the promised pantomime depicting the struggle between good and evil. Evil was represented by the Rangda, a widow-witch with fangs and bulbous eyes and a necklace of guts. Her opponent was a loveable lion-faced cater-pillar. More glaring, whirling deities followed, and other car-nival creatures. There was some frank horsing around with a dildo which amused everyone except Dalu and me.

I stayed at Dalu's side throughout, drinking yoghurt and sirsak juice from a bamboo mug, so that all her friends could come up and tell her we were like mother and daughter. She never demurs, only smiles grimly. A chicken was killed on stage to signal the end of the performance and the old people got up to take refreshments: smoked eel, barbecued pork, roast grasshop-pers, *tape* and palm wine. Then the fire was lit, and the workers paraded around it carrying spades and churns or balancing baskets on their heads. The music changed to a heavy, clumping rhythm and the Conquerors' songs were sung in piercing little Oriental voices. The dancers stamped and clapped vigorously – a good way of keeping the infuriating foot-biting insects at bay.

At first I was wary of dancing with anyone in case it constituted some kind of unwanted contract, but then I saw Mãezinha, who had run home to get changed, being spun into the dance by Benício, whom I know for a fact she despises, so I thought that I would risk it if someone asked me. But no one did. No one wanted to dance with a clumsy foreigner, who didn't know the steps, and I dawdled slowly around the perimeter of the square, keeping to the dark edge so that I wouldn't look as left out and awkward as I felt. I was near to tears. As I circled the little dancers, I fantasized that my ex-boyfriend would come leaping from a helicopter, scattering the enthralled villagers. This fatuous scene sustained me as far as the little wooden bridge over the goldfish pond.

It was one of those rare occasions when reality and fantasy conspire, and fall out, and reality emerges triumphant. As I crossed the bridge someone called me from the foot of the steps.

'Ssssss!'

It was him, the boy.

'You came!'

He said, 'We must be quiet!' He seemed over-heated and he trembled when I touched his hands. In one he had a frangipani flower which he tucked behind my ear as I had seen the boys doing at the dance.

He was not smiling. His rigidity forewarned me of his intention. He blurted out on a note of desperation, 'Kiss my mouth the way they kiss at the *festa*.'

I kissed his mouth very gently. The shock of excitement turned me slightly sick. He pulled me down into a crouch and pushed me before him into the bamboo thicket. We lay down on the broken leaves and embraced and kissed again. I was streaming with sweat but the boy felt dry and hot and very thin; beneath the cotton of his sarong I could already feel what I was going to get.

He rolled me over and pulled up my skirt at the back. Then he tried ineffectually to spear me. He was a bit wild and lacking in finesse, but nothing seemed to matter except getting it in before he gave up. We found the place by a joint effort. He scraped at my stomach with his nails, moving frenetically inside me. I couldn't really participate except by my acquiescence. We were well within earshot of the revelry and I found out at first hand what the pumping beat and thrusting hoe-handles symbolized. He cried out, 'Oh! I can't stop it!', then he came with a little ulu-

106

lation and withdrew at once. I turned and took him in my arms.
I said in English,

'I love you.'

He asked, like a child, 'I didn't do anything bad, did I?'

'No, you did nothing bad.'

He pulled back and looked at me and said, 'You are my girlfriend, aren't you? Say it.'

'I am your girlfriend.'

He had slipped into the intimate form of address which they
use for family. I stroked the ridge of his back and his skinny but-
tocks. His sticky penis lay half-deflated on my thigh. I too was
half-aroused; the mouth of my vagina felt as stiff and hungry as
a fledgeling's beak. At the same time I felt drugged with happi-
ness, because of having him near me and unambiguously mine. I
was flushed and sleepy with love, drunk without wine. We lay
and necked for a long time in a state of trance. Then I remembered
to ask him his name.

'I don't know your name. Mine is Amy.'

He said, 'I know what your name is. Pai told me.'

'Pai told you!' I said indignantly. 'He wouldn't tell me your
name. What is it?'

He averted his eyes, muttering something that sounded like
'Jwangeh.'

'Jwangeh?'

'Don't say it! It's a bad name.'

'But I must call you something.'

He frowned. His mood had changed. He demanded impetu-
ously, 'Stay with me tonight.'

'But I can't. I have to go back to the party. They'll miss me.'

'No,' he said curtly. 'We'll sleep at the waterfall, together. It
won't rain. We'll be safe.'

I wanted to sleep out with him, to sleep in a full embrace and
wake up entwined, in the heat of the morning. But I didn't dare
disappear for the night without Dalu's permission. I wouldn't
have risked it with my own mother, and Dalu didn't strike me as
any more broad-minded. I said helplessly,

'I can't. No one will know where I am; there'll be trouble. I
have to go back.'

'No,' he said sharply. 'You're staying with me tonight. Now
you're my girlfriend and you have to stay with me.'

He had imprisoned me under him and gripped my arms. A

prickly plant was scratching my neck and I struggled to sit up. I said, placating,

'I want to stay. But I can't. Dona Dalu will be worried.'

'If you go back, I'll never see you again.'

Tears came to my eyes. 'How can you say that! How can you?'

'Because it's the truth. You understand nothing. "Dalu will worry!" he mocked. 'You think Dalu will worry about you? She loves you like a daughter, does she?'

I said, 'No, she doesn't and I don't love her. I don't like her. But I live in her house and I have to be courteous at least. She deserves that.'

'Don't tell me what Dalu deserves,' he said furiously.

I didn't understand the rancour, the grim tone. I asked, 'Do you know Dalu?'

'No,' he said bitterly, 'I don't know her. I only know her name.'

I wondered then if there were some kind of caste system on the island and if this was why they all said they didn't know each other when they probably lived a few miles apart. I said,

'Dalu is like the person in the Bible who gives a stone when you ask for bread. But I have to try to be grateful.' I don't know how much he understood of my peculiar Portuguese, but after a moment he started to laugh, which was not a pleasant sound.

I said, 'You think I'm stupid.'

'No, you're not stupid, but you don't understand how things are.'

I had heard this line once too often from Mãezinha and it irritated me. I thought that they were all very good at cryptic utterances but never bothered to explain anything properly.

'I never will understand if you won't explain.'

He bent his head, then he said miserably, 'I want to tell you. But I can't, I can't.'

I said gently, 'Why can't you tell me, *querido*?'

He mumbled, 'I'm afraid.'

I wondered fleetingly about his mental state. His reactions seemed so extreme. He had cried a few involuntary tears which I wiped away with my fingers. I said recklessly, 'If it's so important, I'll come with you tonight.'

'No.'

'I want to come.'

'No. It was wrong of me to ask.'

'You can ask me anything you like.'

'No. It was not fair.'

I put my arms round his bare shoulders, but he stood up at once. 'Forget it. Go back to the party. Go back to Dalu and your cousin.'

'I don't want to leave you,' I said, hurt. 'When shall I see you?'

'I don't know.'

'Tell me how to find the waterfall.'

He hesitated, then said in a mechanical way, 'You go up to the top of the steps and take the path to the left. Then as soon as you can, you take a path up the mountain; keep taking the steepest track until you come to the bridge. Then you'll see the waterfall.'

I said, 'When will you be there?'

'I don't know. Often. Now go back. Be careful of the bridge.'

I said querulously, 'I can't see the bridge. It's too dark.'

The fire had been doused, to howls and shrieks from the boys and girls, though the music went on. He hesitated, then said, 'Hold on to me and keep quiet.'

We crossed the little bridge single-file, my hands on his naked waist. On the other side we nearly collided with someone: a big tea-picker, I think. The boy whispered, 'Now I must go.'

'Don't be angry with me.'

He said, 'It's not your fault.'

He let me cling to him. We swayed for a moment to the music coming from the lighted stage. He was exactly of my height. I wanted to dance with him but I knew he would refuse.

There was a wall of blue flame as some practical joker chose to re-light the fire with the aid of paraffin. Then came a rustling sound and a roar as a great bunch of dry branches, saved up especially for the purpose no doubt, were tossed into the middle. In the flare of light could be seen startled lovers breaking apart, and a number of couples scuttling out of the undergrowth, tugging at their clothes. There was a lot of laughter, embarrassment and indignation; this joke was probably repeated every year.

Who would have thought Dalu could move so fast? Before I knew it she had yanked my head back and hit me across the face with all her force. It was the kind of blow which killed the little monster nanny. Then she wound her claw in my hair and towed me unprotesting across the field behind her like a donkey on a rope. The dancers all stood and stared. I caught sight of Mãez-inha's dismayed face. The flower fell from my hair and I half stooped to reach for it, but Dalu hit me another crack and tugged on my hair. Her lips were frothy with spit. She called me a name I'd not heard before.

The truth is that I'm not a very brave person. I rarely oppose anyone except by stealth, and I allowed Dalu to humiliate me publicly. She prodded me into the cow cart and ordered me to stay. Like a dog I did as I was told. I was trembling. My nose and lip were numb and my face was burning. I've never been slapped so hard before. On the stage there was some kind of commotion but I couldn't see round the corner of the houses.

I could have run off into the dark, but I wasn't brave enough. Perhaps I was just too canny. I knew I needed the shelter of Dalu's house and the goodwill of the community. My chances of surviving alone in the jungle weren't worth a kitten's whisker. Dalu got into the cart and pushed her bony little body up uncomfortably close against mine. We both sat staring ahead, with her elbow digging into my waist. When we hit the bumps we joggled hard together.

I was glumly apprehensive about what my punishment might be, but by the time we reached home her galvanic rage was spent and she had returned to her everyday ill-humour. She ordered me harshly up the ladder, and I went thankfully, to sit alone in the miserable confusion of my thoughts.

Someone must have watched me and the boy making love in the bamboo grove and reported to Dalu. I felt outraged by the spying eyes and I felt ashamed too. I hated to think of my flower being trodden underfoot.

As I write, the lamp is running out of oil. I wish I had gone with him.

XIV

It's raining. No wonder they speak of the rain with such awe. It's not like English rain. The village pathways are canals, everything moveable is floating. The little carts have become boats. A minute ago there were scurrying workers all along the track, carrying baskets on shoulder-poles; now they are all wading waist-deep through the water, baskets bobbing. It's warm rain – the children have come running down in cheering, excited gangs to splash and wallow in the ditches.

I'm not confined to my hutch any more. Dalu called me down last night and lifted the restriction. She said, 'It wasn't your fault, girl'. I wish she wouldn't show traces of human feeling, I'd prefer to hate her unreservedly. 'You must not look at that person, or speak to that person again. Do you understand?'

I said that I understood. I was glad she didn't extract a false promise and force me to lie. Then she said, 'You can stay down here,' but as soon as I decently could I went up to bed. I didn't want to be with Dalu, and that person's semen was still leaking down my leg.

I was nearly asleep when someone squeezed through my window and dropped down lightly beside me. It wasn't my boy, but it was the next best person, Māezinha, who quickly put her finger to her lips and lay down next to me. She said, 'Tell me what happened,' and I did, beginning with the meeting at the Port Stores.

'You invited him to the *festa*? *Meu Deus!*' said Māezinha in a tone of awe. 'And then? At the *festa*?'

She wouldn't accept my evasions and kept pestering me for more details. 'And when you were lying in the bamboo grove, what did he do? Did he put his *coiso* up inside you?'

In the face of such ingenuous frankness, I couldn't lie.

'Yes.'

'*Nossa Senhora!*' said Māezinha. I felt her shudder. Then she said purposefully, 'Look, we have to go to the sulphur baths.'

'To the volcano? What, now? Are you crazy?'

'Listen to me. We have to go at once. You must take an offering, some rice, salted meat, whatever. You must get into the sulphur bath and wash out your inside. That's what the girls do when they don't want babies.'

I was fairly sure it wouldn't work. 'That's all rubbish, Māezinha.'

'It's not!' Māezinha was getting agitated. 'You must do it. It's bad juice. You must wash it out at once.'

Her insistence began to frighten me, and I half rose. I said, 'Why do you say that? Does he have an illness?'

I was beginning to tremble. I was already calculating my chances of getting back to civilization before the disease reached its chronic stage. 'Māezinha! Is he ill?'

She said reluctantly, 'No. I don't know. I don't know if he is ill.'

Downstairs Dalu coughed and we were both still for a moment.

I hissed furiously, 'Then what is it? Tell me!'

She only looked at me dolefully.

'If you won't tell me, I won't go to the sulphur bath. Why do you say bad juice?'

'Bad family,' Māezinha whispered at last.

'Bad family! How do you know? Do you know who he is?'

She looked away. I accused, 'You do! You've been lying to me all this time! I thought you were my friend.' Her lips trembled. I demanded, 'Why did you lie to me?'

'Because of Aunt Dalu. Aunt Dalu hates him. If she knew what you'd done she'd kick you out of the house.'

'Well I don't believe you. You're not afraid of Dona Dalu. Why didn't you tell me you knew him? You could have warned me not to say anything.'

'Oh! All right!' said Māezinha angrily. 'I didn't tell you because I didn't want you to see him again. You were silly. You thought about him too much.'

I asked curiously, 'Were you jealous?'

'Jealous! You're so stupid. If you only knew! If you knew the trouble you're bringing on yourself.'

'If I don't know, why don't you tell me?'

'Come with me to the sulphur bath and wash yourself. Don't say a word to anyone. Don't think about him ever again. When you go home you can marry an educated man. That is the right thing for you.'

'Is your family more important than his, Māezinha?' I ventured. 'I know some families on this island are more important than others.'

'You don't know anything.'

'Then tell me.'

She said haughtily, 'We don't speak of such things in my family.'

'Mãezinha, you're my friend. Tell me. I promise I won't repeat a word of it.'

She said reluctantly, 'If I tell you all I know, will you come to the sulphur bath?'

'Oh heavens! Yes, all right.'

She squatted down then, and her face became gradually solemn with the unwelcome responsibility. She began, 'Well, did you know Tia Dalu had a husband?'

'Yes, I thought he was dead.'

'Tia Dalu's husband went missing one day. He was well-liked in the village; all the men turned out to search for him. But they didn't find him.'

'So what had happened to him?'

'I don't know; some say he escaped, on a small boat, but no one saw him go.'

I laughed. I could well imagine why he went.

'And did you know,' she lowered her voice even further, 'that Tia Dalu had a daughter?'

'Dona Dalu told me she had no children.'

'Well she had. A daughter of twelve called Maria de Conceição. She worked in Dona Rosário's house. And when her father went, at that same time, they found out that the girl was pregnant.'

'At twelve?'

Mãezinha nodded. 'She wouldn't tell them who had done it. They all say she was a very timid girl. She never went far on her own.'

I could well imagine that Dalu's little daughter would be utterly cowed and compliant.

'They all said ... it was her father who did it.'

'Her father!'

'Tia Dalu thought so too. She put her out of the house.'

I struggled with feelings of distaste. I knew Conceição was the victim of her bestial father, but she repelled me too; she was implicated by her own mute, stupid acquiescence. I was being unfair and uncharitable, but I come from a normal family where such things don't happen. I said half-maliciously, 'What a shock that must have been for Dalu!'

'She never talked about it. She sent Conceição up the mountain to live with her paternal grandfather, a forester. He was a

113

crazy old man by all accounts. His wife was dead. Then when the baby was a few months old she brought it down to the village and went to see Tia Dalu. She pleaded with her mother to take them in.'

'And did she?'

'No. All the village heard them, shouting and wailing. Then the girl went off with the baby and Sr. Nestor, the store-keeper, saw them at the port at nightfall. She was washed up in the morning on the shingle.'

'Oh God!'

I thought that this wretched little story explained why Dalu was as she was. And then I thought that perhaps Dalu's being as she was explained the story. But whatever Mãezinha had meant to convey, she had more to tell.

'The old grandfather never came down to the village much after his wife died. He sent the wood down the chute and now and again he took his carvings to the Port Stores. But one day he arrived at the school with a little boy; it was Conceição's child.'

'I thought the baby was drowned!'

'So did everyone. Well the boy only came to school for a little while. Outside he would leap and climb like a goat, but inside he just crouched in a corner of the schoolroom. The children were frightened of him because of what he was.'

'What do you mean?'

'People said he was a monster because of the wrong thing his parents did to make him. Some said he drowned with his mother but the Devil rescued him from the water and flew him up the mountain.'

'What nonsense!' I said indignantly. 'You can't believe that, Mãezinha. His mother must have taken him home herself.'

'She didn't have time.' Mãezinha held out her hands and shrugged. 'Sr. Nestor doesn't tell lies. She couldn't have done it.'

'Then she dropped the baby off somewhere for the grand-father to pick up. What did he say about it?'

'He was a crazy old man. He didn't say much and what he did say didn't make much sense.'

'Well, go on.'

'Some of the children were afraid to go to school if he was there. And the others used to taunt him behind Pai's back. People wanted Pai to send him away but Pai said we had to let him come. Then Pai took him to the village well and baptized him in

114

front of everyone. The old grandfather named him 'João Ninguém'. It means Nobody. But it didn't make any difference. So after a while the old man took him away from the school and they hardly ever came to the village again.'

I thought it was the most miserable tale I had ever heard. I said, 'How could they be so cruel? Didn't anyone take his side?'

'Dona Fátima. She doesn't care about Tia Dalu or anyone.' She looked at my expression and said defensively, 'He's all right. Sr. Onorusco pays him for the wood he cuts and Sr. Nestor serves him at the stores. Pai still goes up the mountain to see him though the old grandfather has been dead three years now. And the people from the other villages call him the *guia* because they say he knows every stone on the mountain. But mostly he keeps himself to himself. If he comes into the village, people cross themselves and keep their fronts to him so he can't call them back.'

'What do you mean, call them back?'

'If someone calls your name from behind they put a curse on you. If it's a powerful curse you can die. That's the old religion.'

It didn't sound like any kind of religion to me. I said, 'But what has he ever done to be treated like that?'

'It's not what he's done,' said Mãezinha inexorably, 'it's what he is. And he can be nasty. Tonight old Wufti threw him a bone and he hurled it back at her. Then he jumped up on the stage and overturned all the trestles.'

I said, 'I've seen him, I'm sure I have. He came running naked into our goat-shed and Dona Dalu made me toss him a bone.'

'That's not João Ninguém.' Mãezinha looked at me uneasily. 'João Ninguém is seventeen years old. You still don't understand, do you? He's your boy. The one who carried you over the mountains.'

Once or twice I've come upon the scene of a road accident, and looked compulsively, with a kind of detached pity and revulsion. This was like catching sight of a familiar car, all buckled up, recognizing the sweater of the person who was lying on the road. I'd felt indignant on behalf of Conceição and her little boy; but now their hurt and disgrace were mine too. They had entered my body with João's semen.

'No!' I said violently.

'Sshh!' Mãezinha put her arms around me, restraining me.

'Let go of me.'

'Sshh! Come on, let's go to the sulphur baths.'

I went rigid with anger. I said, 'Thank you for telling me that horrible story. I'll come to the sulphur baths if you want because I promised. But I won't wash out his juice. I love him and I want to keep it.'

Mãezinha said, 'You don't understand ...'

'Don't ever tell me again that I don't understand. You're ignorant. You don't understand.'

Mãezinha looked at me in consternation.

'I thought we had some stupid, vicious people in my country but thank God they are not as bad as the people in this village. To think I respected you and thought you were my friends!'

I met her eyes and glared. I felt very cold towards her. I said, 'Please go now. I don't want to talk any more.'

'Amy ...'

'Leave me alone!'

After she had gone I cried for a long time with my face pressed into the bamboo floor because the last thing I wanted to do was wake Dalu. I cried for me and I cried for João. It was so much worse than I'd imagined. I'd thought him hysterical; now I wondered that he'd managed to stay sane at all. I wondered if he was crying too. I was glad he had thrown over the food tables.

Then I wondered if he had taken me because I was the only girl ever to offer. I had all night to think about it. I didn't sleep. As soon as it was light I wrote the letter I had been composing in my head. Afterwards I went out to see to the goats. I intended to go up to the waterfall as soon as I had the chance; but I didn't get the chance because it started raining.

six and three-quarter moons gone, six and a quarter moons to go.

As soon as there came a pause in the rain, I begged permission from Dalu to take the goats out to graze. She looked at me suspiciously; she keeps close track of me these days. Then she said reluctantly that I could take them to the back of the factory, where there was shelter if I needed it. So I flew up the ladder to get my letter. I'd hidden it more carefully than I hide my exercise book because it was written in Portuguese. I stuffed it down my blouse and went to rouse the goats. They were all lying down chewing, and didn't look enthusiastic about going out. Their assessment of the weather wasn't optimistic.

The moment we rounded the corner of the batik factory, which is really a shed, Benício came out and invited me in. It was the last thing I wanted to do but I couldn't quickly think of a reason to refuse.

I sat down with the girls and drank some tea. Mãezinha didn't look at me and I felt uncomfortable. I suspected that I'd been unfair to Mãezinha, who had been the unlucky bearer of bad news, and, like a Roman messenger, had suffered the consequences. As soon as I had swallowed down my tea I went. I left Isti in charge of the younger goats and I hared up the Steps. I only had an hour or so. I knew I was sailing pretty close to the wind. By the time I reached the top, my lungs hurt and my legs were shaking. Then I turned left along the track and looked for paths up the mountain. There were plenty of them but they were all overgrown and slithery after the rain. Rattan thorns kept plucking at me and I couldn't see my way ahead, but the letter burning at my breast impelled me on. The sky was as grey as it is over my native Warwickshire. It was a low shifting haze with dark dots which boded ill.

At last I spotted the rope bridge, as João had said I would. I crossed it like a fat tripper on a cakewalk. I could see the waterfall above me. A pale green heron was fishing at the foot of it. The climb was steeper than I had imagined: I remembered João making the ascent in leaps and bounds. I slipped on the boulders, clutching at the ferns, and skinned my shins. The water had been a shower when João had shown me the way behind it. Now it fell in rounded, shining columns with a rumbling sound. The spray clung to me like grease.

A little nutmeg tree hid the entrance to the passage between the rock and the falling water. I stepped into the opening before I could change my mind. The water didn't touch me but made a blinding silvery arc to my left. I felt along the rock face till I came to a fissure and this I squeezed into. It was a short, narrow corridor through the mountain and at the end I could see daylight. The tunnel soon opened out into a kind of room, the floor thinly grassed, half-open to the sky.

He wasn't there, and whatever I had expected it wasn't this. The little cave looked like a rubbish tip, there was sodden debris everywhere. Under the overhanging rock it was still dry: I could see scraps of food and fruit trodden to a mush underfoot, rotting leaves and flower petals, splinters of carved wood which might once have been an item of furniture. I picked up a piece of paper and recognized at once the coastline of France. There were more soggy shreds. They were all part of a map of Europe. I felt disturbed. I didn't know whether to leave the letter or not. In the end I put it on the driest ledge and extricated myself as quickly as I could. I didn't begin to feel safe until I was well clear of the waterfall and hurtling down pathways towards the village.

It was now coming on to rain quite heavily. In a troubled frame of mind I arrived back at the factory to find the goats pacing about under the trees, bleating irritably and wagging their tails. Mãezinha was huddled there watching them.

'What are you doing here?'

'The goats tried to come into the factory.'

'Oh God!'

She permitted herself a giggle. She said, 'It's all right. Benício sent me out to help you.'

She looked up at me anxiously, but she didn't ask me where I'd been.

I said, 'Mãezinha, I'm sorry about what I said. I was upset. Are you still my friend?'

She said, 'Come and sit by me.'

'Don't you have to go back?'

'Benício sent me out, now Benício can call me back.'

We sat down under the banana palms and put our arms around each other. She said, 'Look, when João Ninguém came to the school I was just a little girl. I didn't even know he existed until then. I could see there was something strange about him, and I learnt from the others that it was something dirty and secret. And they said he was my cousin.'

'He is.'

'I was ashamed and I didn't want him to be my cousin, I wanted him to go away. Can you imagine that?'

I could imagine it very well.

'My family never talked about it. It's more difficult for us, you see, because of the disgrace.'

I could see, but I said, 'Imagine what it was like for him at the school.'

'I never thought about him like that.'

Tears came to my eyes. I said, 'He's just a boy, Mãezinha. He's not a devil. He's very gentle. On the mountain he cleaned my injured leg and he held my hand when I was frightened.'

Mãezinha had heard all this many times before.

'How can it be,' I went on indignantly, 'that they won't speak to him in the village but they call on him to help when there are people to be carried over the mountain?'

'Well he came down to the beach because he's a mountain guide,' said Mãezinha. 'If he sees a boat from the mountain, first he goes to the cabin and lights a fire and rings the bell, then he goes down to the beach. He didn't know it was people from our village because he didn't recognize the boat. The soldiers from Weh Tuluk stole the good boat and gave them a poor little one in exchange.'

'What were they doing in Weh Tuluk anyway?'

'They were on their way back from Kawalinggan. Dona Maria do Rosário was very ill. Because she is Sr. Onorusco's wife she is very important so she went to the hospital. Mateus's wife was ill too, and the girl whose place you took. She said they should come with her and she would pay. But the doctors at the hospital said they were all too far gone; the disease was in the blood and there was nothing they could do. They all wanted to go home again, but the girl was so bad that Pai said they must go back by the other route which is quicker but more dangerous. Then the soldiers from Weh Tuluk came out and captured them. They are not our enemies but they wanted the boat. The soldiers didn't keep them long because they were afraid of the sickness. And the girl died. Maybe it was meant to be. If Frei Serafim had gone instead of Pai he'd have left you behind.'

'I know.'

'Some people were angry because they brought you back home instead. They said her ghost would come back to trouble us. Pai said it wouldn't.'

I knew the unburied girl had caused bitterness. Pai, a pragmatic priest, had valued my life above the dignity of the dead. I asked, 'When they got back to the island why didn't they put in at the port?'

'Because they were very tired and didn't want to row through the water-spouts in a little boat. So they beached on the wrong side of the island. And João Ninguém came down. They needed him to show them an easy way across the mountain, carrying the sick people, but no one wanted to be carried by him. So they said he should carry you. But then no one would carry the other end so Pai had to.'

The rain had stopped for the moment and the goats had ventured out from under the trees. I said, 'Why didn't you tell me before, Mãezinha? You knew all this and you never said.'

'I was afraid of what you might do. You think you understand but sometimes you don't. Sometimes you go too fast and say too much. You could bring trouble on yourself.'

I thought of the inexplicable mess at the waterfall and I wondered who might find my letter there. I didn't tell Mãezinha I'd found the waterfall in case it was meant to be a secret. I felt cold and despondent. Mãezinha took my hand. She said, 'What are you going to do?'

'I don't know. I must see him.'

She said, 'When the rain stops I'll take you to his house.'

XV

seven moons gone, six moons to go

We had been sent to the covered market in another village. Dalu had given me some rupiahs. She warned:

'Remember you don't give change with your left hand.'

'Why not?'

'Because it ill-wishes them. Don't you know anything?'

In the market it was as hot as hell. The smell of the fish, the thick, greedy clusters of flies, the clamour, the jostling, all made me feel ill. At the door a naked spastic youth lay weeping on a mat; someone flung him a pork bone. We were skinny, barefoot girls but we were besieged by beggars. A whispering, wraith-like old woman plucked at my skirt, a legless man scooted after us on his bottom.

We shared an illicit drink of juice which we bought from a Chinese lady at a kiosk.

'Mãezinha, does João live right on top of the mountain?'

'More or less.'

'Is it very difficult to climb?'

'No, the first part is all terraces.'

'What about the next part?' I asked gloomily.

Mãezinha looked at me in perplexity. 'Don't you want to go?'

'I do want to go but I'm afraid of getting half-way and not being able to go any further and being stuck.'

She started to laugh and quickly put her hand over her mouth. 'If you get stuck I'll have to fetch the *guia*.'

She called him the *guia* now, but she couldn't bring herself to call him João, which, used on its own, is a common boy's name. It is pronounced like the French 'Jean'; or 'Jwean' to be exact.

I said morosely, 'Perhaps you'd better fetch him down to meet me half-way.'

I had been up to the waterfall twice now. My letter had gone. I had hoped and expected that he would make contact in some way, but he hadn't. I wondered if he still wanted me, and why he hadn't responded, but I didn't say any of this to Mãezinha. I said, 'What about the wild animals?'

'They'll hear you coming and keep out of your way.'

'I hope so.'

Māezinha made an effort to be reassuring. She said, 'There used to be tigers in the jungle but there aren't any now. The snakes don't come out at night. Most of them won't hurt you anyway. There are supposed to be sun-bears but I don't know anybody who's seen one. It'll be all right. There'll be a full moon. It'll be easy.'

This started me thinking on another tack. I remembered filling in the last moon on Onorusco's chart. I had been menstruating at the time. I had been interested in the coincidence. Tomorrow was full moon again.

On the way home we had to collect Mateus's billy. I didn't like Mateus; he was the one who had jeered, or sworn, at João on the mountain. One of Mateus's children was playing in the dirt, teasing a big blue scorpion with a stick. Māezinha picked the child up and carried him in under her arm. She had brought sweets from the market for the children. Mateus smiled at her ruefully. He had been melancholy and listless since his wife died.

The billy was a mighty beast with a beard and chest like a lion. He came out in a frisky mood. I felt jaded and in no temper to cope with a wayward animal. I tussled with him all the way up the track, then gave him a good clout on the head. He turned round and nudged Māezinha hard and all Dalu's shopping went rolling down the path. All of a sudden Mateus started laughing, and chasing and head-butting his children, which made them shriek. Māezinha was pleased to see him in high spirits for once. He was quite funny, but I still didn't like him.

Once he got near our goat-shed, the billy knew the way. He started pulling strongly and towed the two of us along. Isti greeted him coyly by peeing on his nose. He lifted his face in rapture and his tongue peeped out lewdly. Dalu came in to make sure he performed. Just as Mateus' stud was mounting Isti I said impulsively, 'Dona Dalu, is this the same billy as last time?'

She looked at me and seemed to be wondering if I knew something she didn't, but rejected the possibility.

'It's the same one.'

'But Dona Dalu ...' because Māezinha was within earshot I said, 'The last kid died!'

She said dismissively, 'This billy is all right. I always use him.'

'But how long have you been using him? Is he serving his own daughters?'

Dalu turned and gave me a queer, frowning look. At that moment there was the sound of scuffling feet and a voice calling her impressively by her full name, 'Maria Madalena! Maria Madalena!'

It was one of Dalu's cronies, damp and distraught. She spoke to Dalu in the old language and I couldn't even tell where one word ended and another began. Mãezinha had been putting the shopping away. Now she slipped into the shed and stood embracing a pole and listening, with her eyes wide open and her mouth closed. For a moment Dalu looked as she had looked when the twin-headed nanny appeared. Then she pulled herself together and snapped at me, 'Get on with your work.'

She followed her friend out.

I said, 'Mãezinha, what's happened?'

'The Port Stores were damaged in the storms.'

'Oh. Is that all?'

The Port Stores are Portuguese-built and sturdy but the water washes about them constantly. They stand on little stilts in the shingle.

'Sr. Nestor trapped his foot in the boards. Some men from the village went to do repairs and pulled up the floor. There was a lot of dried stuff underneath, washed up by the high tides.'

I imagined pieces of fossil-encrusted driftwood, bits of tarry rope, black tangles of seaweed, lumps of sea-sucked glass.

'And a baby's bones.'

Mãezinha wanted to rush over to the Port Stores at once and so did most of the other villagers. I didn't want to go. Besides, I was in charge of the billy, and mainly out of cussedness I had decided that I was not going to mate him with Matahari, my own little nanny. I saw that the news of the find had frightened Dalu and startled Mãezinha. I had felt a moment's confusion, too. However, the baby could not be Conceição's, so it was someone else's, and I didn't see why 'Maria Madalena' had been called to take the centre stage. In fact I suspected that Dalu and friend were morbid old gossips who would enjoy gloating over the remains.

Dalu came home late with three lugubrious old biddies. She looked drawn, but seemed pleased to find me still at my post. I went upstairs and listened to their conversation through the floor, but I couldn't make much of it. I heard the cadence of consolation and a lot of superstitious whispering. After a while I became angry and felt like shouting something rude. I didn't think Dalu deserved sympathy on any count whatsoever and I wanted to get some sleep. Our moonlight excursion was scheduled for the following night. When I thought about seeing João I felt breathless. My arms and legs tingled as if I'd plunged them into a nettle-patch.

I didn't see Mãezinha at all next day. After dark I waited so long that I became tired and that made me pessimistic. When she finally came I was almost sorry to see her. I said to her miserably, 'If we get caught you'll get into terrible trouble for this.'

She said blithely, 'I won't get caught so I won't get into any trouble. But if I don't take you, you'll still try and find him and you'll definitely get caught.'

'Listen ...'

'Oh come on!' she said, darting ahead. She was in no mood for shirking.

There was a full moon as promised and the first half of our journey was deceptively easy; it was a steep walk, not a climb. Then the going got steadily worse. We had to pull ourselves up by our arms, clutching at bushes and tufts of grass. In places there were only toe-holds, or narrow stone ledges to be negotiated crab-wise. I have no head for heights and I was moving very slowly, sweating and trembling. Mãezinha helped hoist me up onto a small flat rock where I could sit in relative safety.

'Shall I go and fetch the *guia*?'

I was so demoralized that I didn't see how fetching the *guia* would help; he couldn't put me in a sack and carry me over his shoulder. I was still going to have to climb either up or down. What I most wished for was to wake up and find I'd been having a nightmare, but I couldn't question the reality of this experience. Only in dreams is there any doubt. I stood up, clutching at Mãezinha, and said, 'Come on. Let's get it over.'

In fact the worst was already over, for the mountain soon folded into ridges which were easy to climb and offered no view of the drop beneath.

When we got near the top we adopted a hill-walking mode again. We were warm from our exertions but the air was cool and reminded me of home.

'Are there any more steep bits, Mãezinha?'

'No,' she said, sounding subdued. 'Look, I don't think you can go down again tonight.'

'Neither do I. In fact I'm not sure I can go down again at all.'

She said in exasperation, 'Are you going to spend the rest of your life up here?'

'I don't know.'

Now I was worrying about João and how he would receive me and whether he would let me sleep tonight where I most wanted to sleep. When Mãezinha wasn't looking I put my hand between my legs to check for blood, but there wasn't any.

Mãezinha walked alongside me in silence, then she said, 'When do you first see Dalu in the morning?'

'After I've milked the goats.'

'What do you do then?'

'I take her some milk and I help her get up if she needs me.'

'Do you see her at all before you milk the goats?'

'No, not unless she's already stirring. I jump out of the window.'

'Good. Look, this is what we'll do. I'll go there very early and milk the goats, then I'll take her some milk and say you've gone to the Port Stores to look at the baby.'

'Will she believe it?'

'Yes. Everyone else has been to have a look. She may be furious but I'll say it was my idea. Then I'll say I'm taking the goats to graze by the factory. Which one is to be left with the billy?'

'Muftiah, but …'

'Muftiah, all right. Tell the *guia* to bring you back by the *cabana* and the wood-chute. It's easier although it's much longer. You'll end up at the Port Stores. Let Sr. Nestor see you, but don't let anyone see the *guia*. Then run as fast as you can to the factory.'

This plan was as full of potential pitfalls as my school knitting had been of holes. I said, 'It won't work. We'll both get into terrible trouble. I think,' I offered bravely, 'I'd better go back down tonight. I can do it. I got here, after all.'

Mãezinha said soberly, 'Getting up is easy. Going down is difficult.'

I looked at her in dismay.

'Well why don't we both go back by the *cabana*?'

'You don't understand. It's too late for us to go by the *cabana* already. It takes hours.'

'Oh heavens! Why didn't we leave earlier?' I asked peevishly.

'Because my sisters were still awake. Come on, let's hurry.'

We stepped up our pace, not running but marching briskly. We had no breath left for talking. In any case, I was too nervous to speak any more. We turned the corner of a rocky outcrop and paddled through a little stream. A large pot lay on its side in the water. We came abruptly to the back porch of a wooden shack leaning up against a large boulder. The door was hanging crookedly and the verandah was sagging. It looked like a house of cards in danger of imminent collapse. On the porch were stored jars of grain and other foodstuffs. There was a neat semi-circular stack of logs and some coils of rope with hooks.

Mãezinha prompted, 'Here it is. Go on.'

'You're coming in, aren't you?'

She looked at me in amazement, 'It's you who wants to see him.'

'I know, but will he mind me coming here like this?'

'I don't know,' said Mãezinha. 'He's your boyfriend, not mine.'

'It's all dark. He'll be asleep.'

'Well wake him up. Call him.'

She poked me. I stood on the porch, hesitating. Then I knocked timidly. The door was wrenched open almost at once. João looked at us and reeled back as if we had come to attack or accuse him. Mãezinha hissed in my ear, 'Say something.'

I opened my mouth but I was completely out of breath. João had his hands pressed against the cabin wall behind him. His eyes were shifting like a dog about to bite or bolt. All at once I spotted my letter lying on a wooden trunk in the corner. I said, 'Oh, you got my letter. But you didn't answer it.'

He looked at the letter and then at me. I could feel, rather than hear, that Mãezinha was beginning to convulse with laughter. She always laughed with her whole body.

João moved then. He seized the letter and thrust it into my hands. He said, 'I can't read this. You don't write good Portuguese. You need a better teacher.'

Mãezinha put her hands on her hips and curled her lip at him in disdain. She had earth on her face and grass-stains all over her skirt. João drew himself up in his shabby sarong and out-stared her. Had they known it, the family resemblance was strong. They had never looked more alike. Then he grasped my sleeve and yanked me over the threshold. He said imperiously, 'Read the letter.'

The shack had a homely smell of smoked fish. I longed to look round and touch his belongings but I was afraid I wouldn't be allowed to. I was hurt by his criticism of my writing and I thought it had been a mistake to come. I didn't read out the letter. I bent and unbent it in my fingers as I said, 'It says that I'm sorry I made you angry at the *festa*. I didn't understand then. But I do now.'

I looked up at him and suddenly saw from his face how desperately he minded what I said next, so I went on, 'I want to know if you still like me, and what you really think of me.'

He said simply: '*Amo-te*. I love you.'

I felt like a bird newly launched into flight. My insides lurched and my ears buzzed. We had both forgotten about Mãezinha, who was hopping about impatiently in the doorway. She said, 'Look, if you're staying, remember to come back by the *cabana*. And you can't stay long, you must be at the Port Stores by dawn.'

João put a possessive arm around me. He said, 'She's staying. I'll look after her.'

It wasn't a promise, it was a dismissal.

I had never seen Mãezinha look ill-humoured before. She said, 'She can't climb down the cliff. She's hopeless at climbing. And she must be back by dawn or Tia Dalu will skin both of us.'

João looked at her impassively. 'You can go now.'

She said shrilly, 'With the greatest of pleasure.'

As she turned to go, I said, 'Mãezinha, thank you.' She gave me a long, unreadable look.

When she had closed the door I said anxiously, 'Is it safe for her to go down in the dark?'

João said bleakly, 'She came up all right.' After a moment he opened the door again to check that she had really gone. Then he started busily lighting the little wood-stove. I said nervously, 'It's a lovely house.'

'It's poor.'

'It's simple but it's clean and it smells nice. I love wooden houses. Why are you lighting the fire? Don't we have to go now?'

'Don't listen to that girl. She doesn't know anything.'

I wondered if he hated Mãezinha particularly or all of them indiscriminately, and I wondered if I would have to climb down the cliff after all.

João had put a pot on the stove and was preparing something that smelt chemical, like a treatment for hoof-rot. Then he added little seed-pods and honey. He said, 'Put the skins down by the fire.'

He gave me the cup, watching my face as I tasted it.

'It's strong.'

'It's a special drink.'

The fumes made me shudder, but it was just about palatable with the addition of the honey. I think it was a kind of crude rice brandy.

He squatted down beside me and we sipped from the cup in turn. I put my lips on the rim in the place where his had been and felt my cheeks growing hot. Then João handed me my letter and said again, 'Read it!'

I read it out, asking, 'Is that the right word? Is that spelt right?'

He always said yes. So I tested him a couple of times by pointing to one word and reading something different. He didn't correct me and I was soon convinced that he couldn't read at all. When we had finished he laid the letter reverently in his box. I said, 'When I went to the waterfall there was a lot of rubbish there, and ripped-up maps. Were they your great-grandfather's?'

He nodded.

'What happened?'

He said after a moment, 'It was Zé.'

'Zé? Who is Zé?'

'When anything got broken my great-grandfather always said it was Zé.'

'Who is Zé? Was he somebody in a story? Did your great-grandfather invent him?'

He said, 'My great-grandfather was a brilliant story-teller. He used to be the *dalang*, master of the puppet show. The people in the villages would listen to his stories till the sun came up. I can't tell stories but I'll tell you one he used to tell me. It's a legend from these islands about a boy separated from his family by war. When he grew up he came back to his own country without knowing it. He met a woman who was old but still beautiful and he married her. They went out on a boat for their honeymoon and their honeymoon lasted three days.

'At the end of the three days the young man was sleeping and his wife reached down and stroked his hair. As soon as she touched him he knew that she was his mother, because that is what a mother does. The mother always strokes the hair of her son. Then a storm arose on the lake and they were drowned.'

He looked into my face, his eyes frightened. I didn't know how to respond, so I took his hand. He asked, 'Do you think they were wicked?'

'No, I think they were unfortunate.'

'What did your friend tell you about me?'

'I think she told me everything.'

He said half-incredulously, 'It doesn't matter to you?'

I shook my head. 'I love you. I don't care about anything else.'

'How could you love me?'

'How could I stop?'

His skin had a dry, slightly bitter smell which I found arous-ing. We kissed, then lay down on the rugs and stroked, licked and bit each other without awareness of time. I remember that I opened my blouse and knelt over him to make love, my legs on either side of his. He didn't seem shocked, although the sum total of his sexual instruction to date must have been watching the wild goats mounting each other. I wasn't surprised by my unusual lack of inhibition either. I attributed it to love rather than to the amount of rough alcohol I had drunk.

Then I began to feel very sick and João helped me outside, where I vomited sparsely. I washed my face in the stream and drank thirstily from my cupped hands. When I was full of cold water, I felt like the wolf who had stones sewn into his belly and nearly tumbled into the stream. I said I needed to lie down and João took me up the ladder to his loft-bedroom where I lay on the floor. The room was revolving steadily and all the wood-carvings seemed to be jumping and gliding about.

I was shivering, but I felt warmer when João lay down next to me and held me tightly. The next thing I remember is a steady sound intruding upon my dream: a plock plock plock which sounded like someone chopping wood. Then I realized that it was João chopping the wood, and it was broad daylight already.

XVI

I was very perturbed, but at the same time I was happy to wake up in João's bedroom. The little loft seemed to me so luminous that I looked through the window half-expecting the dazzle of snow. What I saw was the mountain, rising to a peak in whorls and spirals like a trumpet shell. Below me was the small plateau where João had made his garden. He was squatting by the stream, slicing wood into neat sticks; his bare arms moved with grace and rhythm. I loved to watch him work.

I ran outside. The early morning was pleasantly hot. The earth didn't burn my feet and the sweat didn't sting my eyes.

'João, why didn't you wake me?'

'You were sick.'

'But what am I going to do? I'll be in such trouble.'

He looked down at his sticks again and muttered, 'I'll take you home.'

'Let's go, then,' I urged. 'I'm very late already.'

He went on stubbornly chopping sticks. He said, 'You can wash under the spring.'

'I haven't got time!'

'First wash, then we'll eat, then we'll go.'

I could see from his set face that nothing I said would make him hurry. I went and stood under the spring. In another moment he had taken off his sarong and sprung in beside me. He said, 'You can't wash like that, take your clothes off; I'll do it for you. Now I'll wash you.'

'We haven't got time to play!'

We washed each other under the cold water, kissed, and rubbed our wet, stinging bodies together. Then we went back to the house and João poured out a measure of the rice brandy. He said, 'If it has made you sick you should drink a little more of it next day, otherwise it knows it is your master. That's what my great-grandfather used to do.'

I said vehemently, 'No, don't give me any more. That's what got me into trouble. You didn't do it on purpose, did you?'

'No, Amy, no. My great-grandfather said it was a special honeymoon drink, that's why I gave it to you.'

'Well, it works.'

We ate rice steamed in a banana leaf and some pieces of a miserable fruit which always reminds me of boiled carrot. I felt a pleasant lassitude from the hangover and I almost gave up fretting and let myself enjoy this unscheduled extension to my visit. When João had finished eating, I stood up and said,

'Now we must go.'

'I think it's too late, Amy.'

'What do you mean?'

'They will know by now that you are missing and your friend will tell them you are with me. Once they know that I have had you, they won't welcome you in the village any more.'

'You said you would take me home.'

'I will take you,' he said angrily, 'but why did you come here if you didn't want to stay? Or is my house too poor for you?'

I said, 'I do want to stay, I want to more than anything, it's the most beautiful place I've ever seen. But I can't, there would be awful trouble.'

He said eagerly, 'No, there wouldn't be any trouble, they would leave us alone. Will you stay?'

I wanted to say yes but I knew in my heart that it could not be so easy. I said, 'Dalu wouldn't let me go, I know she wouldn't.'

'Dalu!' he said scornfully, 'Dalu can't stop you. She had better not try.'

'What will they do to Mãezinha for helping me?'

'She'll be all right, she'll tell them something.'

'João, I don't know, I want to, but I'm afraid.'

'Don't be afraid, Amy, I'll take care of you.'

He stroked my wet hair and kissed my mouth and then, because I didn't move, but sat on the floor biting my lip, he said, 'Come on, I want to show you something.' He lifted me up and led me outside.

'Where are we going?'

'Just come.'

We walked up to the bare tip of the mountain and looked down on the rain- forest which covered the other side of the island. He said, 'The black eagles fly from here. And down there, there are naked savages living by a great lake. They are of the old religion and they speak the old language. They live as tribes in long houses, not like Christian families. On this side is the forest where I work in the day. I'll show you.'

Of course I knew that if we delayed much longer there would

be no need to decide; every moment I stayed away was making it less possible for me to return. We went hand-in-hand to the forestry clearing, where he was cutting *teca* and black persimmon wood. He had made a little shelter of rough poles and leafy branches. We sat in it and ate persimmon fruit for our lunch and then we must have fallen asleep together.

João swore suddenly and I sat up.

'What is it?'

'Listen.'

I could hear them too, men's voices a long way off.

'Stay there and be quiet.'

I watched him swarm like a squirrel up a tree trunk and disappear among the branches. A few moments later he dropped down silently beside me.

'Who are they?'

'Men from the village,' he said curtly. 'Rui, Tino and Mateus.'

'What do they want?'

'I suppose they are looking for you.'

'Are they coming to ask you to search for me?'

'No, not those three. They are coming to cause trouble.' He thought for a moment, scowling. Then he said, 'You had better not stay here. Come with me.' He took me to the edge of the clearing. 'Look down there. Do you see the *cabana*?'

I could just see the roof, far below, jutting out over the sea, on the gentler, western slope of the mountain.

'Go down there and keep hidden until night. Then go into the *cabana* and you can light the fire. If they catch you you had better tell them you were lost on the mountain. I'll come and fetch you after dark.'

'But where are you going?'

'To meet the *sacanas*.' he said with a grim twitch of the mouth.

'João, be careful!'

But he had slunk in amongst the trees and was gone.

I made for the *cabana*. It was a long steady climb down, but not precipitate. It took about two hours. While I was concentrating on where to put my feet I couldn't worry about what was going to happen next. I hid in a thicket a hundred yards from the cabin. I was anxious about João, I was anxious about my own fate, and I was anxious about Mãezinha. I hoped she had had the gumption to stick to our story. I'm not a habitual liar but like most people I'll lie if I have to. If they caught me I decided to say that I had seen a ship on the horizon and climbed up the mountain for a better view. I'd climbed higher and higher and there'd been no further sign of a ship. I'd felt bitterly disappointed; I'd gone wandering about blindly and got myself lost. I didn't think it was one hundred per cent convincing but I thought it might serve its purpose.

The mistake I made was in entering the cabin too soon. I was being eaten alive by insects and I anticipated nightfall. It was a tiny rough cabin made of splintery planks and smelling of kippers, but everything was there to sustain human life. I was just thinking about lighting the fire when I heard tramping feet.

'Ó Pá! Look who we have here!'

It was Mateus's big, rough, exuberant voice. He was in high spirits. Tino was squeezing a bleeding thumb, tightly bound up in a scrap of rag, and cursing: 'Filho da mãe!' I thought, 'If the filho da mãe did that, what did the three of them do to him?' Mateus said kindly,

'Where have you been, Amy? Your cousin-sister is very anxious and your mother is pacing up and down the black beach crying out that you are drowned.'

I thought this scenario highly improbable. He spoke as he would speak to one of his children. 'Where have you been, querida? Were you running away?'

I pretended to cry, which was not difficult because I was thoroughly dismayed by their arrival. Mateus put his arm round me and banged me rhythmically on the shoulder. I was determined to hate Mateus and I was angry with myself for not being able to. I sobbed out my story about the vanishing ship and they exchanged looks. I couldn't tell if the looks meant 'she's lying' or 'she's a bit lacking'. Rui said, 'At least she had the sense to stay in the cabana.'

I wanted to know why they had been looking for me at João's, and what had happened there, but I could only ask obliquely, 'How long have you been looking for me? Have you just come up from the port?' (which I knew they hadn't).

Tino, with the sliced thumb, said sulkily, 'No, we came up the hard way.' He didn't look as if he considered me worth the trouble. 'This hero,' – Mateus – 'wanted to prove himself to his sweetheart.'

They all laughed but I didn't understand the joke.

I didn't want to spend the night in the cabin with the three men, but I wanted to go home and face Dalu even less. In the event Rui tolled the bell twice to signal good news to the people below and then we set off for home. I felt full of dread and pessimism. The men sang noisily, wrestled like schoolboys, boasted about the prowess of their fighting-cocks and made cracks about Mateus's love-life, which he took in good part.

We arrived back at the village about eight hours later. It wasn't yet dawn. The lamp was still lit in our hut and shining out through the bamboo screens: a pretty effect, but not an encouraging sight. Mateus escorted me to my door and called out cheerily,

'Here she is, Dona Dalu!'

Dalu came out into the night. She didn't fall upon me and embrace me. If she had been pacing the shingle weeping she showed no sign of it. She looked at me, assessing my condition, then asked, as if I were a strayed nanny-goat, 'Where did you find her?'

Mateus said, 'She wasn't up the mountain. She was at the *cabana*. She had climbed up the hill looking out for ships and gone too far.'

Dalu nodded. I could see she didn't believe it for a moment. She said to me sarcastically, 'I don't think you climbed too far, *menina*, I don't think you climbed far enough.'

We neglected to thank Mateus for my deliverance. I trailed unwillingly inside and started to apologize for the trouble I had caused. Dalu cut me short. She said in a tone of pure cascara,

'Well, *menina*, you had a long climb up to the *cabana* in the hot sun, didn't you?'

I began on my tale about the ship. I didn't think Mateus had done it justice. Again she ignored me, interrupting in the same arch tone to ask, 'And did you meet anyone on your way up the mountain?'

I was tired of this charade. I said, 'Yes.'

'Well! Who did you meet?'

'Mateus, Tino and Rui.'

She punched me in the mouth. I wondered how her deformed hands, which visibly gave her pain, could perform these sudden acts of violence. I thought about smacking her back but I've never hit anyone in my life and I didn't want to begin with an arthritic old woman.

'And who else did you meet?'

'Nobody,' I said rudely.

'That must have been a disappointment for you.'

If I had really been missing between morning milking and the time Rui tolled the bell, I wouldn't have had time to visit João. Of course she knew it, and it was that which saved me from a worse row. I said, 'I'm going to bed,' and made for the ladder.

'Oh no, not up there you aren't.' She had dropped the heavy irony. 'You'll sleep down here in future where I can see what you're up to.'

I should have ignored her and gone upstairs. I should have said, 'Look, I'm your guest not your slave,' but as usual I didn't protest.

She watched me undress with an assessing look, checking me for love-bites perhaps. Then I watched her undress and lay down beside her with revulsion. I willed my mind away from the claustrophobic little hut, the scrawny old woman, to the cooler air of the mountain and a view of the other side of the island: the steep plunge of forested slopes into marsh-green jungle. João stood at the foot of my bed repeating endlessly, '*Amo-te.*'

These good remembrances comforted me for a sleepless hour, then two by two the bad thoughts started coming. I thought about João, lonely all his life, despised by everyone but the crazy old grandfather with the curious taste in names and bedtime stories. Then I'd arrived, a fellow accident; they'd told him to carry me because I was of no importance. I'd held out my hand to him. How could he have refused it? If I'd been daft Mafalda who exposes herself to the village boys, wouldn't he have loved me anyway?

Dalu seemed to be asleep, although she moaned and whick-ered and blew like a walrus. Gingerly I slid my finger between my legs, then held it up gleaming, but not with blood. In my heart I wanted to have João's baby, some primitive part of me positively rejoiced in the possibility; my rational side looked on in horror. I didn't have to wonder what Dalu would say or do, I had Maria de Conceição as an example.

I thought about Conceição's last journeys, carrying João. I'd just made the same journeys myself. Sr. Nestor had seen her and the baby at nightfall, and found her washed up on the shingle in the dawn light. I didn't see how it had been done either. Had she walked back to the village and climbed up the cliff with the baby in her arms or tied in her clothing? The very thought made me giddy. Then had she climbed back down a steep cliff with the sole intention of drowning herself at the bottom? Why had she gone out of her way to visit the port in the first place? To contemplate the sea and think about drowning? If she had left the baby somewhere on the dark hillside, how had the grandfather managed to find him in time? Had I been misled or lied to? What did I know for sure? That a well-seasoned little skeleton had been found at the port. Logically it would be Conceição's baby. If it was, then who was João?

I gave it up and I slept. I woke when I heard the goats shifting about expectantly next door. Dalu came in while I was straining the milk. Her manner with me had never been pleasant so I could not say that it had deteriorated. Mãezinha's little sister appeared, wooden-faced, in the doorway and Dalu told her to take the goats out to graze.

I was surprised, then very resentful. I learned that this was in fact part of the punishment programme Dalu had devised for me. It was a subtle one. She had noticed which tasks I took pleasure in: they were mostly those that took me out of the hut and away from her supervision. She had found reasons why I couldn't do them any more. Yesterday I had abandoned the goats, so now I was no longer in charge of them. All my jobs were to be in or around the house, where she could keep an eye on me. Mãezinha was considered to be my accomplice so we weren't allowed to see each other any more. Her sister was to have my bedroom and I was to sleep with Dalu.

I felt something approaching panic. I was losing my privacy, my freedom of movement, my friend; she had rightly calculated that these were what I valued most. I could hardly believe that Dalu was prepared to subject herself, out of sheer spite, to so much of my company. I wondered if we'd be eating Matahari for supper next. I was afraid that she'd deprive me of my little exercise book if she knew about it, so when I went up to get my things I stuck it in the waist of my skirt and later I hid it under the straw in the goat-shed.

* * *

seven and a half moons gone, five and a half moons to go

Now I write before and after milking, with a bucket strategically placed where Dalu will fall over it and give me advance warning of her arrival. I've just counted my moons: there are five and a half left.

Mateus's son came round to fetch the billy. I went out with him to the shed and he said in my ear,

'Mãezinha wants to know how you are.'

'Tell her I miss her and I'm sorry I got her into trouble.'

In the evening Dalu and I sit out on the veranda, looking like mother and daughter to all who pass. Yesterday Dona Fátima paused to chat. Dona Fátima is enormously tall; of all the women she is the most European-looking. She would pass as a batty old Englishwoman in Putney. When she stopped and leaned on the rail, Dalu got up in a huff and went indoors. Dona Fátima laughed and said,

'Did you enjoy your walk up the mountain, daughter?'

Her tone was so conspiratorial that I said, 'Yes I did.'

She said, 'Do you know, I used to walk up that mountain myself and for much the same reason.' She came closer and dropped her voice. 'Come to my house and take tea with me. I've got something to show you.'

I said, 'I can't, Dona Fátima, Dona Dalu wouldn't let me.'

She called out in a teasing tone, 'Dalu, I'm inviting your daughter to take tea with me.'

There was no response so she laughed again and whispered, 'I'll tell you something surprising that not many people know. She might know,' jerking her thumb at the hut, 'but nobody else knows unless your Joãozinho does.' She nodded at me enigmatically and strode off.

I called out, 'Come and see us again, Dona Fátima.' She came back and looked at me as if confiding a secret of great importance. 'They say old 'Quim was crazy but he was as sane as you or me.' I wondered if that was much of a recommendation. 'Come and take tea, *filha*, and I'll show you what he wrote. The Lord said it was nonsense. He crumpled the paper up and threw it away, but I've still got it.'

Everyone in the village knew that 'the Lord' referred not to Jesus but to Sr. Onorusco. Fátima loathed him as fanatically as she revered his ailing wife. She had been their servant once but had been pensioned off for being old, dirty and eccentric. I was quite intrigued by Dona Fátima. She had never spoken to me before. However, I couldn't make much sense of her story. I didn't know who old 'Quim was, or why I should care what he wrote.

I don't think Mãezinha's little sister is very happy living with us. She goes home at every opportunity. Mãezinha never uses her to carry messages so I don't either. She has the typical broad, brown, sullen face of the Indo-Chinese peasant. Dalu is impatient with her and I haven't got time for her. I feel depressed, the sun is giving me headaches and making me queasy.

Once I used to panic in crowded supermarkets. I'd rush for the exit, pushing people out of my path, knocking things off the shelves in my flight. Now I keep getting the same sensation in Dalu's hut. I think I've stopped breathing and I feel faint. Dalu can tell from my face. She says sharply,

'What's the matter? Get on with your work.'

∗   ∗   ∗

It's been three weeks now since I saw João, three weeks since the goats mated, three weeks since I crossed off the last moon. Yesterday evening I finished the milking in good time but I only wrote a few lines because Dalu called me out onto the veranda. Mateus's eldest boy was there, and he said Māezinha was asking about the goats, which didn't seem to surprise Dalu at all. I said they were pregnant. Dalu looked up in irritation.

'Matahari was blethering and wagging her tail this morning, wasn't she?'

She had been, but I said, 'I'm not sure.'

Dalu got up with a sigh of exasperation and went to look for herself. I wondered if Māezinha really meant to enquire about my condition or the condition of the goats. I said,

'Is Māezinha at your house?'

He nodded.

'What is she doing there?'

'She's looking after us.'

'That's nice. What did Māezinha say exactly?'

'She said to go and talk to you while you were in the milking-shed, but Dona Dalu called you out. She said to ask if you were all right.'

I said, 'Tell her I'm not all right.'

In another moment Dalu reappeared, saying testily, 'Matahari is on heat. Can't you tell after all this time? Where's the boy? He can take her to the billy now.' I said, 'Mateus hasn't got room for her, Dona Dalu, and his goats have all got horns, they might hurt her.'

She sat down again, shaking her head. 'I think that child does a better job than you.'

Dona Fátima didn't call again but we heard the news that Maria do Rosário was worse, and that reminded me of Fátima and her important information. The only time I am free of Dalu is when she makes her confession. I have to go to confession too. I am a Christian but I'm not a Catholic. I didn't feel this was worth explaining in the beginning when language was such a problem. Perhaps as a consequence I treat confession as a kind of oral examination. I sit at the back of the church, out of earshot, and I wait for Dalu, then I have my turn. She doesn't take long. I suppose she only recites her trivial misdemeanours. Fátima lives in an annexe of Sr. Onorusco's house, which is right next to the church, so I thought I could risk a quick visit while Dalu was at confession.

Fátima was not in the same merry expansive mood. She looked dour and heavy-lidded and seemed reluctant to let me in. I said,

'Dona Fátima, please can we be quick? I only have five minutes while Dalu is in confession. What do you have to show me?'

Fátima's quarters were dark and muddled and smelt of old cauliflower stalks. Today she was limping instead of striding. I suddenly remembered how ill Rosário was and Fátima's reputed devotion to her, and felt insensitive.

I asked, 'How is Dona do Rosário?'

She shook her head and her old jowls wobbled.

'Come next week,' she said thickly. 'Come next week and I'll tell you.'

'I'm sorry. I shouldn't have come. I'll go.'

'No, wait there.'

She was bending over a drawer and rummaging amongst the contents. She found what she wanted and squinted at it.

'Can you read, *filha*?'

'Yes I can.'

She handed me a strip of crumpled paper. I was surprised, but took it politely. It didn't look like anything of consequence. There were only three lines on it. I glanced at them and a name leapt out at me.

'Read it, daughter.'

At first sight the three lines didn't make sense. I read:

'*Eu deixo-vós dois companheiros na vossa escuridão*
João-ninguém para vos guiar
Zé-ninguém para vos chamar de volta.'

'They all said old 'Quim was mad. He was no madder than you or me,' Fátima affirmed. 'When 'Quim was dying, little João came down to the village to call Pai, and that's how the word got around that 'Quim was going.'

'Was 'Quim João's great-grandfather?'

'He was. Well, I could have told them that 'Quim had nothing to leave anybody, but he'd been to foreign countries so they thought he might have some treasures stashed away. The Lord usually goes to write out the wills, but he had his own good reasons, no doubt,' she said direly, 'for not wanting to go visiting up the mountain.'

I didn't want to hear about the Lord. I tried to deflect her, but she was settled into her story and she simply raised her voice and continued,

'So the Kabul boy, Frei Serafim, took it upon himself to go instead. He was always very earnest and a bit pushy. I heard him telling the Lord about it when he got back. Little João let him in and Serafim asked Old 'Quim if he had anything to leave. 'Quim just laughed at him, but then he said,

'You've got your pen out ready, have you? Well you can write this down.' And that's what he wrote, on the paper you've got there.'

He had written:

'I leave you two companions in your darkness,
João-ninguém (Nobody) to lead you forward,
Zé-ninguém (Nobody) to call you back.'

I thought the old man had a nice turn of phrase.

'The Lord just threw it away, but I picked it out, and saved it. Do you know I never thought of it again until they found the baby's bones down under the Stores? Then I thought I would give it to you because you're little João's friend. You can take that and keep it.'

'Thank you, Dona Fátima.'

She said, 'Think nothing of it. If you come next week I'll have something else to tell you, something your João will be interested to hear.'

'Thank you, Dona Fátima, I really do have to go now.' I edged towards the door and she followed me, still talking. She said, 'But what I don't understand is why Conceição took the one baby with her and left the other behind.'

I said, 'I expect it was because she couldn't walk down the mountain with two heavy babies. She took Zé because he was awake and left João because he was sleeping.'

XVII

eight moons gone, five moons to go.

It's full moon again. There are only five moons left. Already there is activity at the Port Stores. The rice, tea and rubber are being crated and stacked; they are getting ready for the arrival of the boat.

I yearn to escape. I hate this stifling hut. The greasy cooking smells disgust me; the smoke makes my eyes sore and itchy. Dalu and I live cheek by jowl in mutual distrust. We do what we can to frustrate one another. I want to go home to my family and be feasted for a week and a day. I want to speak freely and fluently in my own language. I even actively want to go to university. Yet I can't bear the idea of leaving because it means I'll never see João again. I am afraid that the short time we've had together may be all we'll ever have.

I'm still not bleeding. Sometimes I manage to convince myself that I'm not pregnant, and that I've stopped menstruating because I'm over-anxious or undernourished. I can remember sitting with my mother at the kitchen table and listening to some calm, serious woman talking about menstrual problems on the radio, and how periods often stop when girls go away from home. I feel encouraged, but not for long. I only have to look at the goats to make the unthinkable seem inevitable. If females mate, they become pregnant, that's commonplace.

Then I wonder why I let it happen. Perhaps I'm so neurotic that I can't tell reality from fantasy; perhaps I thought nothing I did could have real consequences. Perhaps I secretly intended to do it, and hoodwinked my rational self. When I think about being pregnant, I'm appalled; but when I think about a baby growing in me that is half João's, I melt into a sweet masochistic jelly.

There was to be a party at Mãezinha's house and normally I would have been invited. I could see that Dalu was in a quandary because she didn't want to take me but she didn't dare to leave me behind. So she called in a crony to mind me.

Dalu went off with her niece, who seemed unusually excited. She had been getting in my way all day. I wasn't even allowed to know the nature of the celebration. I sat on the verandah and felt resentful. After a while a man walked by with a hornless billy-kid on a piece of rope. The billy was going to the butcher's to get his throat cut and he was a jaunty little beast. The man stopped to chat and I looked at the kid carefully because sometimes the breeders bite the balls off young males. When I was satisfied that he was intact, I asked if I could take the kid to the goat-shed for a drink. He agreed, with that indulgent look the villagers give me when they think I'm being naïve.

At first the kid showed more interest in the teats of the milking goats than he did in Matahari, but Matahari was persistently coquettish and she finally persuaded him to clamber up on her. As a reward I gave him a drink of milk from a bucket. I was glad that his last hour of life had contained some satisfaction.

After dark, when the party must have been well under way, Mateus's son appeared, bringing food for my minder. It was a piece of roast wild pig, which she audibly enjoyed. He also brought her a drink. She would have liked to refuse it. I saw her wince at the eye-stinging smell, which I identified as rough rice brandy. However, etiquette evidently demanded that she should accept the drink. She smiled and thanked the child and downed it quickly.

Shortly after drinking the brandy she began to fidget uncomfortably, then got up and rushed outside as I used to do when my intestines were still getting accustomed to the local bacteria. She was gone so long that I was considering how I could best take advantage of her absence, but just then she came back, sagged against the screen and closed her eyes. I soon grew bored with watching her sleep. I went out to the shed to collect my exercise book and I took it upstairs with the lantern and wrote for half an hour. I still felt discontented, as though I were missing out on a good opportunity, so I decided to go for an illicit stroll in the dark. I hopped out of the window and tiptoed round to the doorway to peep in at the old lady. She was still asleep, stretched out on the floor.

I visited the monkey, a fellow captive who was kept chained up on a veranda with a melon rind and a piece of broken mirror for company. Then I sat down on the hillside above the house. It was good to be out in the dark; everywhere I could hear the clashing of tiny cymbals. It was like the sound the telegraph wires make, ksheesh ksheesh ksheesh, but there weren't any telegraph wires. At first I felt satisfied to be sitting there in direct contravention of Dalu's orders; then I began to think about my moonlight scramble with Mãezinha and I wished that I could climb the mountain and go and see João. I knew it was impossible. I couldn't manage it alone. I considered going via the port and up past the *cabana*. I wondered how far I could get before the gang of three came after me; or, worse still, Tino and Rui without Mateus's captainship.

I wasn't brave enough to try. I knew I would wait until Dalu noticed I was pregnant and probably let her beat me. Then I would creep up the mountain for refuge, as Conceição had crept; but if Dalu hated me enough she might not throw me out, she might punish me instead by forcing me to stay. João had said: *'Don't be afraid, I'll take care of you,'* and, *'Dalu can't stop you. She had better not try'*; but he hadn't come, he hadn't helped me. Had he been injured by the gang of three? Or did he think that I had left him on purpose?

My courage was at low ebb. I propped my elbows on my knees and put my head in my hands. The lamp was still lit in the upper half of the house and the light filtered out through the screens. As I sat there I distinctly saw a figure moving swiftly, in silhouette, across my old bedroom. I said, 'Damn and blast! They're back!' and ran down the slope to the house. I planned to tell Dalu I had been to the stream to relieve myself.

I slipped in behind the screen. The lower storey was still in darkness. The old woman was snoring, sprawled inelegantly on the floor. There was no sign of Dalu. I looked up uncertainly at the circle of light at the top of the ladder and called, 'Olá!' As I did so the lamp went out. A black shape like a giant bat detached itself from the hole and swooped down at me. It swung momentarily from the ladder and had me pinioned against the wooden wall before I had time to scream.

A hand was pressed hard over my mouth. Then removed.

'Amy!'

I said in disbelief, 'João?'

'Did I hurt you?'

'No, but you nearly frightened me to death.'

'I thought you were Dalu.'

He still had me pressed against the wall, but he stroked my cheeks and mouth with his fingers and thumbs and moved his body against mine. 'Don't cry, don't cry.'

I put my arms round him and pressed small, fast, biting kisses all over his face. I said,

'I was just thinking about you and wanting you to come. How did you know I needed you?' My tears were still running down his face and neck.

He said, 'Don't cry. I've come to take you home.'

As he rubbed against me something hard pressed into my hip-bone and hurt me. I put down my hand and felt it. It was the hilt of a long knife in a scabbard. We went on kissing. João was hot and manic. I said, half-hysterically,

'João, stop. She'll wake up.'

'She won't.'

'Dalu will come back.'

'No, no, she won't come back. Sshh.'

He fumbled for the place and pushed his fingers inside me. I was quite helpless. João took me roughly, up against the wooden wall, and hurt me a little. I think there was something besides love which impelled him to do it in his grandmother's house. Afterwards he said,

'You must light a lamp now and find all your things.'

'She will wake up.'

'She won't, don't worry.'

I lit the lamp and crept around collecting my few clothes, which were all neighbours' cast-offs, my pointed sun-hat, and the horn comb and little hair-slide given to me by Mãezinha. I smelt strongly of sex and sweat: a pungent, spicy smell, like boiled onions. The old lady was still insensible on the floor.

I went upstairs to get my exercise book and pencil. On the wall was a crude picture of the Virgin Mary which I had studied at my leisure, criticizing the perspective, the tawdry crown and doll-like features of the Queen of Heaven. It had been slashed through and through with knife-strokes. The sight of the torn-up face frightened me.

Downstairs, João was pillaging. I saw him pick up a lump of whey cheese wrapped in a leaf and put it in with my belongings, then he drank the milk straight from the pitcher in a single gulp. I didn't protest. I felt that Dalu owed him more than she could ever repay; but at the same time it made me uncomfortable. I said,

'Was it Zé who ripped the picture up?'

He didn't reply. He was busily knotting up all my possessions in a skirt. We left Dalu's house, carrying my light bundle. It felt like a final departure. I held João's hand tightly. I felt dependent and blissfully immune from harm, like a foetus attached to its cord.

We didn't take the main track but went round the back of the house. Matahari called to me from the shed in a low, stuttering voice. We stole up the hillside and through the trees until we came to the top of the Steps.

'Are we going to your house?'

'No, it's too far, and we have things to do in the village tomorrow.'

We climbed the rocks to the waterfall. In the cave behind the ledge he had made us a bed of grass. It smelt chokingly of earth and evoked the sound of lawn-mowers, and memories of Sunday afternoons at home. All the rubbish had gone but the thin soil had sprouted a crop of poisonous toadstools, which they call snake's hat. João lit a small fire to keep the blood-sucking insects away. He said,

'We'll be safe here. No one knows this place but you and me. Go to bed, *amor*, I'm coming.'

He went to wash at the waterfall, then lay down, cool and slippery, in the grass beside me. He threaded his fingers through my hair.

'I would have come to fetch you sooner but your friend had made plans for tonight.'

I said, puzzled, 'Mãezinha? Have you seen her?'

'She came up to my house in the middle of the night. She was very nervous,' he said, sneering, 'she thought I might bite her on the throat.'

'What did she want?'

'She said that the old nanny-goat had locked you up and it was making you ill. She said that you had sent her a message to say you were not well.' I thought Mãezinha had acted bravely. I, on the other hand, am a timorous soul, diffident about revealing the truth. I can procrastinate indefinitely. I didn't tell him the nature of my unwellness.

'She said that I should go and get you. She said tonight would be best because Dalu would be away and there would only be her friend.'

'Aha!' I said, as understanding dawned. 'The fire-water was your idea, wasn't it?'

'She was lucky she came to no harm,' he said shortly.

He paused, and even in the dark I could sense his anxiety.

'Your friend said I should elope with you, just take you and marry you quickly. She said it was what you wanted me to do.'

After the initial jolt I was airborne, ascending gently. It was like the feeling of watching thick snow falling, through a window, and imagining that you are rising instead, effortlessly and noiselessly, in your capsule.

'Do you want to marry me, Amy?'

'Yes, I do.'

João smiled; a rare occurrence. He said, 'Tomorrow we'll go and see Pai.'

João was tired and went to sleep quite quickly in my arms. The angles of his bones stuck into me like coat-hangers, but I didn't like to move him. I stayed awake, listening to the fierce rushing water which curtained us off from our enemies. I was peaceful in my heap of grass. I found myself in a mood of euphoric self-sacrifice, renouncing my family, my education and all for love of João. In my imagination I stood on the mountainside and waved to the departing ferry then I turned away with barely a backward glance.

I dozed, and I thought for a moment I was back in my little loft bedroom, lying on the floor. I looked up at the picture of the Virgin and I saw that her face was changing. Her cheeks and forehead were moving and bulging as if worms burrowed beneath her skin. One eye burst and hung out, like the eye of a rabbit melted in the pot; it looked demurely downwards. Then her lips split into a grin as the tip of the knife protruded between them like a sharp silver tongue.

I came to with a start and clutched at João.

'João, where's your knife?'

'It's here. What is it, Amy?'

'I was afraid we might lie on it and hurt ourselves.'

'No, it's by the side of the bed. Go to sleep.'

I lay in the grass and tried not to see the smile on the face of the Virgin. I didn't feel safe any more.

In the morning we showered, and walked down to the village, holding hands. Pai was just coming out of his house. He looked neither pleased nor surprised to see us together, and that should have forewarned me. He took us into the little sacristy of the church and we sat on a bench. He glanced at our linked hands but did not comment. João said, 'Pai, we would like you to marry us, at once.'

He smiled slightly, but as at a private joke.

'We talked of this before, do you remember, daughter? My answer is still the same.'

'I don't think you gave me an answer, Father.'

He sighed, and said testily, 'I am sure that I made myself perfectly clear. The answer was no. It is still no. If you were married you could not go home when the ferry comes.'

'Of course not. If I were married I wouldn't want to.'

'João.' His tone with me had been tart, a little edgy. Now it changed to one of patient explanation. 'João, I understand that you need a wife, that is very natural, but Amy is only with us for a short while. She has to go back to her own family, to her own country.'

João looked so crestfallen that I said hotly,

'I am to go back to my own country, and what about João? Is he to spend the rest of his life alone?'

Pai tightened his lips and fixed me with a long reproving stare. He said, 'That is exactly the outcome I wish to avoid. We must all pray for patience, so that we don't make mistakes.' He turned again to João, and said gently, 'João, it is possible that a bride might be found for you in time, perhaps on the other side of the island. Have you considered that?'

I thought this suggestion hurtful and insulting. I said furiously,

'Would you like me to leave the room while you discuss it?'

João gripped me by the forearm. He raised his voice and said, 'I don't want to marry a heathen from over the mountain. I want to marry Amy. I am taking her to my house because she has been locked up and she needs me to take care of her.'

Pai looked at me. He said,

'Has Dona Dalu punished you for running away?'

'Yes.'

'What would your own mother have done?'

'My own mother would never treat me the way Dona Dalu does.'

'Dona Dalu gave you food and shelter, didn't she?'

'Yes, in exchange for my labour.'

'She gave you a little nanny-goat of your own, didn't she?'

'Yes, she did, a little sickly nanny.'

He said sharply, 'When you are living amongst poor people such a gift is not to be despised.'

149

João broke in determinedly, 'Father, I am taking her to my house. But first we would like to have the blessing of God.'

Pai said, 'The blessing of God is not mine to bestow.'

'Who can bestow it, Father, if you can't?' I asked mutinously. 'Frei Serafim?'

He looked at me steadily, but his fingers began to beat on the table, and he began to prevaricate.

'Marriage is not merely a question of God's blessing. You would need papers, witnesses, the consent of your parents.'

I said, 'I'm over eighteen. I don't need parental consent.'

He raised his eyebrows and bulged his eyes at me.

'Perhaps in your own country you don't, but this is not your country.'

'If we need witnesses, call Mãezinha and Dona Fátima.'

'Mãezinha certainly won't come. Mateus would not allow it.'

I said in disbelief, 'Mateus would not allow it? Does Mateus employ her, or own her?'

Pai replied levelly, 'They are man and wife; they were married yesterday.'

'Mãezinha and *Mateus*? And no one even told me?'

João said, 'I thought you knew.'

I demanded, 'Did she want to marry Mateus? Was she even consulted? Was this part of her punishment?'

Pai didn't respond. He brushed these questions aside as irrelevant. He said stonily, 'Let us return to your own situation for the moment. Do you have papers, daughter?'

'You know very well I haven't.'

'And João has none, no record of his birth, no family name even. Under these circumstances Sr. Onorusco will certainly not issue a certificate.'

João said, 'We don't need a certificate. We only want a blessing.'

Pai closed his eyes as if in prayer. 'And that, I have told you, I cannot give.'

I said, 'If you won't bless us, we shall have to ask God for his blessing ourselves.'

I meant to convey that we could manage quite well without his help. He said, 'Then that will be between you and God.'

I am not by nature a quarrelsome person, and until then I had had the greatest respect for Pai, but I was upset by his attitude and also by the news about Mãezinha. I accused, 'Aren't you evading your responsibilities, Father?'

He said angrily, 'I hope you are as conscious of yours as I am of mine.'

'You won't marry us, you won't bless us, you don't want to help at all.'

'On the contrary, I will help you in any way I can. If you, daughter, are unhappy with Dona Dalu I will arrange for you to stay with Dona Maria de Lurdes until you leave the island.'

I said witheringly, 'No thank you.'

João stood up. He said with finality, 'I am taking her up the mountain. Tell them to leave us alone. Tell them I will kill the next man who comes near my house.'

I expected Pai to remonstrate but he made a gesture of defeat. He said, 'I have told them, repeatedly, from the pulpit. João, I can understand your feelings, but what you mean to do is not right, and only bad consequences can follow. You are not man and wife and you may not take Amy to live in your house. Amy, you will remain here while I go and speak to Dona Maria de Lurdes.'

'She is coming with me.'

Pai shouted, 'She is not! João, you cannot have her.'

João said, 'I have had her five times already.'

He leapt up and stood in the doorway of the sacristy with his hand on the hilt of his knife. Then he called me with a click of the tongue and a jerk of the head, as you would call a dog. We left.

XVIII

We walked past the main archway, which was crowned with stone pineapples and squatting lions, and round the outside of the great walled garden. João climbed up swiftly among the trees. His eyes and mouth were pulled down in an expression of fury. I stumbled after him. My legs felt as insubstantial as flower stalks and my empty stomach was blown up with gas like a football.

We reached the slope above the *praça*. There the trees thinned out and I could see brown and white goats grazing around the *tuna*, a circular bandstand where the dances are performed. Matahari spotted me at once and came charging purposefully up the hill towards me. She is short in the leg but quite a sturdy little goat. If the truth were known, I always favoured her at feeding time. I called her Matahari, which means 'eye of the day', because she first struggled to her feet as the sun was coming up. Until then she had not looked like surviving. João said,

'Is she in kid?'

'She was mated yesterday.'

He bared his teeth in a little grin. 'Let's take her.'

He went into the wood and cut a length of creeper tendril, with which he quickly improvised a collar and lead for Matahari. Mãezinha's little sister sat on the rail and stared. I called out imperiously,

'Tell Tia Dalu I am taking my goat.'

Matahari didn't need a lead, she had volunteered to come, and would have followed me willingly. We took her to the waterfall. She would not venture behind the water, so we sat outside and João picked a little warm hand of bananas; I fed Matahari the skins.

João lay on his belly in the grass and scowled down upon the village. I knelt up beside him. I could see the *praça*; the huts looked like haystacks. People were congregating, gathering around the *tuna* and waiting for something to happen, perhaps more wedding celebrations. I asked, 'João, do you think Mãezinha was happy about marrying Mateus?'

'She didn't say.'

Mãezinha had considered practically every village boy as a

potential boyfriend but I was certain she had never thought about Mateus. He was too old for her, too crass, and second-hand.

'How did she seem, was she smiling?'

'She didn't smile at me.'

She had risked the displeasure of Mateus by visiting João, alone at night, and by conniving at my escape on the very night of her wedding when all her thoughts should have been on her husband. It proved that I was still her special friend, and eased the hurt of being left out.

'João, why do you think Pai wouldn't marry us?'

'He thinks I am not fit to marry. He thinks my children will be ugly or misshapen, mad, sick creatures.'

I shivered.

'Once twins were born in the village, to an old man and his wife. My great-grandfather told me. They were boy and girl and the priest said they had sinned in the womb, because they were naked together. The husband told the mother to take them up the mountain and leave them for the birds, but she didn't, out of weakness and pity. She took them and left them with the Sisters on the hill by Yogung. They grew up; the boy had a tongue so thick it choked him and he couldn't speak; he died as soon as he became a man. The girl repented. She took the vow of silence. She never uttered a word as long as she lived, but sometimes she cried out in the chapel and waved her arms.'

I wanted to say: 'I have never, in all my life, heard such rubbish.' Instead I said patiently, 'But the twins hadn't done anything wrong. They were defective because they were born to elderly parents. Listen, the doctors in my country are brilliant. They can take a tiny scrap of skin from a baby while it is still inside its mother, and from that scrap of skin they can tell you the sex of the baby and if it has any diseases.' I knew this was true because my brother's wife had had the test. 'They know all about babies and the way they grow. Do you have any weakness or illness in your family, like wheezing or fainting fits or bleeding?'

He shook his head slightly. He was always apprehensive when questioned. 'Then there is no danger, your children will be perfect.'

'Pai told me that the children must pay for the sins of the fathers, and the fathers' fathers.'

I thought, 'That was a pretty cruel thing to tell you.' I said firmly, 'Well in my country we know better, and we don't persecute children for what their parents have done. In my country you would have lived a normal life, like everyone else.'

Privately I suspected that in my country most of the children of incest never saw the light of day. I said,

'Our baby will be fine. It will be a strong, beautiful baby.' As I spoke I remembered how I had prevented Matahari from mating with her grandfather and I knew that I was a hypocrite.

João looked at me fearfully. He had grasped only the salient point.

'Are you going to have a baby?'

'Yes, I think so.'

He recoiled momentarily, then he said, 'When did it happen?'

'The first time, at the *festa dos namorados*.'

'The first time,' he repeated with a touch of pride. 'My great-grandfather told me you had to do it three times.'

'Well nobody is always right.'

'If it is a boy I could teach him to do wood-carving.'

'I'm sure you could teach him lots of things.'

'You could teach him his numbers, Amy, he had better learn to write numbers.'

'Yes.'

He looked curiously at my abdomen and asked:

'How big is he?'

'Still very tiny.'

'Where is he?'

I showed him where I thought the baby was. I said, 'João, should I have told Pai?'

'I don't know.'

'He thinks I shall leave when the boat comes, I'm sure that's why he wouldn't marry us. He might feel differently if he knew about the baby.'

João jerked me round to face him. His eyes were bleak. He had a mottled green rag tied round his head, and a cow-lick of coarse black hair escaped from it. I thought he looked like a young bandit. He said, 'You aren't going on the boat, you're never going to leave.'

'I won't leave, of course I won't.'

'You have to swear it; you have to swear that we'll die together.'

'But how can we promise that?'

'Swear!'

On my arm I had a half-healed scratch with a scab like a thin piece of rind. João lifted it off with the point of his knife. Little beads of blood bubbled up along the pale line. Then he drew the knife lightly across his own forearm and pressed the wound to mine, clasping my hand.

'Swear!'

'I swear.'

My arm was sheathed in João's blood. When I saw the size of his cut I exclaimed, 'Jesus! You crazy boy!'

He pulled the dirty bandana from his head and tied it round his arm. He said, 'Now let's pray for the blessing.'

I hadn't seriously meant to pray for a blessing. I believe in God, but I don't know how to contact him. I don't pray except in church or in grave distress. I had only meant to challenge Pai's authority, because we had invited him to mediate between us and God and instead he had played piggy-in-the-middle. I suggested, 'We could say the words of the wedding service. I know most of them.'

I'd seen my brother Richie married and afterwards, as a jealous twelve-year-old, I'd conducted my own wedding ceremony with the aid of a C of E prayer-book and my mother's big dressing-table mirror. My phantom groom had been a lean, dark BBC actor from a children's serial. I asked,

'Do you know the Latin words?'

'No, I've never been to a wedding.'

'Well,' I said, 'I'll try and tell you the words in Portuguese. We have to promise to love and look after each other, to adore each other with our bodies, and to leave behind all others. Do you promise?' He promised, and I promised too. He asked me if I had had any others in the village and I said that I hadn't. I asked him in turn and he shook his head.

'But you must have wanted one of the pretty girls?'

'Sometimes I used to go down to the padi-fields to catch frogs and I used to hide and watch the girls at the *festas*. But I didn't want to kiss them, I wanted to hurt them. Until I met you, I didn't think I was a man. What else do we promise?'

'We promise to share everything we own.'

'But I don't own anything, I only have this knife. It was my great-grandfather's.'

It was a long thin knife with a wavy blade. I looked at it askance. I said, 'What about your house?'

'It isn't mine. I have to pay the *Senhório* in grain and poultry.'

'Well I don't own anything either, except Matahari. You can have half of her, the front half.'

Matahari was propped up on her horny knees, tearing at the grass on the bank. João stroked her underside, from beard to tail, with the back of his knife. He said,

'Let's cut her this way.'

'Don't, João, you're much too careless with that knife.'

'No, I am very careful with it. What else do we promise?'

'Well at one time a woman had to promise to obey her husband, but now I think she can choose whether to promise or not.'

'What do you choose?'

I said, 'I don't see why the wife has to obey. If she does, it probably means the husband is a bully.'

'I would never hurt you, Amy. I have never hurt anybody.'

'Didn't you hurt Tino?'

'Tino! Tino is a stupid man. He tried to pull my knife from my hand. You can promise to obey me and I will promise not to bully you.'

I should have explained then that there are other ways of bullying. I never pursue understanding if there is a risk of causing dissension instead. Perhaps I'm a self-appointed victim, or, as my mother would say, just a coward.

'You repeat: "I, João, take you, Amy to be my wife, and promise that we'll stay together whether things go well or badly, whether we're rich or poor, whether we're ill or healthy, until we die."'

João promised, then I promised too. He cut me a little ring from a hollow cane and put it on my finger. I wondered if I'd become Amy Ninguém, or perhaps Amy Rabbit of the Bramble Bush, which is Dalu's name. He said, 'I'll make you a proper ring tomorrow, perhaps out of tamarind.'

'Will you carve it for me?'

'Yes. I carved some things for you before. I brought them here, but they got broken.'

'By Zé?'

'Yes.'

'João, do you know who Zé really was?'

He said, 'I'm João, but sometimes Zé comes inside me and then I'm bad.' As he said it, I remembered his first words to me. I knew now that he had said: 'I am not bad, I am not bad, I am not bad'.

'But you are a *minha mulherzinha*, my little wife. Zé wouldn't hurt you.'

I thought, 'This has gone too far. It's a wonder the old man didn't make him schizophrenic.' I said,

'Do you remember when your great-grandfather was dying, and Frei Serafim came to write his will?'

He nodded mutely, swallowing. 'Do you remember what your great-grandfather said? I have got the paper, Dona Fátima gave it to me.

'I leave you two companions in your darkness:
João-ninguém to guide you,
Zé-ninguém to curse you.'

'There were two of you, you see, two boys, twins.'

'No, it was me he meant. I am two.'

'Listen, they found little Zé's skeleton under the Port Stores a month ago. He drowned with your mother. Didn't your great-grandfather tell you about him?'

'My great-grandfather never spoke of it at all, except sometimes, when he drank arak, he would say that he knew the heart of his own son, and that it was never proved.'

'So who told you about your parents?'

'Pai. It was when I went to the school. He told me why they didn't like me, because of what my parents had done. He said it was not my fault.'

'Well now you know about Zé. I think, because your great-grandfather was a story-teller, he told you the truth but he told it to you in stories. You are a more practical person and you believed those stories were real. You aren't two people, bad and good, that wasn't what he meant. You are always João, but sometimes you get angry. You have every right to be angry, anyone would be angry. I was glad when you threw the food-tables over, and cut Tino's thumb. But don't say it was Zé; it wasn't, it was you.'

His face remained impassive. He said, 'If Zé comes, Zé comes. My great-grandfather couldn't stop him and Pai couldn't stop him. Pai said it was a sickness of the heart and we should pray, but it made no difference. When Zé comes, you won't be able to stop him either.'

From the village came the sound of the drum.

'Death,' said João, listening, and I said, 'Dona do Rosário, Senhor Onorusco's wife. That's what they were waiting for.'

João said, 'Good. It will keep them busy and take their minds off us. Now it's time to go home.'

Home used to smell of air-freshener blocks. The toilet had a furry seat cover and the TV talked to itself all day long. Home had shining steel windows with a view of orderly flower tubs and greengrocer's grass. I thought, 'I'll never go home again.' I had a notion that I could hear distant, invisible doors slamming all around me, closing me out or closing me in. The slamming doors caused a dizzy feeling and a stirring of panic. I suppose it was like the misgivings you have on going in to sit an exam, or like walking into the maternity ward with your suitcase. You desire the outcome and you came in of your own free will, but all the same you're frightened and you feel like running away.

XIX

nine moons gone, four moons to go

There are only four moons left. One of them has a crease in it, like a bread roll, and the last has a wobble. It looks like a lemon, or a pendulous breast.

Last week we went shopping. João had credit at the Port Stores, because that's how he is paid for the timber in the chute. We took along some ducks with their legs tied together, to sell at Yogung market. I was going to buy a little cotton jacket to wear in the cool evenings.

Before dawn we started down the mountain with our baskets and shoulder-poles. By the time we reached the Stores I felt so tired and out of sorts that João asked Sr. Nestor if I could wait there in the shade while he walked to Yogung.

'Senhor,' he said with dignity, 'my wife is tired.'

Sr. Nestor looked me up and down with expressionless little eyes, taking in the thickening and swelling, before he nodded assent.

When João had been gone a while I wandered round the Stores, fingering everything. Sr. Nestor didn't speak to me. He has never been a conversationalist, but his flat face and silent stare were unnerving. I felt bored and disappointed. I calculated that João couldn't get back until well after dark, and in that time I could easily pay a visit to Dona Fátima. I said to Sr. Nestor,

'*Obrigadissima*, Senhor. I feel much better now. I'm going to take a walk.'

He said, 'No Senhora, your husband intends you to stay here.' I couldn't tell if the 'Senhora' was meant in mockery or not.

I said, 'That's all right, Sr. Nestor, I'll be back before João.'

'No Senhora, he wishes you to stay.'

My dignity was offended. I didn't think he would actually manhandle me, so I walked out of the shop.

Behind the building was a pile of splintered wood and a heap of sea-debris: broken shells, bleached cuttlefish, strange marine creatures like spiky rubber balls. Perhaps it had been Zé's bier. Sr. Nestor appeared silently at my side while I was kicking through the flotsam and jetsam.

'Where did they bury the baby, Sr. Nestor?' He gestured towards a big swampy flat with sinking mud.

'They threw him in there? And Pai allowed it?'

His eyes moved shiftily.

'They said it could not be a Christian. Will you take some tea with me at the stores, Senhora?'

'No thank you, I want to see Dona Fátima.'

He said flatly, 'I wouldn't go to the village if I were you.'

Nevertheless, I started walking along the hot dirt road. It was about eight miles to the village; I had last travelled this way in Benício's cart on the day of the *festa dos namorados*, thinking of nothing but João. As I neared the village I became strangely anxious about bumping into Dalu. I had to encourage myself with the thought that, hot, tired and pregnant as I was, I could certainly out-run her. The idea of running away from a potential great-grandmother might seem absurd to anyone who has not experienced the chilling power of those pus-green eyes, the irises ringed with metal so that they gleam like acid drops in a certain light.

In the distance I saw Rui, ploughing up the burnt rice stalks with two bullocks in a yoke. At the washing-place I recognized several women I knew by sight. I lifted my hand and called out,

'*Boa tarde!*'

No one spoke or smiled but they all turned and watched me pass like a one-woman procession. I thought, 'Well, now I know my name. It's Amy Ninguém.' Rui eyed me slyly; I didn't greet him.

The very next person I saw was Mãezinha carrying home the water. At first I didn't recognize her from the back because she had pinned her hair around a false bun as befitted her married state. She was about to disappear into Mateus's house so I called out:

'Mãezinha!'

She stopped dead and then she turned round to stare at me. I thought she was frowning in disbelief, then I realized that she was terrified. A small child came running out. Mãezinha clutched him to her skirt with one hand. Then she whirled round and pushed him through the dim opening before her. I couldn't believe what I had just seen. Mãezinha had not been frightened of being seen with me. She had been frightened of me.

I walked on mechanically, feeling sick. All at once I realized what I had done: I'd called her from behind. At first I was disgusted with myself for my stupidity, then I became impatient with Mãezinha for hers. Surely she, of all people, could not believe I would mean to curse her or wish her harm. I had reached the centre of the village. The goats were grazing above the *tuna*; some raised their heads briefly as I passed. Mãezinha's sturdy little sister was minding them. She stared at me raptly with her finger up her nose. My feet were sore and swollen from the heat and I stopped to wet them in the goldfish pond as I had often done before. I could feel rather than see the people peering at me from their houses. It was an odd, lonely feeling like an awareness of threat. I had had it once before in Birmingham bus station late at night, and for a moment I was again running across the oily black station, my high heels striking echoes from the concrete.

Something bowled across the grass and landed harmlessly by my foot. I looked at it. At first I thought it was a joke. It was a good stock bone with a marrow to it. Then I realized it wasn't a joke. I kicked the bone into the pond. It was sharp, and scratched my toes. I turned round to face the watchers but I couldn't see a single one. As a gesture of defiance I crossed myself ostentatiously.

I didn't meet anyone else except a gang of children. I thought I caught a whisper of 'witch', but probably I imagined it. The children giggled and hid under their hut. As I plodded on I felt like the baddie in a Western. The town seemed deserted but they were all spying on me from their houses.

Dona Fátima came out to greet me. She raised her arms and signalled powerfully to the unseen spectators, like a home-going sailor, then she ushered me grandly through the door. The house was dark, all the shutters were closed, and it smelt of wet dog and old men's pyjamas. I was hardly inside before she began on the gossip.

'Well, Miss, what have you been doing to Dalu's goats?'

'Nothing,' I replied stoutly. I thought she was going to accuse me of stealing Matahari.

'Did you come by the *tuna*? Did you see any kids?'

'No. Why?'

'Most of them aborted.'

'The kids?'

'And they didn't eat them, they buried them.'

I pretended to be shocked but in fact I was pleased. I thought of Matahari growing daily broader in the belly. I said smugly,

'I tried to tell Dalu not to go on using that billy. He was serving his own daughters and grand-daughters.' In my imagination the little two-headed nanny bleated at me with both her mouths, and suddenly I was afraid. For a moment I was full of darkness and dread, my body felt empty and insubstantial. I'd promised João our baby would be fine, but what I know about incest could be written on the back of a postcard.

Fátima was fetching me a cup of brackish water. As she put it in my hand she said with glee,

'Of course Dalu says you put a hex on them before you left.'

Her breath reeked of coal tar, suffocating me. I felt faint already and my ears started to sing. I sipped at the water and struggled to regain control of myself. After a moment I managed to say coolly,

'I wish I had such powers, Dona Fátima.'

'Don't let them hear you say that!'

'I'm surprised Dalu told anyone about the kids. Something happened once before and she made me promise to keep it a secret.'

'Ah well, now she has you to blame,' said Fátima shrewdly. 'She says you're the spirit of her dead daughter come back to trouble her.'

I said, irritated, 'Surely even Dalu can't be that stupid. I'm a year older than João for a start. I'd have to be a year younger to be the spirit of her dead daughter. Anyway, isn't Dalu supposed to be a Christian?'

Fátima said, 'Fools, superstitious fools.'

I wondered why Dalu had never expressed such fanciful notions or paced the beach weeping when I was there to watch. Perhaps because it was all an act and she knew I would see through it.

I said, 'Most of them don't believe it, surely?'

I'd been hoping to enlist her help in finding me a midwife in the village but I could see my chances receding. 'When I was washing my feet in the goldfish pond, someone threw me a bone. Who would that be?'

Fátima said, 'Oh, any one of them. I expect they thought you were poisoning the fishes. I'll go and get some before they throw them all out. They're very good fried with a little chilli, you know. Take some home for Joãozinho.'

She gave me another cup of warm water. 'They say you're pregnant.'

'How do they know?'

'They sniff things out,' said Fátima, making a snuffling face. 'You'd better be careful. One devil up the mountain they can put up with, but a breeding pair of them might be a different matter.'

She laughed as if she'd made a grand joke.

I said, 'Do you know anything about delivering babies?'

'No, *filha*, but I expect it's very much like delivering goats, you know. Little João will have to do it. I hope you have more luck than Dalu.'

She laughed again, maddeningly. I had been thinking of Fátima as my friend, but now I decided that she was heartless and I didn't like her.

I had just decided to leave when I remembered the original object of my visit.

'I have to go soon, Dona Fátima. Do you remember asking me to call because you had something to tell me, something about João?'

'I do indeed,' said Dona Fátima, allaying my suspicions that she was shedding her brain cells in excessive quantities. She settled down opposite me, her chin on her large hand, and posed a riddle.

'Tell me this, daughter, when Tiago went missing, who was the only man in this village who didn't go and look for him?'

'I don't know, Dona Fátima.'

She leaned forward like an accusing politician and asked me another. 'And answer me this, where did Dalu get her padi-field and her first nanny-goat?' She rapped the table triumphantly and said, 'The answer's the same in both cases.'

I went on listening because the garbled tale of old 'Quim had proved to have a point in the end.

'Where did she get them, Dona Fátima?'

'Where would she get them, an ignorant farm-worker, wife of an impoverished peasant, mother of a serving-wench? Where would she get the money to buy a padi-field or even a milking goat?'

I couldn't imagine.

'When Tiago went missing every man in the village turned out to look for him. Every man but one. He was laid up with the fever.' She nodded significantly. 'He was laid up all right. I took him cinchona bark tea at three o'clock and he was dozing, with the sheet thrown off him. His chest was slashed like a side of pork.'

I didn't follow, but I was intrigued. I made an intelligent guess. 'Do you mean Senhor Onorusco?'

'You've got it.'

She crouched lower over the table. The loose flesh of her neck poured over her hand. Her hair was coming down and her blouse was unbuttoning itself. She said gruffly, 'My lady Maria do Rosário was not a woman like you and me, she was a pure woman. She should have been a bride of Christ, her father made a mistake in marrying her to the Lord. He worshipped her. You didn't see her when she was well, she was so beautiful. At first she forced herself to do her duty as a wife, but she dreaded him touching her, she found his ways disgusting. And she never conceived, that was a great sorrow for her.'

I felt a little sorry for Onorusco.

'I didn't much like Tiago's daughter, I'll admit. She had a miserable look about her. She wasn't pretty like Mãezinha, she had one of those long noses like you,' said Fátima, who had a longer one. 'She was a poor thing, she flinched if you raised your voice to her, she was always grizzling. I came upon them once. The Lord was sitting in his big chair in the study and he had her trapped between his legs. Conceição had her back to him, pulling away, and he was fondling her front and kissing her neck.'

'Conceição and Senhor Onorusco?'

'He let her go when I came in. 'Poor child,' he said to me, 'poor child, she needs all the affection we can give her.' Well the girl worked in the kitchen and I saw for myself that she was pregnant. If she so much as looked at food she'd change colour and retch. I nearly went up and told my lady there and then, but when it came to it, I hadn't the heart to bring her news like that, she would have felt the shame very deeply, it would have caused her such trouble and hurt. I kept quiet, and now I've kept quiet so long the Lord thinks he's bought me off, I dare say, like he bought Dalu off.'

'Dona Fátima, are you saying that *Senhor Onorusco* is João's father?

'I never doubted it for a moment '

'And Dalu knew?'

'Of course she knew. A girl like that couldn't have kept it a secret. Dalu didn't mind. The Lord paid her a milking-nanny for the use of her daughter. Conceição was a girl with nothing much about her; Dalu was glad to get a good price. But when Tiago found out, then it was a different matter entirely.'

'Tiago was Dalu's husband?' I said, grasping this fact at last.

'I've already told you that. Well I knew old 'Quim, and I knew his boy Tiago. They wouldn't be so ready to slander him if he was here to defend himself, I can tell you.'

Fátima pursed her lips and fingered the whiskers on her chin.

'Well, my guess is, knowing the kind of man he was, that he went to the Senhor and he meant to hack him into pieces and hang him up on hooks in the *praça*. But the Senhor did for him instead, or else he called in his bodyguard to do it for him, and they threw him down a gulley or into the mangrove swamp.'

'Do you have any proof of this, Dona Fátima?'

'Yes, what I saw with my own eyes. And Dalu's padi-field. That was for keeping quiet about her husband's murder and sending the girl up the mountain out of the way.'

'But why did Conceição keep quiet?'

'Because she was terrified, you could see it written on her face. She said nothing, and the more she said nothing, the more they thought it was Tiago. But I'd be surprised if 'Quim believed it.'

I said, 'I don't think he did.'

'Do you believe me, daughter?'

'Yes I do.'

She'd explained all the things I found most puzzling in Mãezinha's story: Conceição's silence, Dalu's implacable rejection of her daughter, a seeming conspiracy to conceal the survival of João. She'd also explained some of the things I hadn't been clever enough to puzzle over: Dalu's comparative affluence, her standing in the community.

'Dona Fátima, what do they believe about the baby's skeleton? Who do they say it was?'

'Oh they believe what they choose to believe, of course. Some say the baby fell off a boat. Some whisper,' – she mimed women gossiping behind their hands – 'that it's Conceição's and your João is a demon without a human body. You could tell them differently, I'm sure.'

'But didn't you tell them about 'Quim's will?'

'They wouldn't pay any attention to old 'Quim. Look, Pai is a very important person in the village, isn't he? When little João turned up at the school (what a shock that was for someone!) Pai told the people to accept the boy. But they wouldn't.

'So Pai baptized him in front of everybody and said, "See, he's a Christian." But someone else was whispering, "No he's not, he's a demon". Someone even more important. Do you see?'

I saw. Who wants to offend the most powerful man on the

island? More prudent to slander Tiago and victimize João, to smile obsequiously at Dona Dalu who has the protection of the Senhor. If Fátima or I tried to disprove the lies, we might be in danger from their original perpetrators. I didn't like Fátima much, but I warned her,

'Dona Fátima, please be careful what you say. Remember you could lose your home, or something even worse could happen to you.'

'Oh, I shan't say anything. I leave that to you now. But I promised myself that one day I'd tell little João, and it can't hurt my lady now. The truth is,' said Fátima, all her animation drained from her, 'that I don't really care any more. It's the kind of callousness that comes with old age.'

I had dreaded walking back along the village street but I walked it unseeingly. I hardly felt the ridges of earth beneath my feet. I didn't care about the passers-by, or rather the absence of them. The street was so empty that it might have been the day of silence. My fists were clenched and I muttered under my breath. 'It's monstrous! Monstrous!' I must have looked just like a witch putting hexes on the rice-terraces as I stalked past. I was almost at the pond before I realized it. I didn't mean to go fishing; I thought their goldfish would stick in my throat.

At the corner of the *praça* is a large tree. Two men were sheltering beneath it, half-hidden amongst the snarled roots. They were holding a hoe and a rake and they had pieces of cloth tied over their mouths and noses. I walked on a couple of paces. Then the head of the hoe struck me hard on the back of the neck and I fell on my face in the dust on the path.

I felt full of helpless surprise. I thought I had had an accident. Next moment I was grasped by the ankles and thrown onto my back. One of the men looked down at me. He had cold amber eyes, like a dog; the whites were pink with irritation. He trod heavily on my face with his bare foot, and at the same time the other man swung his rake and brought it down on my belly.

The dusty foot of the first man was in my mouth and over my nose, choking off my screams. The second man jerked my legs apart and held me up by the heels. His companion grasped the handle of his hoe and rammed it up hard between my legs.

I didn't scream; I didn't have the breath or saliva. Instead I protested hopelessly,

'No! No! Please!'

The hoe-handle entered me. I arched my back and rose up on my shoulder-blades. The thick, splintery shaft intruded intolerably and the pain was so preposterous that I thought it was the end for my baby. I thought I was as good as dead myself.

They thrust it inside me three or four times. Then they held me between them as we used to do in a children's game, 'Shake the bed, shake the bed, and turn the blanket over', and they tossed me in the direction of the goldfish pond, where I landed on the stones, half in and half out of the water. As I squatted there I saw a barefoot boy in a sarong come running swiftly down the path. He was skinny and angular with wild black hair. His elbows and knees were working furiously and his eyes were rolling like the eyes of a crazy person. For a moment I didn't recognize João.

He bounced on the bridge as if it were a springboard and leapt high into the air. He landed on top of Pink-eye, and as he landed he struck him hard on the jaw with his foot. The man reeled and fell back against the bole of the tree.

João seized the handle of the rake and swung it around him with all his might. He spun round in frenzied circles, like a Highlander throwing the hammer. A hush had fallen. Pink-eye was motionless by the tree. I sat and stared like a picnicker who has had too much wine and sun. All of a sudden the rake head thudded into the bark and embedded itself there. João wrenched it free with a yell and swung again. This time the tines impaled the ear of the pink-eyed man and he hooted like a chimp.

The other man was running. João flew after him and swung again. There was the clack of wood on wood; the man had turned to defend himself, chopping downwards with his hoe. João crouched and swept the rake from side to side in a low arc, and the man jumped, again and again, as children do in skipping games. As he tried to retreat, his legs tangled. He tripped over the rake handle and he went down in the grass. The rake hit the hoe with a clang and sent it skimming away through the seed-heads.

João struck the man two blows on the skull: two iron shots. Then he clawed at him with the tines of the rake, first lifting him by the clothes and shaking him, then hacking at the flesh of his face as he would hack at hard earth. I could not watch.

João flung down the rake and ran back to the tree, where Pink-eye had slid to the ground. He bent over him, knife in hand, and slashed at the cotton mask. For a moment the man's face was exposed, then a bright symmetrical pattern appeared upon it as if drawn in thin red ink.

'João!'

I tried to stand. As I did so I had a familiar but shocking sensation. A thick warm rivulet oozed out between my legs. I pressed my hand there and withdrew it, glossy with blood.

João came running, sheathing his knife. He looked at me through half-closed eyes, like a child expecting punishment.

'João, I'm bleeding.'

He said quickly, 'It's all right, it's all right, I'll take care of you. Can you walk, Amy?'

'I don't know.'

He picked me up and carried me in his arms. I closed my eyes and pressed my face into his neck.

'João, are those two men dead?'

'No, they are resting.' He said ironically, 'I know those two. That is their favourite sport. They must learn to lose a game or two without complaining.'

'They won't follow us, will they?'

'No, I would hear them. If they stepped on my grave I would hear them.'

He carried me up a path to the waterfall. I opened my eyes and looked back and I saw dark splashes of blood on the stones.

'João, I'm frightened.'

He put me down in the hay, where I curled up, quivering like a dog, and closed my eyes again. João took off his sarong and soaked it in water.

'Come on, Amy, let me see where you are hurt. There, they are only scratches. The skin is broken, that's all.'

'I'm bleeding inside. I think my baby might be dead.'

'No, no, Amy, let me see. It's just a little fall of blood, just a little cleansing blood, we can stop it with a cloth.'

I said, weeping, 'The baby is hurt, João.'

'No. Do you think babies can be hurt so easily? He is very well-protected. He is safe inside you, as safe as we are in this cave.'

I lay and stared sickly, unseeingly, at the rock corridor. I was expecting a warm rush of blood or a racking pain at any moment. More than anything I longed for an ambulance, its blue light flashing, to take me away to hospital, to be put on a high white bed and piped for a transfusion.

We stayed at the waterfall for three days. Sometimes João left me, to fetch food and see to our stock. The blood trickled out steadily. I cried for the baby that was inside me, and I cried for myself, for the child I no longer was. The two sportsmen had done to me what the soldiers on Tuluk had not. They had spoiled me. They had entered my secret passage and touched some vital part of me which could never recover.

I didn't tell João.

XX

On the fourth day João carried me home. I sat in the house and dribbled blood. The next day was the same, and so was the one after. I felt gloomy and irritable. I said fretfully,

'I wish there was someone to tell me what to do.'

'My great-grandfather said that when his wife was ill she went every day to the shrine of Nossa Senhora da Saúde.'

'But she died anyway.'

'Yes.'

I felt like saying, 'Well that was no bloody use then, was it?' I said fractiously, 'Why do you tell me that? It didn't make her better, did it?'

'God didn't will her to get better.'

'So if God wills you to live, you live. If God wills you to die you die. You can't change his mind by lighting candles to Nossa Senhora.'

João had made *nasi goreng* and we ate it with our fingers from the same bowl. Afterwards I ran my hand down his slim brown arm.

'I'm sorry. Tell me about the shrine.'

He took me to the door and pointed to a square outcrop of ochre-coloured rock. He said, 'Do you see that rock down there? The shrine of Nossa Senhora da Saúde is on the other side. Every four years the village people make a carpet of fennel and flower-petals stretching from the church to the Steps. Then they carry the statue of Nossa Senhora all the way up the mountain by candlelight. The penitents walk on their knees from the church to the Steps.'

'Onorusco and Dalu?' I wondered. I thought it was more likely to be Dalu's old crony, atoning for her one drink of arak. I hadn't told João about Onorusco and Conceição; I had meant to tell him, but, as is my cowardly habit, I was putting it off.

'What do they do when they get to the shrine?'

'They have a picnic, then they go back again.'

Matahari was in kid. She had to be tethered because, in the absence of other goats, she thought we were her herd and kept following João home. She hated being tied up. She called constantly on a high note of desperation, her face irritable and pathetic. Out of obstinacy, it seemed, she kept binding herself to trees by winding her rope round the trunks. João was indifferent to her problems. He treated her as he would treat a sheep or a duck.

I went out of the house next morning because I could hear Matahari blethering inanely. I crept along like an old lady, expecting a gush of blood at any moment. I could see João irrigating the garden from a brimming bowl under the spring; he had scratched a network of channels in the thin dry soil. Matahari was standing on three legs. One front leg was so neatly bandaged in rope, it was hard to believe she hadn't done it on purpose. She had knocked over her water bucket. I said in disgust, 'Well, really!' I shouted,

'João, she has been calling for an hour or more, couldn't you see she was caught up in her rope? And she has to have a stone in her bucket or she knocks it over. I told you.'

He heard, but looked inscrutable, so that I went on shrewishly, 'If you can't take care of her properly, I'll do it myself.' He came over then and looked at me. His eyes were narrowed and his mouth drawn down, giving him a look of sexual arousal. He said, '*Cala-te*! Shut up.'

I loosed Matahari and sat down in the sun. She came and lay next to me. She hadn't seen me for a long time and she was as fussy as a bitch on heat. The ducks were lying in a line with their heads on their backs. In response to a secret signal they all stood up, side-stepped, and faced in another direction, more perfectly synchronized than any ballet troupe. When I looked again João had disappeared. I went to the shack to look for him and Matahari followed me. The shack was empty. He had gone off to the forest without saying goodbye. My bravado evaporated and I felt miserable.

The idea came to me that I would walk to the shrine today because it would please João. There hadn't been any gush of blood, only a stale brown spattering, so I hoped it would do me no harm. I could see the rock quite clearly from the garden and there was a path of sorts. I would have taken Matahari but she had lain down thankfully in her shed, so I shut her door. I took some pink guavas and a rambutan with silky auburn hair and on the way downhill I picked some big gaudy flowers like jungle birds. These were for my offering to Nossa Senhora.

There was not much to see at the shrine, no soapstone curlicues or dragon-heads: only a crude stone altar and a shapeless effigy, the features worn smooth and mongoloid. The altar was strewn with offerings, scraps of chequered cloth, wizened fruit, plaited coconut leaves, melted candles, a handful of sago. A monitor lizard lay along the stone. It had a shining turquoise helmet and a lime green body. I knelt down and prayed to the lizard,

'Nossa Senhora, please let me stop bleeding and let my baby be all right.'

The lizard twitched. Its tongue flicked out between its lips like the blade of a knife. It wore an enigmatic smile on its little scaly face. I thought, *the smile on the face of the Virgin*, and I began to feel uneasy, so I crossed myself and quickly arranged my flowers and fruit.

The pilgrimage took longer than I'd anticipated. The terrain is so steep that landmarks miles distant are clearly visible and look deceptively close. It must have been quite late in the afternoon when I got home. João was standing on the path, his face strained. I ran to him and he seized me. I said,

'I'm so sorry. I should never have spoken to you like that. I've been to the shrine.'

'Don't ever go off without telling me. It frightens me.'

I said, 'Oh my love, I'm sorry. I thought you'd gone to the forest.'

'I did go to the forest. I've just come back.'

For supper we had a duck cooked in coconut milk. João seemed subdued. When I went to the door he said,

'Don't go out again. You rest. I'll do whatever needs doing.'

'I'm only going to the toilet.'

The toilet was a trench which João had dug behind the house. Unknown to him I shunned it because of the smell and the flies buzzing round my bottom and when I was well I had often wandered down off the track and found my own place amongst the trees. That is what I was doing when I stumbled over something solid in the long grass. I looked at it in surprise. At first I thought it was a lamb, then I saw it was a white kid, lying in a heap of offal. It was very small. Its eyes had never opened and it was still brown and sticky from its mother's waters.

In another moment I started running back to the house shouting,

'Matahari! Matahari! Matahari!'

Her shed door was closed but her shed was empty.

'Amy, what is it? What's the matter?'

'Matahari's not here and I found her kid dead in the trees.'

He said, 'You stay here. I'll go and look for her.'

I followed him anyway to the edge of the trees. Quite soon he came back up. He was carrying her over his shoulder like a slain deer. Her body had been ripped down the middle from the throat to the tail and her intestines were hanging out. She looked more like a traffic accident than a butcher's carcase. Crowds of flies were feasting on the bright pink tissue and viscous clots. I asked,

'Was it deliberate? Did someone do this on purpose?'

'Yes.'

'Monsters! Monsters! Damn their eyes! Why, João, why would anyone want to do such a thing?'

I looked into Matahari's eyes, and her panic and suffering registered in my own body. Then a cool wind began to curl around my shoulders and back, turning me gooseflesh. I thought, 'When they ripped open Matahari, they had another gravid body in mind.'

'It was a message for me, wasn't it?'

'No, Amy.'

'Yes. Because she was pregnant. They mean to cut me open and kill my baby too.'

'No.'

I went on hysterically,

'Who was it? Was it those two men? Or did Onrousco send one of his paid thugs?'

He said in disbelief, 'What are you saying? Onorusco? Why do you say that?'

'I don't know. Don't ask me now.'

'But why did you say Onorusco?'

'Please João,' I said, 'let's bury her first.'

He dug a hole under the trees and we put Matahari in it. I said silently, 'Goodbye, Flower. I loved you.' I said it silently because João was there and he had never liked me talking to her in English. He held me tightly and he didn't say, 'It's only a goat', or suggest that we should eat the kid, although we would normally have eaten it, because it was a little billy. He said,

'There's no need to be afraid, Amy, believe me. Come into the house now.' As I slumped down by the fire I remembered that I had so nearly taken Matahari with me to the shrine and that started me crying again. João took my hand and shook me gently. He said,

'Amy, why did you say Onorusco?'

I saw that it was no use trying to bluff him. I had meant to tell him anyway. At the right time I could have chosen my words with much greater care, but I'd just suffered another shock and my thoughts slid around out of control.

'Fátima knew your mother when she got pregnant. She said Onorusco was your father, not Tiago. She saw them together.'

He didn't speak. His mouth fell open and he narrowed his eyes.

'Fátima said Tiago went to challenge Onorusco and Onorusco fought with him and killed him. She said Dalu knew all about it. Onorusco gave her a rice-field to keep quiet.'

He was quite motionless, frowning. Then he said,

'Tell me everything she told you.'

'Oh João, I can't, not now.'

'Try.'

I saw that he hadn't received this news with indifference, as he'd received Fátima's revelation about Zé, but I was too distracted to care. I related Fátima's story as nearly as I could and he listened to me carefully. He said,

'Do you think it's true?'

'Yes, if she saw what she says she saw. We only have her word for it.'

'She was a friend of my great-grandfather's. He thought well of her.'

I was very selfish. I should have thought more about João and the shock he had received, but my bereavement was fresh, whilst Conceição and Tiago had been dead seventeen years and João hadn't had to witness their end. Besides, João hadn't known either of them but Matahari had been leaning on me that very morning. I'd felt the kid move in her firm belly and her harsh brown coat hot under my hands.

It was still early but João said we should go to bed and I was glad to, all the crying had made me sleepy and I hoped for oblivion. I slept almost at once but not for long. When I woke up I was alone. I remembered Matahari and there was a clutch of grief at my stomach. Then I remembered what João had learned that evening and all at once I was fully awake and aware. It was like being very drunk and becoming for an instant perfectly sober. In that moment of clarity I knew that João had gone down into the village.

I went and checked that he wasn't downstairs or at the trench. Then I put on the cotton jacket he had bought me at Yogung and filled the lamp. He had said, 'Don't ever go off without telling me,' but if I left him a note he wouldn't be able to read it, so after a moment's thought I tore a page out of my exercise book and drew a picture of the waterfall, and left it lying on the trunk.

I started running down the path. I knew I should climb down the cliff to save time, but I also knew that I couldn't do it. So I ran down the hill, lantern swinging, falling over clumps of grass. I tried not to cry because it wasted precious breath. I suppose it was panic that sent me hurtling on and not any coherent plan at all. I was full of dread and urgency.

By the time I reached the *cabana*, I had to slow down because my calves were aching and trembling uncontrollably. The lantern was more of a hindrance than a help, so I left it at the cabin. I drank water at the stream and plunged on. There were no more landmarks then, only the patch of blurry grey sea slowly enlarging and coming into focus, taking on a metallic sheen, and the speck, becoming a promontory, becoming a dark, squat building, the Port Stores.

I slithered down the last few feet on my thighs and bottom. As I started up the flat road into the village, my legs were bending under me like bananas and I had to sit down on the shingle and rest. All the while I scanned the sky fearfully for intimations of dawn. I wanted to get to the village in the dark, but I had no plan. I had keyhole vision. My mind was concentrated on its one objective: to get there fast.

Dawn came while I was on the road. The sun comes up swiftly here, all falsely-smiling benevolence. The first hour of light is pleasant, like a summer's day in England. When the light came, I felt despair, that whatever was to be done had already been done. I nearly went back then, but instead I thought that I would go to Fátima. I met no one on the road except a small boy riding a water-buffalo, but as I came into the *praça* three things happened in swift succession. I saw that the water-spout where they fill the jars was gushing red. While I was doubting my own eyes I heard men's voices in the *praça*.

I had got there just in time, or rather, at the worst possible time. There was a twang and a swish, like an arrow being loosed from a bow, and a solid red mass fell from the sky, landing wetly and heavily at my feet, spattering me all over. Next moment, another sodden missile came rolling down the bank towards me, and lay on the path unfurling its arms. My scream must have woken every sleeper in every hut around the *praça*.

The two bodies were quite featureless but for the tufts of dark hair on one of them. They were bloody from top to toe, shining red all over. My jacket was soaked in blood.

There were three men in the praça: two up the tree and one below it. It was Tino. I fled up the hill. The sound I made when I ran was somewhere between a sob and a scream. As I ran I prayed, 'No! Don't let it be him. Please don't let it be him!' I tore up through the trees and along a goat-track to the top of the Steps. As I scrambled up the paths to the waterfall I changed my prayer to, 'Let him be there. Please let him be there.'

The rope bridge writhed under my running feet like a caterpillar. I sprang onto the wet boulders, but slithered off them; clutching at the ferns, I hauled myself up again. I was breathing in great gulps, like an infant exhausted by crying. I squeezed into the passage between the rock and the water, moving crabwise until I came to the fissure in the mountain, and entered the cave. My prayer hadn't been answered. The little cave was empty but for the heap of hay that had been our eve-of-wedding bed.

I went out and stood under the pounding, hammering water. Then I took my blood-soaked jacket off and put it into a pool, weighted down by a stone. When I came out I was shaking violently. My teeth were chattering so hard that I kept biting my lip. I went back to the cave. I ordered myself. 'Think, girl, think!' I forced myself to recall the scene at the *praça*, the moment when the two bleeding bodies had come tumbling down. One had been bigger than the other. One had had a tuft of black hair: that didn't mean anything. If one was João, who was the other? Dona Fátima.

To sit and wait seemed intolerable. Waiting at the waterfall was harder than running down the mountain. In my imagination I climbed the cliff and ran to the shack; but the shack was empty and my picture was still lying there on the trunk.

From the village came the sound of the drum. Then João appeared in the mouth of the cave.

XXI

João held me tightly. He said,

'Be quiet! Be quiet or you'll make yourself ill.'

We lay down in the dried grass. Under my breath I gabbled the words of rhymes and prayers as I used to do when I was a little girl: Ding dong dell, pussy's in the well, Our Father which art in heaven, Lazy Elsie Marley. The grass was busy with insects and the dried stalks and leaves scratched my arms. When I had stopped shaking, we got up to go. João tied my wet jacket round my head because I hadn't brought my hat.

'Amy, hold still, you've got blood in your hair. Now you keep this on and when you get home you can throw it away. I'll buy you another one.'

To rejoin the mountain path we took a steep track high above the sea. Below us the little fishing boats looked like floating insects with spindly legs and folded wings. João took my hand and pointed them out.

'Look, that's the Three Marias, that's César's boat, Our Lady of the Sea.'

'Where's your knife?' I asked in sudden panic.

'It's here.' He held it up, clean and coruscating. 'Amy, I told you, it wasn't me.'

I saw that he had a thin line of blood in the hem of his sarong, but that probably meant nothing. I scratch the top off an insect bite nearly every day.

'Who were they, João?'

'You don't need to know that. If only you'd waited for me! Before you came I often used to go to the forest at night. Sometimes I stayed there till morning. Didn't you promise me never to go to the village again?'

'I thought you were in danger!'

'If I were in danger, you couldn't do anything to help me. Now we really may be in danger. Who saw you?'

'Tino,' I said in dismay. 'I shouldn't have been there, should I?'

'No. Listen, Amy, when we get home you are not to leave my side for a minute, not even for half a minute, unless I tell you. If they come, they'll come soon. And this time there'll be more than three of them.'

'Then let's not go home, let's sleep in the forest,' I begged.

'No, I think we must go home and go about our work as usual.'

It was still daylight when we reached the house. For our supper we ate bowls of cold fried noodles, sitting on the porch. As soon as night fell João said,

'Get the skins from the house, you had better sleep out here tonight.'

He imitated the call of a night-bird: a series of metallic clicks and a loud whirr. It sounded like someone winding up a clockwork toy. 'If you hear that call, go down behind the cabin and hide in the trees. Don't come out until you hear it again.'

I wrapped myself in the skins and leant, shivering, against the cabin wall. I felt too frightened and dismal to cry. I had taken a wrong turning at the Port Stores when I had chosen to walk to Costassol. Ever since, circumstances had lined up against me, sliding one by one from dark doorways like a gang of assailants. I was very tired, but each time I started to doze I woke with a jerk. From time to time I put my hand inside my clothes and felt for blood, but none was coming. Despite all the distress and exertion of the past two days, the channel was sealed again, the baby had become quiet inside me.

In the middle of the night I saw something slinking stealthily through the plants around the cabin. I whispered, 'João!'

His voice came from the top of the boulder. 'It's all right. It's only a little leopard-cat. Go to sleep.'

I fell asleep for an hour as the sun rose. I thought, 'It's morning, they won't come now.' João woke me. He said,

'Fetch some food from the house. We're going to the forest.'

We gave the ducks grain and water in their shed and we walked up to the forestry clearing in the morning sunshine. While João worked I sat on a branch and looked down over the tree-tops. Nothing was stirring. I could see the curve of the coastline and the sea fanning out all around. This became the pattern of our days and nights for a week or more. Then one day João said,

'They won't come now.'

'Perhaps they have caught the murderer.'

'They were not murders.' I looked at him. He said, 'When people are killed the way you saw, it is a punishment, not a murder.'

That afternoon I fell asleep in the forest shelter. I dreamt of the water running red from the village spout, and that woke me.

João was lifting my skirt up above my waist. He was poised above me, his own sarong pulled aside in readiness. He said,

'Amy, I must. Just lie still. I won't push hard.' I closed my eyes and gritted my teeth. He put his penis in and moved it gently up and down. Almost at once, I felt a small pulsing as his semen spurted into me. He kissed me and undid my blouse, meaning to give me pleasure. I jerked and made an incoherent noise. In my mind was the image of bleeding, rolling bodies.

✳   ✳   ✳

ten and a half moons gone, two and a half moons to go

Our simple pattern of life showed through again like a waxed pattern on cloth. João went to Yogung market. He said,

'There's no need for you to come. It's too far for you. I'll bring you a jacket.'

'Bring me a green one. Can you buy some things at the Stores?'
He hesitated.

'Yes, if I have time.'

'But you'll be going that way.'

'I might not.'

I thought, 'He's worried about the money, about who'll take over now Onorusco is dead and whether they'll pay his wages.' I was tired of thinking such thoughts.

I went and took my exercise book from its hiding-place and sat down on the porch. I never wrote in front of João any more. Once he had looked over my shoulder and asked,

'Who is it to?'

'It's not a letter.' I added, 'It's in English,' so that he wouldn't have to pretend that he could read it.

'Why are you writing in English?'

'Why?' I said in surprise. 'Because it's my own language.'

'Well it isn't mine.' He went back and crouched over his piece of *jaca* wood, holding it still with his feet and whittling viciously.

When my baby is born, I want to teach her nursery rhymes and sing her lullabies. I want her to read and speak English.

I used to see Richie's wife come home from the antenatal clinic with her card giving the latest information on the foetus: his size, position and heart-rate. We all knitted pram-sets, which she accepted, and suggested names, which she rejected. My baby

183

doesn't possess a bib or a bootee, and she has never had her sonic picture taken. I feel sorry for her already.

I want my daughter delivered on a hospital bed. I want someone to come and take flash photos of her in her plastic crib. I want her to have width-fitted shoes, ice-lollies and magic-painting books. I want her to play in the snow and grizzle with the pain in her little mittened fingers. I know these things don't matter and she won't miss them, but I'll miss them for her.

As for me, I want to eat sausages, and chip-shop chips, and watch a football match with my dad and play the juke-boxes with a friend. I want to go to the library and borrow six books in plastic jackets. I want to be Amy again, if I can still remember who Amy is. The truth is that I want to go home.

When I'd finished writing, I walked down amongst the trees and came across the picked bones of the unborn billy-kid."From his mother's womb untimely ripp'd," I quoted. I turned away quickly, but not before I had pictured the knife slicing into Matahari's belly. I thought compulsively, 'How did they keep her still? I hope they stunned her first.' The image was succeeded, without my volition, by another: João, sitting in the grass, a green-patterned rag tied round his brown arm, in front of him the corrugated green hills and behind him the bald, flat-topped volcano. He'd drawn the back of his knife along her pink, freckled belly, between the tiny udders, and said,

'Let's cut her this way.'

He'd been jealous of her even then.

I walked away quickly, trying to escape from the thought which was pursuing me, but the thought kept up with me easily, buzzing behind my ear. I couldn't rid myself of it however hard I tried. I thought, 'João killed her himself. I wonder why it took me so long to suspect him.'

João brought me a turquoise jacket from Yogung. It was made of raw silk and had a soft, rubbery feel. He brought all my shopping from the Port Stores, and fruit from the market. He squatted down and sliced up a rosy mango, neatly removing the stone. I thought, 'That's the knife that killed Matahari.' I had to force myself to eat the mango.

'Are you unwell?'

'No, it's just heartburn.'

He smoothed the buffalo skin beside him and said 'Come here. I sat down next to him and he took my hands.

'Kiss me.'

I kissed his lips. It was like kissing a stranger. He said,

'Let's go to bed, you look tired.'

I lay on my back with my knees drawn up and my arms crossed over my chest. I tried tricks to calm my mind. I imagined a long, boring day at school; getting into my uniform, the bus journey, assembly, lunch in the canteen, every detail. It didn't work. My thoughts kept reverting to Matahari and the shambles in the *praça*. It was like an endless court case, in which I argued for the prosecution and the defence in turn.

In the small hours of the morning I made a decision. The next time João went to Yogung, I would go into the village and hear the news from Fátima. Having a plan of action gave me a little respite from my exhausting internal dialogue. João was asleep beside me. I looked down at his face and remembered that I had said to Mãezinha, 'He's not a devil, he's just a boy.'

✳   ✳   ✳

twelve moons gone, one moon to go

Most mornings I feign sleep until João has gone to work. Then I clean the house, take the ducks to the stream and go to work in the garden. On that particular morning, I was thinning out seedlings, squatting on my haunches. The baby was big enough to obstruct me; it formed a hard ball between my ribs and my thighs. I heard a bell ringing.

João usually came home at midday. He was late and I thought I would walk up to the edge of the forest and meet him. After I'd toiled uphill for a mile or so I stopped for a rest. At midday it's too hot to walk far. The sweat of my brow was running into my eyes and the waist of my skirt was so wet, I could have wrung it out. I sat down and looked over the ocean and I saw the reason why João was late and the reason he was ringing the bell at the *cabana*.

It was almost too tiny to focus on, a mere tea-leaf on the horizon. The boat was a month early by my reckoning. Once it had docked, I knew it would stay in the port for three days.

The following afternoon, I had my first visitor. It was Pai. He sat down and drank tea. When I offered him food he would take only rice and salt. Then he said,

185

'Compose yourself. I have some bad news for you, unless you have heard it already. I don't want you to distress yourself because it might harm the unborn.'

I looked at him speechlessly.

'Dona Maria Madalena was killed some weeks ago, senselessly killed. She was in the wrong place at the time, that's all.'

My reaction must have been all he expected because he said, 'Calma, filha, calma.'

'What happened?'

'She asked to see Senhor Onorusco late in the evening. He mentioned it in passing to Dona Maria de Fátima. I think she visited him late because she wanted to keep the visit a secret; perhaps she wanted him to write out her will. Late that night Dona Fátima heard a noise. She saw robbers dragging two bodies from Sr. Onorusco's house. They were Dona Dalu and Sr. Onorusco.

'Dona Fátima is an old lady. She was distraught. She didn't raise the alarm, she locked herself in a store-cupboard for a night and a day. In the morning the bodies were found hanging in the praça. The bandidos do it to terrorize the people; then, when they come back, the people hand over their goods without a struggle. They will be camped in the jungle not far from here. That's why I tell you this. You must take care, daughter.'

'I'll tell João. He'll be home soon.'

'It was you I came to see,' he said, 'I brought you here and so I feel some responsibility for you.' He spoke coldly; he remembered that I had once accused him of evading responsibility. 'You see, the boat docked today. Has João told you?'

He hadn't, but I nodded. 'In the ordinary way they take fare-paying passengers as far as Kawalinggan, but you don't have your fare, do you?'

'No.'

'Also you must have papers to board, and you have none. You would need to see the British consul before you could land on Kawalinggan. But, if you wish, I can speak to the captain of the ship on your behalf.'

I said nothing. Instead, helpless tears welled up in my eyes. He looked at me for a moment. He said, 'On the other hand, if you still wish to stay, I will speak to Senhor Jerónimo. For the sake of the coming child I might persuade him to issue a wedding certificate for you and João. He is a more flexible man than Senhor Onorusco was.'

I said woodenly, 'Thank you, Father.'

'You don't have to decide anything right now. But don't leave it too long. The boat will leave in three days' time.'

I said nothing, so he stood up. 'Tell João that Senhor Jerónimo is temporarily in charge of Senhor Onorusco's affairs; rent is being collected and wages are being paid as usual. A letter will be going out on the ferry for posting in Kawalinggan informing Senhor Onorusco's solicitors in Europe of his death. Beyond that we know nothing as yet.'

'I'll tell him.'

'Now I must go or I won't be home before tomorrow.'

'You have a long way to walk.'

He nodded and patted me briskly on the shoulder. I said, 'How is Mãezinha?'

'She is well.'

'Pai, when I saw her in the village, I called her from behind. In my country it doesn't mean anything so I simply forgot. If you see her alone, will you tell her that I didn't mean to frighten her. Tell her I love her and wish her well. Will you give her that message?'

He looked at me wryly. He had a dark, squashed-up face and little lewd elephant eyes. He said, 'I will, but I ought to give her a smack round the ear.'

After he had gone, I sat down on the floor with my head in my hands. I remembered our previous conversation and the words I had said: 'Is he to spend the rest of his life alone?'

When João appeared in the doorway, I stared up at him silently. 'What is it?'

'Pai was here.'

He cringed, and folded his arms protectively around his body. I said, 'Shall I tell you the news from the village? Dona Fátima says Dalu had arranged to go to Onorusco's house on the night of the murders. She says she saw robbers dragging the bodies out.'

'It wasn't me! Amy!' He leapt forward and stood over me, prodding himself in the chest.

'Amy, I am João. I am not bad. I never hurt anybody.'

'So the *bandidos* killed Onorusco and Dalu and they happened to choose that night to do it?'

'No! No, it was him! He comes, and I can't stop him.'

'It was Zé.'

'Yes!'

I had known it all along. I said cruelly, 'Either you are a liar, or else you are quite mad. Anyway, they are just as dead whatever name you call yourself, and we might be dead, too, if Dona Fátima hadn't lied to protect us.'

'Amy!' he said in anguish. He stood in front of me, gesticulating hopelessly. His eyes were brimming with tears. 'You must believe me, you must! It's not me who does these things. He does them.'

In my mind's eye I saw him stripping off Dalu's clothes, taking hold of the loose, yellowing skin and sparse hair of her intimate parts, skinning her like a boiler chicken. I said in revulsion,

'Tell me, who killed Matahari? Was that Zé too?'

For the first time he looked angry. He shouted,

'Why do you speak of that now? Why do you speak of it, huh? She was just a little *cabra*.' On the island, *cabra* is a term of abuse.

'Yes she was only a *cabra*, but I could have drunk her milk, and we could have bred from her and had a whole herd of goats. Or else I could have sold her and paid my fare to Kawalinggan.'

We stared at each other's faces. Then João flung out of the house and ran off into the forest. I had been filled with anger but I had poured it all out and now I was empty. I thought, 'I can never forget what he did to Dalu, and I can never forgive what he did to Matahari. If I'm leaving, now is my chance.' I sat there for an hour or more, hopeless but indecisive. Later he slunk back. He had been crying and the sight of that hurt me. He climbed the ladder, avoiding my eye. When I went to bed he was lying face down on the floor in a posture of dejection. His back looked very thin; his shoulder-blades stuck out. I wanted to stroke them but I held back.

In the morning João went out early and I supposed he had gone to the forest. I swept the house, emptied the ashes and fetched the water then I collected six grey duck-eggs from the shed. I let the ducks paddle and shovel and ruffle up their skirts under the spring for a minute or two and afterwards I drove them down the stream.

I kept on walking. I never made a conscious decision to leave but my legs carried me down the hill. My heart was thudding. He had sworn that he would never hurt me, but he had also made me swear that we would die together. I was afraid he might come after me with his knife. Until I reached the *cabana* I kept looking compulsively over my shoulder.

After I passed the *cabana* I looked back up the mountain and saw smoke rising from our chimney. It was a strangely forlorn sight. He knew now that I had left and he was already leading his own lonely, private existence without me. I couldn't even imagine what his thoughts were.

It was a very long walk to the Port, and I had plenty of time to think. I thought about Fátima and the clever story she had cooked up in her store-cupboard to obscure the real connection between Dalu and Onorusco. Fátima had said: "Tiago meant to hack him to pieces and hang him on hooks in the praça." She had not been shocked by the butchery; João had done exactly what she expected of him. I thought, 'They are not really Portuguese and they are not really Christians. Here there are no courts. All the executioners are self-appointed. João had said, "They were not murders, they were punishments."

Here death sleeps with you in your cradle, eats with you at mealtimes and walks with you on the mountain. Survival is not a right, it's a matter of luck or divine intervention. The wispy, toothless old women squatting patiently on their verandas are probably only forty years old. Childbirth is a time of great peril for mother and baby. A special region of heaven is designated for women who die in childbirth; there they celebrate endlessly with warriors killed in battle. As for the life of a little goat, it has only a market value. I thought, 'I can excuse everything except the killing of Matahari. Perhaps that makes me a crazy person too.'

Up till then I'd been riding high on a wave of moral indignation. Now I began to founder. The fact is that I'm ordinary. My parents are ordinary and I'm used to an ordinary life. When my fate becomes extraordinary, I don't know how to cope. I want to head back at once for the dry shore of normality.

Once I used to extol the tenets of the Women's Movement. I read a lot of books, chiefly to irritate my mother, who held traditional views. The strong women they celebrated were the ones who left and scratched out an independent existence. The weak stayed because they were too cowed to shift for themselves. But perhaps some of the ones who stayed had been brave: heroines, not masochists, however blurry the line that divides the two. We make solemn promises: 'for better or for worse, till death do us part.' Should we all cross our fingers and regard the vows as a meaningless ritual like the drunken Okey Cokey at the end of the wedding reception? I thought, 'If I were in England there would be someone to give me answers. But out here, who is there to advise me, or Mãezinha, or Conceição? You don't have to be stupid to be ignorant, and I don't know what I ought to do.'

I'd always thought of myself as a weak person but perhaps that was only my mother's prejudice. Perhaps I was really a strong person wrongly labelled at birth. Perhaps I wasn't ordinary at all, but extraordinary. Supposing that I was a woman of extraordinary courage and that I decided to stay: would I ever be able to let João touch me without remembering that his hands were the same hands that had skinned Dalu and slit open Matahari? Would I ever dare let João mind the baby?

The boat was in front of the Port Stores. Seen at close quarters it wasn't as big as they had all led me to believe. Nor were my feelings as expectant and eager as I had thought they would be. I wondered, not for the first time, how my mother would receive such a conspicuously pregnant daughter, once the first thrill of reunion was over. I would tell her that João and I were married, as I truly believed in my heart that we were, but five minutes of her cross-questioning would extract the uncomfortable facts. Seen through her eyes, my baby was an embarrassment; it was of mixed race and probably of a luteous tint. She is a hard-line Conservative, my mother, considerably less liberal than Pai, much less flexible than Jerónimo.

There would be no university course. I wouldn't be going to any more Late Nite Discos. I'd be minding my baby, parking the pram where the neighbours couldn't see the colour of it, hoovering and pegging out nappies in foggy Walsall under my mother's reproachful eye, dreaming hopelessly of *festas* and waterfalls and smoky-smelling shacks, and João. And Zé.

By this time I was standing on the fine black shingle. This was where Zé had entered the water, trusting in his mother's arms. Then the water had closed over her head and they had parted for ever. There, between the legs of the Stores, was the dark space where he'd lain in wait, and over there was the swamp into which someone had thrown his bones, hoping to be rid of him for good. In his will, Old 'Quim had left the villagers two companions in their darkness. Now I was in the dark, too. I'd married João for better and Zé for worse and I didn't know whether they were one or two.

I wondered why Conceição hadn't taken her baby to the sisters at Yogung. Then I wondered if that was where she had been going; if someone had followed her along the dark road and stopped her for ever. Was that what Zé was trying to tell us?

The boat was still tied up, but it was thrumming and giving off the oily smell of hot engines. There was a small crowd there: gawpers with dark, vacant faces. Mãezinha wasn't amongst them. I stood at the barrier and called out:

'O! Senhor Capitão!'

In response, a fair man in a white shirt and cap came down the ramp. As soon as I had begun on my explanation I realized that he was Dutch, and, like most Dutchmen, spoke excellent English. He listened to me courteously, with a slight frown of curiosity, then he lifted the barrier and took me up the gangway and into the air-conditioned passenger saloon. After a moment's hesitation he gave me a glass of refrigerated beer; it tasted like the drink they give the souls of the righteous on arrival in heaven.

I asked to go to the toilet. It had a proper flush with a fierce swish and suck. There were little tilting goldfish bowls of liquid soap and a roller towel. I saw myself in a big neon-lit mirror. I was very thin and brown and my hair looked rough: Amy Rabbit of the Bramble-Bush.

XXII

The Captain, if he was the Captain, brought me three sheets of stationery and lent me a biro. He was a cool but kindly man and I enjoyed the time I spent on his ship. I wrote the letter quickly; I was afraid I might start to waver if I read it through so I sealed it in the envelope and gave it to the Captain.

The air outside was thick with the heat of afternoon. There was a little stir amongst the crowd as I plodded down the gangway. One woman, hugely pregnant under her tea-picker's overall, looked up at me with bright, blank eyes and crossed herself. I didn't take the mountain path. I walked round the end of the spit and then inland until I was out of sight.

The swamp smelt of graves and urinals and cabbage-water. As I walked, the tepid mud oozed between my toes. Here there were watchers too. A hundred pairs of eyes protruded from the surface of the mud. I saw something white trapped among the rushes and I waded out towards it. The mud shifted beneath my feet and I was soon thigh-deep in the evil-smelling water. I thought I had found Zé but what I had found was only a severed bird-wing.

I had come with the intention of baptizing Zé. I was afraid that he, if he existed at all, might have still more scores to settle, that two murders might not satisfy him. I wanted to appease him, if he could be appeased.

I knew the words: 'N, I baptize you in the name of the Father and of the Son, and of the Holy Ghost', and I knew that any Christian might pronounce them. I stood at the edge of the swamp, in the failing light and called out loudly,

'Zé ...'

The baby tapped, with its tiny fists, on the wall of my womb.

The mud-bank heaved. A big blister formed on top and burst with a loud sucking sound. Inside the crater, the silt began to seethe like lava. I was transfixed. I thought the swamp was going to disgorge his bones. I thought Zé would rear up out of the stinking mud before my eyes. Then the bubbling ceased and I saw João running towards me along the edge of the water.

I was not frightened. Perhaps I was too weary to be frightened, or perhaps there was nothing menacing in the way he ran. When he reached me he stood stock still. He said,

'I watched you get on the boat. Then you got off again.'

I put my hands on his warm shoulders and he clasped them at once with his. He said longingly,

'Are you coming home, Amy?'

'Let's go and sleep at the waterfall. Tomorrow we'll ask Pai to marry us. This time I think he will.'

He kissed me, just a soft touch; his lips were trembling. He pulled out the knife and said,

'Amy, I swear to you, I promise you, I will never spill blood with this again, unless it is from my own body.'

'Throw it in the swamp.'

'I can't do that, it was my great-grandfather's. I have to keep it for my son.'

'Keep it at the waterfall.'

He nodded. His eyes were full of tears. He said, 'Come away from here, Amy. This is a bad place, it can give you a fever.'

We walked away from the stench of the foul water. I said, 'João, put your hand just here and see if you can feel the baby moving.'

Dark was falling fast and the little frogs were sending their rattling love-calls across the swamp ... '

* * *

XXIII

That was all. There was one more notebook, but it was badly scorched. A hole had been burnt right through the middle, as though a piece of flaming wood had dropped on it. I could read some of the words but I couldn't make sense of the text, and, like Richard, I abandoned the attempt.

Some days later, Philip turned up, knocking at the front door as one does in normal houses. He smiled at me foxily, like a favourite uncle arriving for Christmas, and kissed me chastely. He said,

'I got your letter. Don't feel too badly about what happened. He was a very disturbed young man. Do you know his history?'

I said angrily, 'No, and I don't want you to tell me.'

He strolled round the house, stiff-legged, and bulky in his green waxed winter jacket. He said suddenly,

'Isn't it about time you came home?'

'Home?'

'You can't live like this.' He looked down distastefully at what he was treading in. 'You might as well be miserable in comfort.'

I said defensively, 'The local kids got in and vandalized the place while we were away.'

'I miss you, Sandy.'

'I'm pregnant.'

He said with a twist of the lips, 'Yes. All right.'

Sometimes if I can't sleep I go downstairs and read Amy's diary, which I keep in a basket of old napkins and table-runners. Philip has never looked at it. If I mention the island of Macak, he frowns and looks puzzled. He forgets, or pretends to forget, everything I did with Jamie. My three-month aberration has been packed away in the linen hamper with a dead woman's trousseau.

It bothers me that Amy's story is incomplete. I would like to write an ending to it. I think perhaps I witnessed the final scene when I followed the brown rats along the rock ledge and encountered the skeletal guardian of the knife.

What follows is all supposition, and it's based, as the policeman would say, on village tittle-tattle. I think it was Mãezinha who climbed up to the cabin and talked to me and I believe she knew who was missing from his bed on the night Amy's house burned down; she had good reason to know.

According to the legend, the Devil rescued João from the water; now they probably say the Devil rescued Jamie from the fire. I don't think it was the Devil, or one of Ceu's saints. I think Jamie and João were out on one of their midnight rambles when the house caught fire, a ramble which ended with a crazy race down the mountainside in a vain attempt to rescue Amy.

So I think it was João who locked the baby in the church and left him in the care of Pai. Then he went to the waterfall, where I found him, twenty years later and one day too late. He had said, "Swear that we'll die together!" and, "Amy, I swear to you, I promise you, I will never spill blood with this again unless it is from my own body." I think he honoured both those promises.

Jamie's daughter Joana was born on May 31st with the sun in Gemini. She was born prematurely, by Caesarean section. She is small and skinny and has wavy black hair and gappy teeth. She suffers from debilitating headaches but otherwise she seems to be entirely normal. Sometimes Philip forgets that she isn't his child.

In her Christmas stocking she had a pair of hand puppets with oversized heads and frayed cotton dresses. Once I watched her playing with them. She was sitting at the table opposite Philip, who was reading the newspaper. On her left hand she wore the surly puppet in green gingham and on her right the smiling puppet dressed in yellow and black stars. As I watched, the green puppet pounced on the yellow puppet. The yellow puppet, still smiling, shot up in the air and then swooped down in retaliation. The two plastic heads smacked furiously together.

Joana screamed, and Philip looked at her over his glasses in mild reproof.

Renée Smith was born in Birmingham in 1945. She left school at sixteen, believing that for a writer, experience was more important than education. She has lived mainly in the wilder regions of Wales and Scotland with her three sons, born so widely spaced apart that she has spent most of her life actively mothering. She has had a great variety of jobs, of which she liked farming and cooking best. She now lives on a smallholding in the mountains of Northern Portugal with her husband, Peter. They write, produce wine, and keep goats and poultry. *Zé* is Renée Smith's first novel.